THE BLACK BIRD MURDERS

Also by Ray E. Aquitania, M.D.

*Jock-Docs: World-Class Athletes
Wearing White Coats*

Taking the Bull by the Horns

THE

BLACK

BIRD

MURDERS

Ray E. Aquitania, M.D.

BookLocker

Saint Petersburg, Florida

Published by Booklocker.com
The Black Bird Murders
Copyright © 2021 by Ray E. Aquitania, M.D.
All rights reserved

Library of Congress Control Number: 2021911947
ISBN: 978-1-64719-675-2
First printing

Publisher's Note: This is a work of fiction. Names, characters,
places, and incidents either are the product of the author's
imagination or are used fictitiously, and any resemblance to
actual persons, living or dead, events, business
establishments, or locales is entirely coincidental.

Printed on acid-free paper.

Credits: Vecteezy.com for black bird vectors
(downloaded 6-10-21)

Dedicated to those who actually

penned the books they authored

Writing a book is an adventure. To begin with it is a toy then an amusement. Then it becomes a mistress, and then it becomes a master, and then it becomes a tyrant and, in the last stage, just as you are about to be reconciled to your servitude, you kill the monster and fling him to the public.

— Winston Churchill

1

The brilliant blue sky is picturesque on this spring Saturday afternoon, less than a week from St. Patrick's Day.

"I am on fire today!" yells Erik, a local restaurateur, as his ball rattles into the hole on the practice green.

He is talking to his long-time friend Manuel as he rolls one more ball toward the cup before their tee time. Erik misses the target this time, by about three feet.

"Not by the looks of that last putt," jokes Manuel, who is a chemical engineer from the Pacific Northwest.

They join two others, Garry and Mick, on the first tee and say their pleasantries. It is 3 p.m. and sounds of chirping hummingbirds can be heard on this cloudless day. Most of this foursome are regulars at the Olympic Torch Golf Links, and each one now takes out his driver before the order of the upcoming tee shots is determined.

Mick, the sole lefty in the group, is elected to go first, and he hits his Titleist down the center of the fairway. Manuel follows with a grip-it-and-rip-it style, smashing his golf ball just past Mick's. Erik and Garry, a fitness instructor, proceed with their drives, ending up short of Mick's and Manuel's balls.

"A fine March afternoon for a round of golf," remarks Manuel, the tallest and also the longest hitter off the tee. The four chums engage in unpretentious conversation as they stroll down the fairway.

"I guess it's me," says Erik, whose golf ball is the farthest from the hole. After a practice swing with his 4-iron, he addresses his ball and then sails it toward the green about 180 yards away. It is well-struck, landing just on the putting surface.

"Helluva shot!" shouts his buddy Mick, who is a local neurologist. "I guess you had your Wheaties today!"

None of the others can match Erik's second shot, each landing short of the green, with Manuel having the worst luck, ending up in the deep crescent-shaped bunker. As a squirrel passes in front of them, the weekend warriors lug their golf bags as they walk down the first fairway toward the green.

Erik lays down his bag behind the green, taking out his putter and then walking over to mark his ball. Garry and Mick, still in the fairway, short of the green, drop their bags and take out pitching wedges. They wait for Manuel, who is now the farthest from the first hole's flagstick.

After plucking a sand wedge from his golf bag, Manuel walks into the sand trap, eyeing his ball near the back edge. The golf ball is buried about halfway in the sand, so he knows he must forcefully hit the sand just behind the ball first. This should propel the ball over the lip of the bunker and onto the green. He takes a couple of practice half-swings, careful not to touch the sand.

Once ready, the dark-haired and self-assured sportsman crouches over his ball. He takes a short backswing with his club and then rapidly moves it toward the sand behind the ball. But instead of the gentler sound of sand and then the ball flying into the air, a noticeable thud is heard. He has missed his ball completely.

The other three are amused, all snickering as Manuel blushes in shame. Usually a solid player in hitting out of the bunker, he is surprised at his failed shot and embarrassed at missing his ball altogether.

He again looks at his golf ball and prepares to swing at it once more. Something catches his eye, though.

Behind his ball, peeking through the sand, a black button is noted by the golfer. Not having seen the small disk before his shot, he carefully reaches down to pick it up. He is unable to lift the small button off the sand, though, as if something is holding it down.

Manuel decides to get a better grip on the button with all the fingers of his right hand, and he pulls mightily. This time, the button is lifted off the sand ever so slightly, exposing some green fabric that seems to be connected to it. Pulling harder, the now frustrated golfer sees another button connected to the cloth.

"Guys, some prankster buried a shirt in the sand trap."

The other three smile and slowly walk toward Manuel with their golf clubs, ready to ridicule him for blaming his terrible shot on a shirt in the sand.

Garry takes his pitching wedge and moves away some of the sand in the area of the green cloth and buttons. A polo shirt is exposed.

A chalk-white pallor then comes across the face of the tanned golfer as he suddenly stops what he's doing.

"Gentlemen, I see some skin next to the shirt! It looks like someone's neck!"

All four players look on in consternation as an Adam's apple appears next to the collar of the green shirt.

"Well, boys, that's all the sand I'll be clearing today," Garry deadpans.

Both curious and horrified, Mick tells the others to step back. He uses his golf club and both hands to reveal a body buried in the bunker. Soon, all four help him in the gruesome task of uncovering the entire corpse. They see a medium-framed man with light brown hair. He is wearing a forest green polo shirt, shorts, and sneakers.

By this time, the foursome of golfers playing behind Manuel and company is asking about the delay in play and the apparent commotion.

"Uhhh, sorry for the slow play, but I think we found a dead body!" exclaims Erik.

All the players in the group before Manuel's are silent, eyebrows arched and jaws dropped.

2

"What kind of a name is that anyway?"

Freckled Rex Rhombus, ready in his white uniform, defends his surname by joking, "I think it is a mixture of Latin and geometry."

The sabres clash as the men begin their bout at the Intrepid Fencing Club on Eastmoor Avenue. The first touch is scored by the nimble Rhombus, just near the xiphoid process of his adversary.

"Lucky first blow!" shouts Derek Treadwell, the more experienced fencer of the two and an attorney. "En-garde! Prêt? Allez!" (On guard! Ready? Let's go!)

When they resume, the mildly stout Treadwell is the aggressor moving along the piste, methodically inching nearer. But Rhombus parries and then follows with a riposte. He now goes on the offensive and powerfully lunges with a counterattack, slashing his opponent across the chest.

Immediately, both are in position to begin the next point. This time, the faster Rhombus does not hesitate and catches Treadwell on the left arm for a 3-0 lead.

The men briefly remove their masks to reveal their sweating faces and disheveled hair in the well-ventilated studio. Just as quickly, the masks are donned, with each fencer returning to his starting mark on the piste.

"Looks like a shutout in the making," Rhombus boasts. "When was the last time that happened?"

"I would say, never," answers the attorney in a chummy way. He next asks in French, "Es-tu prêt?" (Are you ready?)

"Oui, monsieur. Allez!" answers the athletic and lean redhead.

Both fencers lunge forward slightly before retreating. They tap swords several times as they traverse the mat, each trying to see an opening in the other's defenses.

The brunet executes an indirect maneuver under Rhombus' sabre, followed by an attempted stab into the abdominal area. However, the redhead quickly performs a diagonal parry to avoid the attack.

Now on the offensive, the faster sabreur does a sidestep to his right before moving forward with a balestra. The retreating Treadwell is then slashed in the left flank area by the lunging Rhombus.

"I don't think this is your day, Derek," remarks his rival as they return to their starting positions.

"Au contraire! I suggest you get ready for my comeback, Rex. I'm just warming up!"

Immediately after both get back to the en-garde position, "Fence!" is declared by the freckled athlete.

Rhombus decides to break ground at a slow pace. In reply, his more portly opponent advances slowly along the mat, sabre pointing slightly upward. Afterwards, the more agile fencer starts to dart forward and then backward, repeating the movements several times.

Treadwell then seemingly loses his concentration given the regular tempo of his adversary's motions. Suddenly, the redhead stops on a dime, catching the brunet momentarily off-guard. Rhombus then rushes forward, leaves his feet, and performs a flying lunge. His sabre catches the mask of his buddy, elevating the score to 5-0.

At that point, the staccato ring sound of Rhombus' cell interrupts the match. He lays down his sabre before taking off his mask and glove.

"Yes, I understand. Please repeat the location once again. Thank you -- I am on the way," he answers on his phone.

"Rex, does duty call?" asks his jaunty friend.

"I'm afraid so, my good compadre. But we will continue this battle later with the current score."

"Wouldn't have it any other way. Be ready for an onslaught next time!" promises the still confident Treadwell.

Rhombus casually responds, "Derek, not to dispirit you, but I plan to keep up my dominant play when our contest resumes."

"We'll see about that, Rex. Hasta la vista!"

3

Manuel briskly walks back to the clubhouse and tells
the staff about the corpse in the bunker next to the first green.
Someone calls 911, and within several minutes, an ambulance and a
police car arrive. The area around the first green of the golf course
and nearby second tee box is cordoned off with yellow police tape.

Half an hour later, members of the crime scene unit are now at
work. The local red-haired lieutenant, Rex Rhombus, in his
signature dark blue pants and blazer, is also present. He is discussing
matters with his smartly-dressed brunette medical examiner.

"Who might be our victim today, Dr. Paris?"

"His driver's license identifies him as Jackson Moreau,
Lieutenant. Just 25."

"And how was his body found?"

"Believe it or not, he was discovered buried in a sand trap near
the first green! The sand is usually 12 inches deep in a typical bunker,
so the murderer had just enough room to completely cover the
victim."

"An unusual location for a body to say the least, Doctor. Have
you determined the time of death?" asks Rhombus, staring up at the
cobalt sky through his aviators.

"Based on the body's condition, I would estimate between eight
and eleven hours ago. After the autopsy, I can be more precise on the
time window."

"That puts time of death sometime in the early morning to midmorning. The golf course starter tells me the first foursome today began play around 7 a.m. So the murder likely happened before 7."

"Sounds reasonable, Rex. It would have been quite conspicuous for the killer to bury the body with golfers already on the course."

"Agreed. And how about cause of death, Danica?"

"I can't really say at this point. No bullet wounds or other obvious signs of major injury are seen. But I do detect a bruise in the occiput indicating blunt force injury on this poor soul."

"Could that have killed him?"

"Unlikely, since it is not that large."

"Point taken."

"I did find something else noteworthy, Rex. This item was attached to his shirt."

In a small plastic evidence bag, a lapel pin with the image of a black-colored bird is handed to Lt. Rhombus. There is no inscription or identifying information on the object.

"What do you make of this article, Doctor?"

"Given that the pin was attached to his polo shirt, I do not think it belongs to the deceased. These pins are conventionally placed on a dress shirt or jacket."

"Then it is likely that the killer planted this pin on the victim."

"I would have to concur. It probably holds some significance to the assailant. Perhaps he is an ornithologist."

"That is possible, Danica. Make sure the lab checks the lapel pin for fingerprints. And tell me when you are able to determine the reason he died."

Soon, the body is placed into a white body bag to be transported to the morgue. Samples of the sand in the bunker crime scene are collected.

Rhombus looks for the officer first on the scene.

"Officer Bloom, was this man robbed after he was murdered?"

"There are no indications of a theft, Lieutenant. His wallet contains about $80 and two credit cards, and his fairly nice Seiko watch wasn't taken."

"So it appears we don't have a clear motive at this time."

"Also, I talked to the golf course operations manager. He states that a golf cart was found near the first tee box when he arrived this morning. Usually, these carts are kept together in the storage/parking area."

The lieutenant says, "A reasonable conclusion is the killer used the golf cart to move the body to the bunker, which is at least 400 yards from the first tee. Make sure they check that cart for blood and dust it for fingerprints, Officer."

"Right away, sir."

Finally, Lt. Rhombus asks Manuel and his three golf buddies about their story.

"Did any of you know the victim?" asks the lieutenant with the caterpillar eyebrows. "And do you have any ideas on how his body got on the golf course?"

"We just met -- I mean discovered -- him in the sand trap this afternoon," replies Garry. "I don't think any of us have seen him before. The golf course is not gated, so most anyone can sneak on. Do you know what killed him?"

"That is police business, sir. Do all of you live here in the town of Quai Natia?"

"Yes," says Mick, the only man wearing a distinctive newsboy cap in the group, "except for Manuel, who is here on business from the state of Washington."

Rhombus turns toward Manuel and shakes his hand.

"I can tell you're a good man, Manuel. Like you, I also hail from the Evergreen State. What part?"

"Just east of Yakima, Lieutenant."

"I know the area well. It has some of the state's best biking trails."

"No argument there, sir."

"Very well. Thank you, gentlemen, for bringing this body to our attention. Please give the officer your cell phone numbers. We'll call you if we need to. Have a good day."

They all nod and say their goodbyes.

4

A few hours later, Lt. Rhombus gets a call on his cell.

"Rex, this is Eli. We had no luck with fingerprints on the lapel pin. Not even a trace of blood was detected in the sand from the golf course bunker. Also, at the bunker, there were no clear footprints left by the assailant -- he covered his tracks pretty well, literally and figuratively."

"What about the victim? Does the toxicology screen indicate any alcohol or prohibited substances?"

"According to Danica, those tests are all normal."

"Eli, does she have a C.O.D. at this time?"

"So far all she saw was the head bruise, which she said would not have killed him. She should get to the full autopsy in the next 24 hours."

"Thank you, Detective. And make sure to ask Officer Bloom if any blood or suspicious fingerprint was detected on that misplaced golf cart."

"I'm on it. Over and out."

Rhombus is troubled by still not knowing the immediate cause of death in the apparent homicide. He looks at his notes and decides to pay a visit to the deceased's widow, Hanna Moreau. She resides in the tranquil district of Calais in Quai Natia.

Arriving at Mrs. Moreau's front door, the lieutenant knocks and then sees the weeping widow as she opens the door. She has just returned from the morgue, appearing to be in the throes of despair.

Showing his shield, he says, "Good evening, ma'am. I am Lt. Rhombus of the Quai Natia Police Department. My deepest sympathies go out to you and your family. May I come in?"

Straining to talk because of her sobbing, she welcomes him in. Understandably, Mrs. Moreau is not herself, her blouse not fully tucked into her skirt. A couple, Jon and Elise Blakemore, sit in the living room.

"This is my sister and her husband, Lieutenant."

He shakes their hands, offering his condolences.

After he sits down with the widow, Rhombus says, "I am sure today's events have been horrible, Mrs. Moreau. Could you tell me when you last saw your husband alive?"

Wiping away her tears, the green-eyed blonde mumbles, "Around 5 a.m. today, just before Jackson left for his early workout at the local gym. He doesn't usually go so early on a Saturday, but we had plans to see our son's Little League baseball game later in the morning."

"Could you tell me what gym he went to?"

"The Fitness Zone on Grant Street."

"Thank you, ma'am. As you may know, your husband's body was found buried at Olympic Torch Golf Links. Was he an avid golfer?"

"He loved to play at Olympic Torch whenever he had the time. But he was often too busy."

"I see. Would you say your husband acted peculiarly earlier today or in the last week?"

"He appeared to be his usual self, Lieutenant."

"What about any recent arguments with anyone, ma'am?"

"Not as far as I am aware."

"And did he have any enemies? Or did anyone rub him the wrong way?"

"I thought everyone liked my husband, sir. And I know of no one who holds a grudge against him. Do you have any idea what type of person would kill him and then bury him in a bunker?"

"Not at this time, Mrs. Moreau, but we are actively investigating what we found at the crime scene. I would also like to say that a black bird lapel pin was attached to your husband's shirt."

"Black bird? What does it mean?"

"I was hoping you could tell me. Did Mr. Moreau have any special interest in birds?"

She ponders for a moment before responding, "If he did, I never knew about it."

"Fair enough. Ma'am, did your husband work in Quai Natia?"

"Yes, Lieutenant. He was a junior accountant in the firm Binnington & Kane."

"I am familiar with the business. And are you aware if he was having any problems at work?"

"Not to my knowledge, no."

"Okay. Now Mrs. Moreau, don't take this the wrong way, but I need to ask if you think your husband may have been having an affair."

She is offended by Rhombus' question.

"That is impossible! Our marriage was very solid."

"Sorry, ma'am, but I just need to get that on the record. Only a few more questions, so please bear with me. Can you tell me who knew of your son's game today?"

"I guess all the kids, parents, and coaches involved would have been aware of it."

"That sounds reasonable. Have you noticed any odd or suspicious behavior in any of them recently, Mrs. Moreau?"

"I know most of the parents and kids, Lieutenant. Everything has been fine."

"What about the team coaches?"

"I don't recall any friction between any of them and my husband."

"That is good to hear. Where does your son attend school, ma'am?"

"Franklin Delano Roosevelt Elementary School, on Korpi Street."

"Got it. Finally, did your husband have any siblings or living parents?"

"His only sister Emma lives in Pennsylvania. Cliff, his father, died of melanoma about four years ago, but his mother Astrid is alive and relatively well. She lives down the coast, in Green Springs. I can get her number for you if you like."

"Thank you, that would be great. I much appreciate your time on this very difficult day, Mrs. Moreau. Here is my card with my personal cell phone. If you think of anything important, please don't hesitate to call. My team will keep you informed about the investigation."

The grieving widow makes an earnest request to the lieutenant.

"Lt. Rhombus, you need to find who killed my Jackson! He or she can't get away with this! I still can't believe it."

"I promise you – I will do everything in my power to do so."

She thanks the lieutenant before showing him to the door.

5

Danica Paris. Magna cum laude in her class at the
University of Texas at Austin, with a major in biochemistry. Near the
top of her medical school class at the Baylor College of Medicine.
Everyone knew she could write her own ticket to almost any
residency, and she opted to enter the pathology program at Baylor.

Steffi Jordan, a diminutive dark-haired lady wearing a canary
yellow dress and a sunhat, asks Paris, "Tell me again how you got
into forensic pathology and all those dead bodies."

The doctor, brown-eyed with chestnut hair, is dressed in snug
maroon jeans and a gossamer ivory blouse. She returns the menu to
the waiter at the Edible Potato and smiles.

"You know, call me crazy, but I liked the smell of formaldehyde
in that first anatomy class at Baylor," she jests.

"Come on, Danica. Tell me the real reason."

"Okay, here it is. Sometime during medical school, I was told
that 90% of a pathologist's work is interesting, while only 10% of a
clinician's is. I have definitely found that to be the case."

But Mrs. Jordan, sipping her peppermint iced tea, pries further.

"That can't be the only reason."

"Plus, I don't have to worry about noncompliant patients!"

"I still think there is some screw loose in your pretty little head,
but I still love you."

"Love you too. It seems like just yesterday when we were
roommates at Austin. Weren't those great times?"

"The best! Now we are all grown up, or at least we are supposed to be," she says with some sarcasm.

"So what brings you to Quai Natia this weekend?"

"As you would expect, a pharmaceutical representatives convention. Plus it gives Troy the opportunity to long for me."

"Are things going well with your better half?"

"Swimmingly. After his elbow fracture healed, he decided to start his own construction firm in Houston. He loves the autonomy, but not the hours."

Dr. Paris suddenly appears pensive.

"What's wrong?" asks her bright-eyed friend. "Does it involve the murder two days ago at the golf course? The news is all over town."

"It sure does. And it bothers me that I haven't yet been able to find an immediate cause of death."

"I'll leave the dead body talk to you and your colleagues, thank you very much."

"Sorry, Steffi. Sometimes I take my work home with me. Admittedly, I usually do."

"I know. But I was wondering: Is there anything else or anyone else you are taking home with you these days?"

"Well, there is this guy at the police department."

"Tell me all about him, and I want details!"

6

News involving the bizarre homicide at Olympic Torch
Golf Links has dominated the headlines of the *Quai Natia Gazette*.
The usually quiet town of Quai Natia in California's Central Coast is
now rampant with speculation, gossip, and palpable fear. The four
golfers who discovered the body are becoming minor celebrities on
local news outlets. And the unique nature of the crime is playing to
people's imaginations.

Mrs. Moreau continues to tell reporters that her husband was
liked by everyone she knows and loved by his family. In this difficult
time, her parents can not be with her since they are not well enough
to travel. Fortunately, Mrs. Moreau's mother-in-law Astrid is able to
drive up from Green Springs and stay with her for several days.

Meanwhile, at the Quai Natia police headquarters, Dr. Paris is
summarizing the postmortem results to Lt. Rhombus.

"On my external examination, there is evidence of blunt closed
head trauma in the occiput. No defensive wounds are seen in the
arms or hands, so the perpetrator was a friend or someone not
perceived as a threat. Or he or she snuck up on the victim."

"Did the head injury kill him, Doctor?"

"Not likely. The bruise is not that large. And there is no
hemorrhage in the brain."

"So is the cause of death still unclear at this time?"

"Actually, the internal examination showed swelling of the
brain, lungs, and liver, with venous congestion. And blood tests

28

showed lactic acidosis. Hence, I would say asphyxiation, or inadequate oxygenation of body tissues, caused his death."

"But what could have caused this loss of oxygen?"

"I saw some petechiae in the conjunctivae and periorbital skin. In other words, some tiny areas of bleeding on the eyeball surfaces and around the eyes."

"Doesn't that usually happen during strangulation, Danica?"

"Very good, Rex. However, there were no ligature marks and no signs of neck injury. Consequently, we can eliminate strangulation. Smothering is also unlikely since there is no bruising around the nose and mouth. But using a soft pillow could have prevented this bruising."

"So it is still possible that the killer smothered the victim. Anything else?"

"Yes. I didn't see the traditional cherry red lividity of carbon monoxide poisoning, nor did I sense the bitter almond scent of cyanide poisoning. But I am still waiting on special tests looking for other causes of asphyxiation."

"I understand. For now, let's keep the autopsy results confidential. I will obtain a court order to that effect today."

"Mum's the word, Rex."

"And Danica, have you any new insight on the black bird lapel pin found on the victim?"

"Rex, the most common black-colored birds in America are the raven, the crow, and of course, the blackbird. The rook is black-feathered, but its face has a prominent whitish area. The raven and crow are seen all over the U.S., but it is rare to see a blackbird in these parts."

"Can you tell which one it is based on the lapel pin?" asks the lieutenant.

"I showed the pin to a local ornithologist. He says the image looks more like a crow, but he's not positive."

"Doesn't a crow generally symbolize a dark omen?"

"To most of the world, yes, but Native Americans consider them a sign of good fortune. This bird also stands for personal transformation as well as death."

"Doctor, a simple explanation is that the killer is marking his victim with a symbol of death. But do you believe the pin tells us anything specific about the assailant?"

"As I said to you earlier, he or she may just be a bird-lover. But I talked to the director of the only birdwatching club in Quai Natia, and she can't think of a suspicious member or one with a special affinity for black birds."

"There is one other possibility."

"What is it, Rex?"

"Are you familiar with the SR-71 supersonic aircraft?"

"I can't say that I am."

"Well, it was developed by the Lockheed Corporation and was in service from the 1960's to just before 2000. And because of its primary color, it was called the 'Blackbird'."

"That is quite insightful. So our killer may work with or is fascinated by advanced military aircraft."

"Just something to ponder, Danica. At this time, I will inform the captain of the status of our case so far."

"All right. And when I find something more specific on those special body fluid tests, I will let you know."

"Thank you, Doctor. You have my number."

7

Suddenly bursting into his lane, Eli Stiles swims the length of the pool using the butterfly stroke. He takes in a huge breath as he touches the concrete wall at lane's end, taking off his goggles.

"Show-off!" shouts his girlfriend Jaqueline from the opposite end of the pool.

In her turquoise skintight one-piece suit, she resumes doing freestyle laps while Stiles takes a break between his sprints in the water. They have been members of The Fitness Zone for about a year and a half now, and they met at this very swimming pool about nine months ago. Both are spent after 45 minutes and leave the pool together, chatting before entering the locker rooms.

"Eli, are we still on for that mystery dinner performance?" she asks.

Sporting a five-o'clock shadow, he answers, "Front row table as I've been told."

The two have been a couple for about seven months now, but planning the specifics for a date is not like him – he prefers to set the day and time, then the two can agree on something. Today, he would make an exception for her birthday.

"You know, I thought you had forgotten how to make a reservation," Jaqueline says kiddingly, drying her hair.

"Just for that, I am going to cancel the birthday cake I had set up for the dinner."

She suspects, though, that he has not ordered any cake, since he knows she has Type 1 diabetes.

"Always the troublemaker, aren't you? Have you always been this rambunctious?"

"No, ma'am. I am just a simple southpaw from the Midwest, at your service."

"Well, sir, I am relieved to hear that," she says in a kittenish manner.

Eli Stiles entered the University of Illinois at Champaign in 2000 with a major in computer science. Near the end of his third year, though, his raison d'être would change.

On the way to his dormitory on a Tuesday evening, he heard the murmur of a small crowd. Seeing the gathering outside a nearby building, he asked what the fuss was about. Soon after, he fought through the crowd to get to the room of a coed he knew on the second floor.

There, his good friend Rebecca was on the ground, partially unclothed, surrounded by police and the crime scene unit. She had been sexually assaulted by an unknown assailant.

Rather than being shell-shocked at the scene, Mr. Stiles experienced anger toward the rapist as well as a rush of adrenaline. He asked one of the police officers everything he knew about what had happened. He even talked to the paramedics about any details they could give him.

A few weeks after the incident, the perpetrator still hadn't been caught. Stiles' friend Rebecca was still going through psychological counseling and having nightmares. And he felt powerless to help her.

Amidst this turmoil, Mr. Stiles changed his major to criminal justice. He eventually graduated with his bachelor's degree in 2005 and enrolled in the Illinois State Police Academy in Springfield. Since then, he has never looked back.

Standing near the pool, after a few more minutes of repartee, Stiles hugs his girlfriend and they kiss.

"I can pick you up at your place in about an hour. Will that be enough time?"

"I guess you will find out in an hour," Jaqueline responds coyly with a smile.

He pats her on the behind as they hit the showers.

8

The March or vernal equinox of 2019 is soon to be upon the town of Quai Natia. This celebration is more prevalent in Europe than in America, but Quai Natia has a sizable French and Spanish community and usually hosts various special events during this time of the year. In fact, the town's name roughly translates in French to Nadia's Landing.

The local semiprofessional soccer team, the Penalty Kicks, is also heading into the playoffs, and sports bars are expected to be at capacity for today's game. In Pamplona, a suburb of Quai Natia, Viola is up early to prepare her local watering hole, the Just Win! tavern, for the sports aficionados soon to arrive.

Before this Chicago native has the chance to insert her key into the front door, though, she realizes that it is already open. She is fairly sure she had locked up the place the night before.

"Is anyone here? I just called the police and I have a gun," she bluffs to anyone who may be listening.

But all she hears is quiet. Slowly moving through her establishment, Viola glimpses that the chairs and tables are all in place and the pool tables look normal, except for the last one.

Suddenly, she lets out a piercing scream as she beholds a casually dressed brunet laid out on the cloth of the billiards table. His hands and feet are tied securely to the legs of the Olhausen. She can detect no pulse, and she notices that his body is cold. He is not moving or breathing.

Hyperventilating, Viola runs to the phone behind the bar. There is the sound of a siren several minutes later, and Officer McNamara enters the Pamplona tavern. The name on the victim's identification is Matt Pitcairn, age 24, a local resident who works in Quai Natia. Paramedics also arrive and confirm the death of the man on the pool table. They detect no stab or gunshot wounds as they await the medical examiner.

Broad-shouldered Eli Stiles, one of Lt. Rhombus' trusted underlings, is seen at the bar before the M.E. He looks for any indication of a struggle or fisticuffs, but none is found.

"Anything interesting to report, Eli?" asks Dr. Paris as she enters the pub. She is a little surprised that he beat her to the crime scene.

"See for yourself. The victim was securely tied down to the pool table with some rope. Not your everyday homicide."

"I see what you mean. What do you think killed him?"

"Danica, no murder weapon has been recovered, but I did turn up this little nugget – a lapel pin with the image of a black bird on the victim's shirt."

Paris' eyes open wide as she sees the trinket. The whites of her eyes are a stark contrast to her off-black trouser pants and dark green sweater.

Carefully looking at the pin, she says, "This lapel pin is not exactly the same as the one on the other victim, but a black-colored bird is clearly seen. Do you know what that means, Eli?"

"Sure do. It seems we have a possible spree or serial killer on our hands. And he or she apparently wants to give us a message."

"What message is that?" queries Lt. Rhombus, who arrives at the bar.

"Unfortunately, we can't be sure yet," answers the doctor.

Dr. Paris then talks to the paramedics and performs a cursory examination of the corpse.

Detective Stiles suggests, "You know, Rex, the good news is this black bird lapel pin may lead us to the murderer's identity. On the other hand, it may represent an attempt to distract us from more important evidence."

"At this juncture, Eli, I believe the lapel pin either represents the signature of a serial killer or an item left by a copycat killer. Either way, how do you suppose the perpetrator got into the bar?"

"It appears the front door was forced open with a chisel or small crowbar."

"Detective, are there any signs of a scuffle in the tavern?"

"Not that I can see, R-double. And everything is in place according to the owner."

"How about motive? Could this have been a robbery gone bad?"

"Watch, wallet, and wedding band are still on the victim. So we can eliminate theft."

"I agree, Detective Stiles."

"So that would leave lust, love, or loathing as the possible motive."

"Very good, Eli. I also notice the victim was discovered tied down to the pool table."

"Affirmative. Another peculiar crime scene, just like last week."

Paris returns and says, "Rex, as in the murder victim at the golf course, I again see a small- to medium-sized bruise indicating something dull hitting the back of the victim's head. There is also a little redness in the eyes."

"What about time of death?"

"By the pattern of lividity, he died about six to eight hours ago. I'll work on the body as soon as possible."

"Thank you, Danica."

Stiles remarks, "Two murder victims in about a week, turning up dead in unusual circumstances. Could today's victim also have been suffocated?"

"It's possible. I won't know for sure until the autopsy."

"Doctor, have those special tests you mentioned on the first victim come back?"

"Not all of them, Rex. I had to send some samples to a state forensic crime laboratory outside Quai Natia."

The Black Bird Murders

"Please follow-up with the lab. And Eli, pay a visit to Mr. Pitcairn's widow. Try to find a connection to our first victim."

As he puts on his aviators and leaves the building, the lieutenant can feel it in his bones that this killing spree is not over.

9

Minutes later, Detective Stiles is en route to see Mrs.
Pitcairn. He finally arrives at her apartment, which has a distinctive
hexagon design on the front door. After ringing the doorbell, he waits
a short while.

"Hello, who is it?" she asks as she looks through the peephole.

"Mrs. Maya Pitcairn, I am Detective Stiles of the Quai Natia
Police Department. I am here to see you about your husband Matt.
May I please come in?"

He shows her his badge before she opens the door.

"Good morning, Detective," she says with a concerned look.
"Please come in."

The petite widow with dirty blonde hair welcomes him inside as
they sit down in the living room.

"There is no easy way to put this, ma'am. We just found a person
named Matt Pitcairn murdered at the Just Win! tavern."

Stiles presents to her Mr. Pitcairn's driver's license in a plastic
bag. A digital photo of the body at the bar is also displayed.

She immediately recognizes her husband's identification and
the picture of him on the pool table. Suddenly, unable to believe what
she just heard, she is overcome with emotion and her body collapses
on the sofa.

The detective consoles her, saying, "I am very sorry for your
terrible loss, Mrs. Pitcairn."

She is uncontrollably weeping as she takes shallow breaths. Detective Stiles gives her a tissue from the coffee table. After a minute or so, she is trying to calm herself down.

"I want to see him! Where is his body?"

"Ma'am, I will be happy to tell you in a few minutes. But first, do you know who would want to hurt your husband?"

"He was a decent man, with no real enemies that I can think of. How can this appalling event happen?"

"Various people are at the Just Win! tavern looking for clues now. Your deceased husband was discovered tied down to a pool table at the pub. Did he play pool there often?"

She takes a moment to catch her breath and dry her face.

"Oh, he loved to play billiards with the boys at that place. And he was quite skillful."

"So would you say he was a regular there?"

"That bar was a favorite haunt of his. We actually met there."

"Okay. Mrs. Pitcairn, can you tell me when you last saw your husband?"

"Last night, around 7 p.m. He was going back to his office to work so we could enjoy the weekend. Matt called me around 11 p.m. and said he would probably work through the night and just sleep on the couch there."

"Did he do that a lot, ma'am?"

"Not really. But a major presentation was planned for Monday."

"I see. Do you know if anyone was with your husband at the office?"

"No. He told me he was working alone. He may have called some colleagues, but I'm not sure."

"Can you tell me what car he drove?"

"Yes. It is a blue Saab sedan."

"Thank you. We came upon a lapel pin with the image of a black bird on your husband's shirt. Did he have a special interest in birds, Mrs. Pitcairn?"

"Birds? I know nothing about that, Detective. And I can't remember the last time he wore a lapel pin."

"Of note, we found the same type of pin on the murder victim at the golf course last week."

"That's very strange. What can it mean? I don't understand."

"We are still looking into different possibilities, ma'am."

"Detective Stiles, do you know how my husband died? Was it painful?"

"The medical examiner has not reached a conclusion yet. But I don't think he suffered."

"How do you know?"

"We are still straightening out the details, but there were no major bruises or injuries to the outside of his body. Forgive me for asking, but did your husband drink much alcohol or was he addicted to any drugs?"

"Oh, heavens no! Matt was in pretty good health, and he would only have a few beers for the occasion. Only rarely did he smoke."

"That's good to hear. Also, I was wondering if he was having any problems at work or with debts or gambling?"

"For the last year, Matt has been working in the marketing department for the local soccer team. He was excited about our future. And we have been doing okay with money."

She covers her mouth and mildly coughs into her hand.

"Is there something else you wanted to say, Mrs. Pitcairn?"

"I didn't want to mention it, but Matt did some gambling off and on, mostly on football and baseball games."

"Did he ever lose more than he could afford to?"

"Sometimes. He just liked the excitement of it all. I had to put limits on his betting after a while."

"When you did so, did he harbor any resentment towards you? Or did he ever hurt you?"

"Oh, he shouted at times. And once or twice, he slapped me -- nothing serious. Not to the point I had to report him or press charges."

"Nonetheless, I am sorry he assaulted you, ma'am. As far as you know, did he have any outstanding debts due to his gambling?"

"No. We recently took care of that."

There is silence for a few seconds.

"On a different note, Mrs. Pitcairn, what about family? Are his parents doing well? And does he have brothers or sisters?"

"His brother Murray lives in D.C., born to a different father. And his mother Alicia has a house in Arizona. I believe his dad was killed in a car accident."

"All right. I would appreciate their phone numbers if you have them."

"Of course. I will get those for you."

She picks up her cell phone, looks up some numbers, and gives them to the detective.

"You've been very patient, ma'am, and I thank you. But I will ask you one more time: Have you any idea of anyone who might want to harm your husband?"

Sadly, she says, "I honestly can't think of anyone. Detective, can you give me any reason why someone would kill my husband and then tie him down? What did he do to deserve that?"

"Like I said, we are looking into various possibilities. No one should die like that, but rest assured that I will keep you abreast of any new information."

Detective Stiles writes down something on the back of his card.

"Here is my card, Mrs. Pitcairn. I wrote down the name of the hospital where your husband's body was taken to. Just ask for Dr. Paris."

Despondent and mildly discouraged, she shakes Stiles' hand as he leaves and she prepares to drive to the hospital.

10

At the precinct, awaiting the final postmortem report on the first victim Mr. Jackson Moreau, Lt. Rhombus carefully reviews the police reports and criminal records involving both recent murder victims. He finds some traffic violations, but neither had ever been arrested for a crime or misdemeanor. After a few hours, he decides to go home for a short break.

Once there, he relaxes on the black leather couch as he flips through one of the aviation magazines that litter his coffee table. But he is forced to accept the fact that the two recent murders have disrupted a long period of calm in Quai Natia.

As he was growing up, Rex Rhombus' favorite television programs were *Hawaii Five-O* reruns and *Hill Street Blues*, as his father worked in law enforcement. At the University of Washington at Tacoma in 1989, he could not decide between the fields of criminal justice and forensic science. He ended up taking both.

His mother, who had a career as a research chemist, was afflicted with lupus in 1990. Her health rapidly deteriorated to the point at which she was no longer able to do her job. In 1991, his father was injured during a shoot-out while he was on duty. His full recovery would take more than half a year.

To make ends meet, Rex decided to drop out of the university and enter the Seattle Police Academy in 1992. After graduating from the academy, he chose to join the nearby Olympia Police Department. Eventually, he advanced to become the lead lieutenant of the detective unit in 2001.

On many occasions, the opportunity to become captain presented itself. However, he has always felt most satisfied when overseeing good detective work in crime investigations. The administrative duties required in the position of captain are not his cup of tea.

In Olympia, Lt. Rhombus married his wife Isla in 1993. They raised two children, Crawford and Terry, who still live in Washington. Rhombus was told of an opening in the lieutenant position to supervise the Quai Natia homicide unit in 2013. Soon after, he and his wife decided to move to the California town near the coast.

The lieutenant's respite at his home is interrupted by his buzzing cell phone.

"What do you have for me, Danica?"

"Rex, I will soon be starting the autopsy on Matt Pitcairn. But I now have all the lab results on our first victim, including some specialized fluid tests. As you may recall, I found evidence of asphyxiation on the postmortem."

"Yes, I remember. Did you find out how he was suffocated?"

"I can now say that a special test called alveolar fluid analysis demonstrates very high nitrogen levels and very low oxygen levels."

"What do those findings mean, Doctor?"

"They prove unequivocally that Jackson Moreau died of pure nitrogen gas asphyxiation. Someone forced him to breathe in pure nitrogen, which killed him within a few minutes."

"That is intriguing. How does the nitrogen harm someone? Doesn't air have nitrogen?"

"Yes it does. As you know, air is normally 78% nitrogen and 21% oxygen, with negligible amounts of other gases. But if one breathes in almost pure nitrogen instead of air, the nitrogen displaces the oxygen in the airways and blood, rapidly dropping the oxygen levels."

"Is that similar to carbon monoxide poisoning?"

"The manner of death is different with that gas. Carbon monoxide combines with normal hemoglobin in our blood to decrease its oxygen-carrying ability."

"So, they are both deadly gases. But can we tell those two apart in your tests?"

"Yes. Both gases can dangerously lower your blood oxygen levels. But the high nitrogen level in the alveolar fluid combined with normal carbon monoxide levels in the blood point to nitrogen gas asphyxiation."

"Good work, Doctor. Is that alveolar fluid test for nitrogen levels the only one that detects this cause of death?"

"Not the only one. Other laboratories have also measured nitrogen levels in the heart or inferior vena cava, a large vein in the abdomen."

"Once again, you have enlightened me, Danica. I have not had a case involving this cause of death. Is it rare?"

"You can definitely say that. Less than a hundred deaths due to accidental pure nitrogen gas inhalation occurred in the U.S. in a recent 10-year period. Suicides using this method have also been reported throughout the world."

"What about homicides?"

"To my knowledge, this instance is the first I know of."

"Fascinating, Doctor. Do you think you will be able to confirm this cause of death for our second victim as well?"

"Possibly. After the general autopsy, I will order the special tests, which should come back in several days."

"Danica, if nitrogen-induced asphyxiation killed our first victim, that begs the question: Why did he have a bruise in the back of the head?"

"My guess is that the assailant first knocked him out so that pure nitrogen could be easily administered as the coup de grâce. Less likely, the victim could have fallen on the back of his head after dying from nitrogen asphyxiation."

"Those are both reasonable explanations. Let's talk again after you are finished with our second victim. And I have obtained the court order to keep the autopsy results and cause of death nonpublic until further notice."

"Understood. I'll keep you informed, Rex."

After he hangs up, Lt. Rhombus rings Detective Stiles. "Eli, our top-notch forensic pathologist has concluded that the first murder victim succumbed to pure nitrogen gas asphyxiation."

"Wow. I have not heard of that."

"Neither have I, until today. How was your visit with Mrs. Maya Pitcairn, our second victim's widow?"

"R-double, she is the last known person to have seen him alive."

"Would you say she is a suspect, Eli?"

"She is a petite lady who appears genuinely saddened by his death, so I don't think so. Incidently, I have been told that the victim's car was found intact at his office."

"So he must have been abducted from his workplace. Did his widow give you any information that links Mr. Pitcairn to our first victim?"

"Unfortunately, no. He has a brother in Washington, D.C., and a mother in Arizona. His father was killed in some type of car accident."

"I will note that, Detective. For now, let me give you the number of Mrs. Astrid Moreau, the mother of our first murder victim. Please pay her a visit in Green Springs."

"I'll drive down there tomorrow, Rex. Anything else?"

"Yes. Do not tell anyone about the C.O.D. for the time being."

"Got it. Stiles out."

11

Jackson Moreau's Jeep Renegade is discovered by the police near the Olympic Torch Golf Links. The golf course is on the way from Moreau's home to his gym. Lt. Rhombus calls The Fitness Zone and finds that the victim never checked in on the morning he was murdered. Hence, his killer must have kidnapped him on his way there.

Rhombus hypothesizes that the assailant managed to capture Moreau, murder him, use the golf cart to move his body to the bunker, and then bury the body there, all in the span of a few hours. He concludes that the murderer must possess both strength and stamina, unless there is more than one culprit.

But many questions remain unanswered about the two recent murders. Why was the rare method of nitrogen gas asphyxiation used to murder the first, and possibly the second, victim? What meaning does the black bird lapel pin hold? And why were both murder scenes so outlandish?

To gain another perspective, the lieutenant gives a jingle to his long-time friend from the police academy. She graduated the same year as him and is now a seasoned lieutenant at the Esplanade Police Department about 250 miles away.

"Rex!" she exclaims. "I was just thinking of you. And the time we spent on that vacation in New Orleans during Mardi Gras."

The two had been an item in the past, after they graduated from the police academy. Their romance was short-lived, but their lifelong friendship has stood the test of time.

"How's my favorite Southern California crime-fighter? That time in the Big Easy seems not too long ago."

"You're quite the quipster, aren't you? You know it's been over 25 years since we went to New Orleans. But on a serious note, how have you been managing since we last talked?"

He is reminded of a somber time several months ago.

"Taking it day by day, Bianca. You can probably imagine."

Lt. Bianca Durso witnessed the sudden death of Rhombus' wife last September. Isla Rhombus, a vivacious and limber occupational therapist, was wall climbing with her the day after Labor Day when she experienced a sudden cardiac arrest. Doctors diagnosed the rare Brugada syndrome afterwards, but it was too late.

The Quai Natia lieutenant still feels the pain. But he wants to change the subject.

"Is Joss, your personal financial advisor, doing well?"

"Very. But you know he advises his many clients too, right?"

"I am just joking. He is the only Marine I know who now tells people how to invest their money."

"He enjoys it, Rex. And people aren't throwing grenades or shooting at him anymore, so that makes me happy."

"You know I am very proud of your husband, Bianca. Oh, is he still flying his single-engine aircraft to places unknown?"

"That Cessna is like a mistress to him sometimes," she kids. "And when we go on the occasional jaunt, you can see the gleam in his eyes."

"But not as bright as the gleam when he sees you, I take it."

"Not yet! But enough about me. Let me guess – you are calling about the so-called Black Bird Murders?"

"I guess the cat's out of the bag. Who spilled the beans?"

"Your lovely medical examiner Danica, of course. When are you two going to give it a go?" she asks in jest.

"Not anytime soon, I gather. It would get weird at the department, you know. Plus she may be seeing someone."

"I am just giving you a hard time. You know I have tremendous respect for your judgment and reputation. But back to your investigation."

"Have you seen anything like this, Bianca? It seems as if the killer is giving us some message with the lapel pins planted on the bodies. And what do you think about the black-colored birds?"

"Danica sent me images of those two pins. She said that a local expert identified the birds as possibly crows, not ravens or blackbirds. I was just looking into it, and the crow can symbolize 'the other world' and mysticism. Furthermore, the crow is usually not a good omen, unlike the raven or blackbird."

"Do you have any thoughts on how a crow could help us find the perpetrator?"

"The killer may just be marking his actions with a symbol often associated with death. These lapel pins may be his way of getting attention. Do you have any theories, Rex?"

"I have considered what you just suggested. But has anything else come across your brilliant mind?"

"Well, we know that placing the lapel pins on the victims is not necessary in committing the murders – doing so actually slows down the murderer's getaway. So these black bird lapel pins are likely the killer's signature. They are not part of his modus operandi."

"I agree. By the way, did Danica tell you about the cause of death for the first victim?"

"She was still waiting on some tests when we last talked."

"Those test results came in, and she says the C.O.D. is now clear: a little-used method called pure nitrogen gas asphyxiation."

"Believe it or not, I have heard of that but have never seen a case of it."

"Danica tells me this is the first homicide she knows of that involves this technique. Bianca, we are keeping the information regarding the cause of death confidential for now. And if you are available, I would appreciate your help on these head-scratching crimes, when the time comes."

"Anytime and anywhere, Rex, if I am able. Recently, it has been quiet in my neck of the woods."

"And let's have a friendly dinner soon -- on me."

"How can I turn down that offer?"

"I am sure we'll be talking again in the near future. So long for now."

"Ciao."

12

In his pearl white Mustang, Detective Stiles drives along the winding road down the coast to Green Springs. About an hour later, he makes a turn and finds Mrs. Moreau's modest one-story red and light blue house.

Surveying the immediate area, he parks his Mustang in the driveway. Once at the front door, he rings the doorbell. The creaky door opens and a bespectacled middle-aged woman with dark brown hair emerges. She is wearing an apricot sweater with blue jeans.

"Mrs. Astrid Moreau, I presume. I am Detective Stiles from the Quai Natia Police Department. We talked briefly on the phone earlier."

"Yes, I remember. Please excuse the mess in the house. I haven't done much cleaning recently."

"That is quite all right," says Stiles as she welcomes him in.

"What can I do for you, Detective?"

"First of all, I want to express my sincere condolences for your son's death, ma'am. I am sure it is very hard to lose one's child."

"I appreciate that," she says with a downhearted tone. "Jackson was always a responsible husband and father. I hope his wife Hanna is keeping it together. Once my wrist is better, I plan to visit her again next week."

"Oh, did you have a recent injury or fall?"

"If you must know, I fell several weeks ago, and I fractured my wrist when I tried to break my fall. I'm recovering from wrist surgery, but I accidentally banged the same wrist on a counter yesterday."

She grimaces as she sits down and reaches for a glass of water.

"I hope it is not too painful, Mrs. Moreau. If I may, I would first like to ask about your son. Do you know of any recent problems in his personal life, for example?"

"Not really. The last few times I talked to him, he said everything was hunky-dory. And his marriage had been fine."

"His wife tells us that he was well-liked. Was he always popular growing up?"

"It was a long time ago, but he was in fact quite obstreperous as a child. He always had to have his way. In middle school, Jackson was even involved in a few brawls."

"That's interesting. Had he had any heated arguments or fistfights recently?"

"It's funny, but ever since he started dating girls in high school, he became more mellow. To my knowledge, he has never laid a hand on my daughter-in-law Hanna."

"I am very glad to hear that. Let me now ask about your husband Cliff. We were told by Hanna that he died of melanoma about four years ago."

"Yes, that's right. Cliff loved to go cycling when he could, but that sun exposure probably did him in."

"Sorry about your husband's death, Mrs. Moreau. Is there anything else I should know about him? Did Jackson resemble him?"

For a few seconds, she looks up and to her right at a photograph of her husband. Then, she lets out a sigh.

"What is it, ma'am?"

"Well, it has nothing to do with the melanoma."

"Please tell me. It might help."

"Well, we were going to tell Jackson, but now it's too late."

"Tell him what, Mrs. Moreau?"

"That my husband was not his biological father."

"Really? How do you mean?"

The widow hesitates for several moments before slowly walking over to the fireplace mantle. She shows Detective Stiles the portrait of a tanned man with medium brown hair and a narrow face.

"We had our first child Emma without any difficulty. She has turned out to be a lovely woman, and we are blessed for that."

"And how about your son?"

"A few years after Emma was born, we tried to have another child, but it was not so easy. The reason was Cliff's sperm count became extremely low."

"I see. So what did you end up doing?"

"Cliff tried all these fertility treatments but to no avail. Adoption was not what we wanted, so that narrowed down our options."

"What are you trying to say, Mrs. Moreau?"

"Do you know about the Constellation Fertility Center in Cinnamon Meadows?"

"I can't say that I do."

"Well, it is quite a facility. My husband and I went there to discuss the remaining possibilities -- various fertility procedures I could go through."

"In the end, what did you both decide, ma'am?"

"After a lot of discussion, we went with something called intrauterine insemination using donor sperm. It seemed to have the best success rate for our situation."

"So let me get this straight. Are you saying that your son Jackson was born after donor sperm was implanted in you?"

"That's right, sir. Cliff and I went through the donor profiles and found the man who was most similar to Cliff with regards to physical, intellectual, and personality characteristics."

"I get it. To try to ensure that your child would turn out like your husband and you."

"Precisely. And Jackson did. He was never told of his true biological father. Cliff and I agreed that someday, the truth would be revealed to our son, but that day never came."

She sheds a tear.

"Ma'am, does anyone know about your son's true biological father? Do you?"

"I wish I did. But the people at CFC keep the identity of the donor confidential, not even telling me, the recipient. It was all well and good, though, because Jackson was born without problems and grew up to become a fine gentleman. But now he's gone."

Her sobbing becomes more pronounced. Comforting Mrs. Moreau, Detective Stiles reassures her that he and his team will find out who is responsible for taking her son away from her.

"Would it be okay if I talked to the people at the fertility center about your son and the sperm donor?"

"You have been such a pleasant and courteous man, and I thank you. If you feel that speaking with the people at the center can help you find my son's killer, you have my full consent."

"I appreciate it. I would also like to ask you if you can think of anyone who would want to hurt your son."

After reflecting for a few moments, she says, "No, I really can't."

"On another note, did your son mention any financial problems or difficulties at work recently?"

"Nothing like that, sir. Oh, I miss him already," she says as she snivels.

"I have one final question, ma'am. Do you or did your son know a person named Matt Pitcairn?"

The detective shows her a digital photo of the second murder victim.

After pondering for a short while, she says, "Matt Pitcairn? I don't recall that name. And I don't recognize the man in the photo. Who is he?"

"He was found murdered a few days ago, with a black bird lapel pin attached to his shirt -- just like your son."

"Oh my! But I don't get it. How is he connected to my Jackson, Detective?"

"That is one thing we are trying to find out, ma'am. Well, I am grateful for your time today, Mrs. Moreau. Here is my card. And I hope your wrist heals quickly."

Detective Stiles briefly hugs her before seeing himself out.

Once he reaches his car, he takes out his cell.

"R-double, I just met our first victim's mother Mrs. Astrid Moreau. She's a very pleasant lady, and nothing she said clearly links her son with our second victim. However, it seems Jackson Moreau was somewhat of a hothead when he was growing up."

"I am surprised, Eli. We checked his criminal record and it was fairly spotless."

"That's understandable, because Mrs. Moreau said his personality changed in high school. He became more of a lover than a fighter, if you know what I mean."

"Fair enough. And when I spoke with her, his widow did not report any abuse by him."

"There is something else, Rex, regarding Jackson's biological father."

"What of him? Jackson Moreau's widow told me his father Cliff died of melanoma a few years ago."

"That's true. But listen to this: Emma, Jackson's older sister, was born to Cliff and Astrid Moreau. But Cliff became infertile a few years after. The bottom line is Jackson Moreau was born after Astrid Moreau was implanted with donor sperm."

"Intriguing. Where did she go for this procedure?"

"The Constellation Fertility Center in Cinnamon Meadows. Only about 90 minutes from Green Springs."

"Eli, please make the fertility center your next stop, and look into the person who supplied the donor sperm. I will call you when I get a search warrant for any information involving Jackson Moreau and his mother."

"Okay, Rex. If you don't mind, I'll also call Lt. Durso to see if she can tell me more about CFC. She works and lives less than two hours from Cinnamon Meadows."

"That would be fine."

"Please send me the e-warrant as soon as you can. And I hope my visit to Cinnamon Meadows turns out to be fruitful."

"So do I, Detective. Any clue is welcome at this point."

13

Rivulets of sweat flow down the back of her shoulders
and thighs as the blazing sun warms her olive skin.

As she puts one ball in her pocket and the other in her left hand, Bianca Durso looks at her opponent before tossing the tennis ball upward. What follows is a well-placed slice serve that results in an ace.

"That's the game!" she shouts to her adversary on the opposite side of the net. "Now I have you where I want you -- one set apiece and the momentum on my side. Ready for set three?"

"Bring it on, Bianca. It's all even now. And I'm just getting my second wind."

"I saw how you were struggling with my groundstrokes in that last game. I know you better than you think!"

The two battle evenly in the third and final set. She plays with finesse and well-placed shots, while he executes his power game with big serves and frequent approach shots setting him up at the net.

The score is now five games to four in her favor after he double-faults on his serve. Now she could win the set and match by holding her own serve. She is trying to stay as cool as possible on this humid day in her microfiber crimson red top with white shorts.

Her first serve is smashed back to her near the baseline, with her barely getting a swing at the ball. She dictates the next three points, though, including two surprise drop shots that just clear the net.

In her first match point with the score 40-15, Durso decides to play the net game herself. It works to perfection. She swings her racket and hits a flat serve straight at the body of her opponent.

He is unprepared, only barely able to get his racket on the ball, which just clears the net. She quickly sprints toward the net and drives the ball down the line, out of his reach. Arms raised high, she has defeated her stronger opponent.

"An invigorating match, my lady. I believe I now owe you a relaxing massage. Can I meet you in the lounge in about 20 minutes?"

"How forward of you, sir. I am a married woman. But I am not against trying something for the first time."

She brushes his arm and then gestures the come hither motion with her index finger.

Two staff members overhearing the conversation at the tennis club smile as the two walk past them toward the locker rooms.

"That lady is quite the athlete, as well as a looker. But does she always flirt with the other members like that, her being married and all?"

"Oh, you mean Mrs. Durso. And by the way, that is Mr. Durso along with her!"

In the locker room, Bianca Durso receives a call.

"How good to hear from you, Eli."

"Likewise, Lt. Durso. How have you been? Are you still playing tennis?"

"Please, call me Bianca. Yes, I actually just defeated my husband in a match. You know I played on the college tennis team, don't you?"

"That I did not, but I have heard rumors about your athleticism. While you were competing on the courts, I was probably in the computer lab or swimming pool during college."

"I am well aware of your computer skills, Eli. But I am glad you decided on a career in criminal justice instead. Otherwise, I would have never gotten to know you."

"I think it has turned out well for both of us, Bianca."

"Agreed. But I am sure you didn't call me just to congratulate me on my victory."

"You read my mind."

"Let me guess. You need some help on the recent mysterious murders?"

"Yes, if you can. Has Rex or Danica told you about the two crimes?"

"At the golf course and bar as I recall."

"That's right. I am working on a lead that may prove to be a big deal, or not. Have you heard of the Constellation Fertility Center in Cinnamon Meadows?"

"I certainly have. It is located less than two hours from my office. And a good reputation it maintains, as far as I am aware."

"That is good to know. I am on my way there to look into one of the donors. It turns out the recent murder victim at the Olympic Torch golf course was born from donor sperm."

"Now that's not something you hear every day. Do you care to tell me what you are suspecting?"

"At this point, I am just trying to determine if the murder victim Jackson Moreau ever met this sperm donor. But I realize that this biological connection between them may just turn out to be a red herring."

"I see. Did you already call the facility?"

"Yes, I did. And Rex is getting an electronic warrant so I can review any of their records involving him."

"So what can I do for you?"

"If you would, please contact the medical director and ask him to give me his fullest cooperation."

"I would be glad to, Eli. Hmm."

She pauses for a moment.

"Hello. Are you still there, Bianca?"

"Eli, if I remember correctly, the Constellation Fertility Center was targeted in a computer hacking operation or scheme a few months ago. You might want to look into it."

"I definitely will. Thank you so much. Bye now."

14

Making good time on the highway toward the town of
Cinnamon Meadows, Detective Stiles finally takes the off-ramp and
drives a few more blocks. He arrives at the entrance to the
Constellation Fertility Center, a four-story cubic structure with a
diagonal orange stripe as its company logo.

"Dr. Normando Sanchez is expecting me," says the detective to
the receptionist at the lobby.

He signs in, and a few minutes later, a clean-shaven silver-
haired man in a white lab coat cordially greets him.

"I assume you are Detective Stiles."

"How do you do, Doctor?"

"Very well, thank you. I suspect you found our facility without
difficulty. Let's go to my office, shall we?"

Dr. Sanchez, at least three inches shorter than the detective,
walks with a mild limp. They pass through two short nondescript
corridors before taking the lift to the second floor.

"Do all your clients and donors go to this building, Doctor?"

"That's right. Lessens the overhead, you know."

Reaching his office, the doctor invites the detective to sit down.

"I talked to Lt. Durso, who said I may be of service to you."

Stiles shows his electronic search warrant to the doctor.

"Dr. Sanchez, I wonder if you have a file on Mrs. Astrid Moreau.
With the help of sperm implanted by a doctor in your company, she
gave birth to Jackson Moreau, a recent homicide victim."

"Let me look at my records. The client was Mrs. Astrid Moreau in 1994. What are you investigating, if I may ask?"

"Two recent murders in and near Quai Natia, one of which involves Jackson Moreau."

"Oh yes. I have read about the disturbing killings in your town. I am sorry to hear of Mr. Moreau's death. But how are those murders in any way linked to this center?"

"They may or may not be, but I would like to know about your organization as well as who the sperm donor was."

"Well, we have been up and running for almost 30 years now, offering options for willing women to conceive when there are headwinds in the process."

"Do you test both the prospective mother and her partner?"

"Naturally. A first-class laboratory in this building can determine sperm counts and quality, hormone imbalances, and the like. In addition, various physicians, such as urologists, gynecologists, and endocrinologists work here full-time."

"And what of Jackson Moreau's father Cliff? Why couldn't he help his wife have a second child?"

"When we tested him, the sperm count was quite low, possibly from his years of frequent cycling. And I was told that he eventually died of melanoma."

"Yes, I am aware. Now, can you tell me about the donor whose sperm was implanted into Mrs. Moreau?"

"Jackson Moreau was the product of the sperm of a Winston Banks and the ovum of Astrid Moreau. She was implanted with donor sperm from Banks, and Jackson was born at term nine months later."

"What else can you say about Mr. Banks, Doctor?"

"He was born and raised in Missouri before moving to California in his teens. At his high school in San Jose, he played quarterback. Mr. Banks later obtained a business degree from the University of Santa Clara. Afterwards, he went to work for the financial firm Tannenbaum Enterprises in Monterey."

"Did he donate sperm often, Dr. Sanchez?"

"On the contrary -- my files indicate that he donated sperm on only one occasion to the Constellation Fertility Center."

"Does he have any connection with Mr. Jackson Moreau, other than contributing to his DNA?"

"Not that I am aware of. There is no indication in the file that the two men ever met or knew of each other."

"Thank you. You have been very helpful, Doctor. Also, Lt. Durso mentioned a computer crime that occurred here a few months ago."

"I am glad you mention that. Give me a few minutes please."

15

A couple of minutes later, Dr. Sanchez returns to his office and signals Detective Stiles to follow him. They take the elevator up to the top level.

Entering a spacious and cool room filled with racks of computer servers, cables, computers, and monitors, the doctor says, "Let me first introduce you to my main computer savants, Katy and Duncan, who are hard at work."

"Hello, Dr. Sanchez. Who is this?" asks Katy, a slim 30-something casually dressed in neat jeans and a cerulean blue blouse.

"This is Detective Stiles from the Quai Natia Police Department."

Both computer scientists introduce themselves, with Katy clearly infatuated.

"Good afternoon. Glad to meet both of you. Can you tell me about the recent breach into your computer security system?"

"Sure, Detective," answers Duncan, Katy's colleague with the angular physique. "About three months ago, someone hacked into our system and gained access to an undetermined amount of data. It is unclear which information was exposed, but we were able to fix the problem within a day or two."

"I totally understand. Do you suspect that the hacker was a white, black, or grey hat?"

Katy says, "I am impressed! It looks like you know your way around computers, Detective."

"I took some classes in college," says Stiles with a grin. "Now, about the hacker."

"The culprit was not a white hat, since we were not testing our system at the time. If I had to guess, I would favor a black hat hacker, since this person has not contacted us since the break-in."

"Can you tell me anything else?"

Duncan adds, "The question is what the accessed information was used for. I doubt it was just some script kiddie playing around."

"So can I assume your computer network has been running without problems since then?"

"That's right, Detective. I am surprised you came here just to hear about this resolved cybercrime," says Katy.

"Actually, I am investigating some murders, and I was told of the security problem in the course of my investigation."

"Wow! Murders. As in homicides?" asks a very interested Katy.

"You got it. But I can't discuss them any further at this point. Sorry."

"Gotcha. But you can come back any time, Detective."

"You can call me Eli."

"I hope you found your time here useful, Eli."

"Definitely. If another breach occurs, please let me know."

At that point, Katy gets up from her chair and shakes the detective's hand. After the handshake, Stiles realizes that she has left a small piece of paper with a telephone number in his palm. They smile at each other as he walks out the door with Dr. Sanchez.

16

Diana dons her black and purple wetsuit on this somewhat chilly Friday morning. It is only about three weeks away from the competition, and this lissome strawberry blonde is about to start her morning swim in Biscay Bay, two miles south of Quai Natia.

Her training partner, Sabrina, is running on the beach nearby. Both are preparing for the 10th annual Pacific Warriors Olympic Triathlon to be held down the coast in the hamlet of Anchor Beach.

After adjusting her goggles, Diana inhales deeply before diving into the water. She is an excellent swimmer, but she is mindful of the danger of open water. The bay is serene on this day, and she easily reaches the large navigation buoy situated about 300 yards from the beach.

Taking a break by holding on to the red buoy, she could see Sabrina stretching on the sand after completing her five-mile run. The spring zephyr blows gently on their faces.

Sabrina, an auburn-haired native of Quai Natia, waves at her friend, who yells, "I will head back there in a minute!"

Ready to return to shore, Diana begins to circle the large buoy as she usually does before swimming back to the beach. But as she reaches the side of the structure facing away from shore, she makes a ghastly discovery. A blond man, eyes closed and body not moving, is seen tied down to the buoy. He is wearing a wet grey T-shirt and soaked dark blue khakis.

Diana is both shocked and frightened, but she musters up the courage to touch and then shake the body. Seeing no response, she feels for a pulse in the neck and can't get one. His body is very cold. Immediately, she swims back to the beach.

Finally reaching land, she catches her breath with her heart racing and runs to her friend.

"A dead body! Tied to the red buoy! I think I'm going to be sick."

"Take some deep breaths and count to ten," Sabrina says, clearly apprehensive.

"Okay, that's a little better," utters Diana nervously. "There is a man out there tied with some rope to the large buoy. He is not moving and I couldn't feel a pulse. He appears to be dead!"

Processing what she just heard, Sabrina now realizes the gravity of the matter.

"Stay right here, sweetie. I'll call for help."

About 15 minutes after she calls 911, a police siren could be heard as the black and white comes into view. As he reaches Biscay Bay and jumps out of his car, the officer sees the two young women waving to him. He comes to their aid as both wait in their sweatsuits, comforting each other.

"Good morning, ladies. Did one of you report finding a dead body?" asks Officer Lee.

"Yes, Officer. Tied to that large red buoy about 300 yards away," says a spooked Diana, pointing toward the ocean. "I don't know how he got there."

"Do either of you recognize who he is?"

"All I saw was a blond man wearing khakis and a T-shirt, and he was not moving and had no pulse. Some rope was used to tie him to the far side of the buoy."

"I'll get the Coast Guard here ASAP. Are you sure he's dead?"

"Pretty sure. I am a nursing student in Quai Natia."

"That's good to know. Are either of you hurt? Do you need a paramedic?"

"We'll be fine, sir. Both of us are still trying to recover from the shock of it all. One minute, we're training for the upcoming triathlon. And the next thing you know, we're talking about a dead body fastened onto a navigation buoy!"

"I can imagine how you feel. That's definitely not something you see every day."

More than half an hour later, a U.S. Coast Guard rescue boat appears in the bay and its men spot the wet lifeless body. The boat slows down near the red navigation buoy and a couple of Guardsmen dive in.

Someone takes photographs before the ropes are untied, after which the body is pulled into the vessel. No signs of life are detected by a crewmember.

"This situation is really eerie," says one of the men. "I've never seen anything quite like this."

"Can you tell if any items were stolen, gentlemen?"

"Sir, I don't think so – all his valuables seem to be on him."

"Do you notice any injuries or a gunshot wound?" asks the commander of the vessel.

"That's a negative on both, sir. I see no lacerations or other indications of trauma on the body. But someone clearly tied him to the red buoy with some rope, possibly after he was killed."

"Can you tell what type of knots were used?"

"As far as I can see, nothing fancy. We took some photos before untying the rope – it looks like a bunch of simple square knots. I don't even see anything secure like a bow line knot."

The commander remarks, "It is a wonder the body didn't come loose off the buoy. I guess our murderer wasn't a Boy Scout. Let's get our victim to the hospital on the double. We might get lucky on determining T.O.D. and C.O.D."

"Aye-aye, sir."

17

Within one hour of being notified of the latest homicide, Dr. Paris goes to the hospital to examine the corpse. The new victim arrives in a body bag and is placed on the autopsy bay. Mr. Carl Zimmerman, date of birth November 22nd 1975. A 44-year-old blue-eyed blond, with a black bird lapel pin attached to his shirt.

The latest in this string of murder victims was an automotive mechanic at a local foreign car repair shop. He had been divorced for three years, with his ex-wife living in Utah now with their daughter. The next of kin are his parents in Missouri, along with a brother in Arkansas and sister also in Missouri.

The decedent is dressed in damp clothes – a T-shirt and khaki pants. His wristwatch still tells the correct time. After removing the clothes of the victim, the medical examiner sees no gunshot, puncture, or stab wounds. However, occipital blunt force injury is evident.

Hair samples and some residue under the fingernails are removed. There are no signs of the body being submerged for an extended period of time.

Routine blood and urine samples are collected before Dr. Paris makes a meticulous typical large Y-shaped incision to begin the internal body examination. About three hours later, the fastidious forensic pathologist completes the autopsy and sends off fluids and tissue for special analysis.

The Black Bird Murders

At European Car Care, Lt. Rhombus is interviewing Mr. Polar, the last person at the shop to see Mr. Zimmerman alive the day before.

"After work, we went to a local tavern to watch the game and have a beer. Then he had to leave."

"When was that, sir?"

"I would say he left the place around 6:30 p.m., give or take 15 minutes."

"Do you recall how many drinks Mr. Zimmerman had?"

"Only one. He said he would be meeting his girlfriend later."

"I see. Please give me her name and phone number if you would."

"Her name is Cristina Braga, but I don't know her number."

Others at European Car Care tell the lieutenant that Zimmerman appeared to be his usual self yesterday, and he didn't seem troubled or anxious.

Lt. Rhombus then calls Miss Braga after tracking down her phone. She informs the lieutenant that she was supposed to see Mr. Zimmerman at her place around 7:30 p.m. last night, but he never showed.

At Rhombus' behest, Detective Novo goes to Zimmerman's condominium. The victim's car is found locked in the assigned parking spot. Novo is able to pick the lock of Mr. Zimmerman's condo's front door, and he enters the dwelling. He finds everything in place, with no indications of a struggle.

Reynold Novo is the newest addition to the Quai Natia police homicide unit. Burly but still fast on his feet, he joined the team only about seven months ago. While playing some club rugby in mid-February, he tore his right lateral meniscus and required arthroscopic surgical repair. He estimates his knee to be about 70-80% normal at this time.

Novo grew up in the San Joaquin Valley and graduated from the California State University at Fresno. The first in his family to attain a college degree, he was in the top 15% of his criminology program. He excelled at the police academy in the city of Fresno.

A little over 24 hours after Mr. Zimmerman's body was discovered, Lt. Rhombus is sitting at Dr. Paris' office.

"Doctor, I appreciate you making time for the autopsy so quickly."

"You're welcome, Rex. Before I discuss Mr. Zimmerman, I want to give you the special test results on our second murder victim. I can now verify that Matt Pitcairn was also killed by asphyxiation due to forced exposure to pure nitrogen gas."

"That's remarkable. We now have a serial killer on our hands with a preferred M.O. And a rare one at that."

"I am as intrigued as you because of how incredibly uncommon this method is used in homicides."

"Didn't you say last time that Jackson Moreau's death may have been the first known homicide due to nitrogen-induced asphyxiation?"

"As far as I know. And now we have two confirmed cases."

"But bear in mind – this information is only useful if it helps us find the killer. So tell me, Doctor: Who has access to pure nitrogen gas?"

"Unfortunately, many people. It is used for making various products in the chemical industry, such as food preservatives, fertilizers, and explosives. This substance is also important in the manufacture of stainless steel, electronics, and pharmaceuticals."

"Does that mean only someone working in these industries can get it?"

"Not really. You can buy it in various stores by the canister or tank, or one can just purchase it online with a credit card."

"Even so, I will instruct Detective Novo to contact local hardware and general supply stores about recent sales of pure nitrogen gas. Something important might turn up."

"Good thinking, Rex. Chemical supply stores would also be a good source."

"Those will be checked as well. So Danica, what do you have on our third victim? Have you determined when he was killed?"

"Because the body was submerged for some period of time, the time of death is harder to ascertain. But I would estimate Mr. Zimmerman was murdered either Thursday evening or in the early morning hours of Friday."

"Do you believe he was drowned?"

"Actually, this was a rare instance of 'dry drowning,' Rex."

"I am only somewhat familiar with that term. Please explain."

"Sure. Usually, when someone drowns, the lungs fill up with water and a special substance called lung surfactant is destroyed. This surfactant lines the surface of the alveoli, or air sacs."

"And what is different in our third victim?"

"His lung surfactant was normal. And the most likely reason is when he was submerged, his vocal cords closed up and blocked the water from entering the airways in his lungs."

"Are you saying he didn't drown?"

"Not in the traditional sense. But the vocal cord spasm deprived him of oxygen nonetheless, causing death by asphyxiation."

"I understand someone can die like this during waterboarding."

"As it happens, I think you would be correct, Rex. Do you have any experience with that?"

"That is a topic for another day, Doctor. But I am curious. Could he have been killed before being submerged in the water?"

"Much to my dismay, there is no way to know based on the general autopsy. He may have been suffocated before being submerged, or he was drowned in the bay and laryngospasm blocked the inflow of water and air into his lungs. Either way, the loss of oxygen eventually caused respiratory depression followed by death."

"It appears that we can't distinguish the two possibilities quite yet. Did the postmortem demonstrate anything else?"

"As in our first two victims, I detected a small occipital bruise, along with widespread signs of asphyxiation, including swelling and venous congestion in his brain, lungs, liver, and heart."

"And is suffocation with pure nitrogen gas still a possibility?"

"Definitely. I won't be able to confirm that until the special alveolar fluid test results come back. But my guess is he was killed on land, after which his body was pulled underwater by the perpetrator as he swam to the navigation buoy. This conjecture best fits the modus operandi shown so far by the Black Bird Killer."

The lieutenant reviews what they know so far.

"We have two or probably three deaths due to pure nitrogen gas asphyxiation, with a small- to medium-sized head bruise on each body. All corpses were discovered at unusual crime scenes. The three male victims between ages 24 and 44 were in apparently good health otherwise. Robbery was not the motive. And finally, a distinctive lapel pin was found on each one."

"That pretty much summarizes it, Rex. I already called this victim's parents in Missouri to identify his body. They were overwhelmed to hear the terrible news, but they agreed to fly here in a day or so."

"Very good, Danica. The unknown menace continues to plague our fine town. And we still lack a good suspect."

"Given the lack of fingerprints, DNA, or murder weapons at the crime scenes, I hope we catch a break when you look into those stores for nitrogen gas buyers."

"My thoughts exactly, Doctor."

"And do we have any eyewitnesses who have come forward so far?"

"No one yet. At this point, I'm afraid we will just have to play the hand that we've been dealt."

18

Slowly making their way through the hospital, the elderly husband and wife are directed to the morgue. The medical examiner is told of their arrival and meets them there.

"You must be Mr. and Mrs. Zimmerman. I am Dr. Paris. My deepest condolences for both of you. Do you need a minute?"

"No. That's okay, Doctor. Please show us our son."

Both are aquiver with anticipation as the curtain is pulled to the side, revealing the body of Carl Zimmerman. His parents immediately recognize their son. Mrs. Zimmerman's heart drops, while her husband clearly mourns but tries to hide his emotions.

Dr. Paris only briefly talks with them before they insist on leaving. The doctor understands and gets them to sign the necessary papers.

Once they have departed, the doctor gets the chance to call her good friend from college who now lives in Huntington Beach.

"Katana, is that you?"

"Danica Paris! It's been a while. Have you started surfing yet?"

"Oh, you and your water sports! No, I haven't. But I do see the ocean almost every day."

"How's my favorite medical examiner?"

"Busy with work, and some play. Are you still sailing these days?"

"Yup. My Catalina Capri is still going strong. All 26 feet of her. Is this a friendly call, or do you have a puzzle for me?"

"A little of both, Katana. Would you mind looking over some photos for me?"

"Are they part of an active criminal case you're working on?"

"Why yes! Some serial murders in Quai Natia over the last few weeks."

"That being so, please send them over. I would be glad to give you my input, Doctor."

"That would be fantastic. I will text them to you now."

"So Danica, are you seeing someone special?"

"I had a feeling you couldn't resist bringing that up. As a matter of fact, I am. His name is Rafa – he's a crime analyst at the Quai Natia Police Department."

"Now what did I say about office relationships, Danica?"

"I know, I know. But I only go to the police precinct sporadically, and we've been able to keep it professional when I am there. As far as I can tell, no one else knows."

"Sunshine, I suspect that everyone knows by now."

"I hope you're wrong, Katana, but you may well be right," she says playfully. "How is Russell?"

"He is doing well. Still running and training for his marathons as you probably remember. He has run a total of 23 races now."

"That is very impressive. As for me, it gives me a leg cramp just thinking of running 26 miles."

"Me too! Oh, I just got your pictures. Let me look at them for a little while."

"Take your time."

A minute later, Katana gives her verdict.

"Definitely a lefty. No doubt in my mind. And the person just used square knots, which are not the best. He is clearly not a sailor or a mountain climber, for example."

"I really appreciate it, Katana. I'll tell you what – next time I'm in Huntington Beach, we'll have a fancy dinner, on me. I'll convince Rafa to come with."

"That would be excellent. But before dinner, we'll take you both for a ride on the sailboat."

"Sure. Definitely before the dinner. Incidently, is it big enough to be called a yacht?" Paris asks lightheartedly.

"Not quite. It technically has to be 33 feet or longer to officially be called a yacht."

"Really? I did not know that. Anyway, it was great talking to you. See you real soon!"

"Likewise. And I hope my assessment helps in your investigation."

"It definitely does. Take care, Katana."

After she hangs up, Dr. Paris calls her lieutenant.

"Rex, the Zimmermans from Missouri identified their son this morning. And I talked with a friend of mine from college. I believe I can now say a few things with confidence about the man responsible for the recent homicides."

"Can we be sure it is a man, Danica?"

"Almost 90% sure. Most American serial killers are men -- about 85-90% -- and the physical strength needed to place the bodies where we found them is more likely that of a man."

"That makes perfect sense."

"Also, I am certain he is left-handed. I talked to my friend, Katana Gibbs. She is the civil engineering technician who is also a forensic knot specialist."

"I remember Miss Gibbs. She has been involved in some of our cases in the past."

"You're right. And just now, she looked at photos of the knots of the rope used to tie Carl Zimmerman to the buoy and Matt Pitcairn to the pool table."

"And does she have a conclusion?"

"Yes. She says the knots were tied by a southpaw for sure."

"Very helpful, Danica."

"There is more. She also said the knots used for both victims were not the most secure. Therefore, our perpetrator can't be a sailor or climber, for example."

"All these inferences do help narrow down the list of possible culprits, but do you have anything more specific, Doctor?"

"Not yet, but I noted something odd in my brief encounter with the Zimmermans today."

"Pray tell."

"Well, both parents are dark-haired and greying, while the victim was blond. So they admitted to adopting Carl. That seemed reasonable, but then they said they had two more children of their own after Carl."

"That's unusual. Did you ask them to explain?"

"I intended to, but they were so bereaved at the time and insisted on leaving as soon as possible."

"There may be a perfectly good explanation, but I would call them to clarify."

"I definitely will, Rex. On a side note, I heard Eli took a recent trip."

"You heard correctly. He went to Green Springs followed by Cinnamon Meadows. He is back in Quai Natia now."

"Has he made any progress in the investigation?"

"Perhaps. It turns out the biological father of our first victim was a sperm donor, but Eli hasn't been able to reach this person of interest yet. Also, the fertility center involved was the target of a computer breach a few months ago."

"Interesting. I wonder what it all means?"

"Detective Stiles is following up on these clues as we speak, as the body count rises."

"Understood. As for me, I will try to reach the Zimmermans."

"Keep me informed, Danica."

19

A review of the records at the police station indicates that Carl Zimmerman was divorced three years ago from Sierra Cîrstea. She now lives in Park City, Utah, with their daughter Nina. Lt. Rhombus decides to give the ex-wife a call.

"Can you get that, Ray?" asks the shapely woman as the house phone rings.

"Sure can, Sierra," her boyfriend replies. He asks jokingly, "Should I tell the caller that he or she has reached the Jagger residence?"

"Please don't – this is still my place and we aren't married yet," she says friskily as she leaves the shower, putting on a bathrobe.

"Oh, all right," Ray says to her. He then answers the phone: "How can I help you?"

"Good afternoon, this is Lt. Rhombus. Can I speak with Sierra Cîrstea please?"

"She is right here, but what should I say this is about?"

"Police business, sir. Can you please put Miss Cîrstea on the line?"

"Yeah, hold on a minute."

Mr. Jagger then walks to his barefoot girlfriend in the next room.

"Some police lieutenant is on the phone. Did you forget to pay your parking ticket?"

She rolls her eyes and continues drying her ash brown mane. Before entering the living room, Miss Cîrstea pinches her boyfriend's sides to get him to laugh.

"You know I'm not ticklish, don't you?"

"Oh, go finish the laundry, you big macho man."

He plants a smooch on her neck.

"Yes, Lieutenant, this is Sierra Cîrstea. What can I do for you?"

"Miss, I am Lt. Rhombus of the Quai Natia Police Department. I am calling about your ex-husband, Carl Zimmerman."

"Carl? Is he okay?"

"Apparently, his parents haven't contacted you."

"No, I haven't heard from them for about two months. They last called around mid-to-late January to talk to their granddaughter."

"I hate to be the messenger of bad news, but Mr. Carl Zimmerman was found murdered a few days ago near Quai Natia, California, in Biscay Bay."

She is aghast and overcome with sadness.

"What? Are you serious?"

"Very much so. I am very sorry for your loss. Mr. Zimmerman's parents already identified his body."

She is forced to accept the reality that her daughter's father is gone.

"I wish they had told me. Have you apprehended who is responsible?"

"Not yet. The records tell me that Carl was an auto mechanic and his parents are named Randy and Tammy. Does that sound like the Carl you know?"

"Yes. I still can't believe it! Our two-year marriage was not all that great, but he was a good man. He never physically hurt me."

"Miss Cîrstea, did your ex-husband ever have any trouble with the law?"

"No, not that I know of. But he had been in small fights in bars."

"You don't say! About how many of them?"

"I only know of two while we were married. On each occasion, he was defending my honor, if you will."

"And he was never arrested for these fights?"

"No, Lieutenant. Nobody was seriously injured."

"Very well. Miss Cîrstea, when was the last time you spoke to your ex-husband?"

"In early February and before that, the day before Christmas. We mostly discussed how our daughter Nina was doing."

"Did he seem concerned or troubled by anything either time?"

"Not that I remember. He said his job was going well."

"Was he having any problems with anyone?"

"No, nothing like that. I think he had just met someone."

"Ma'am, when we came across your ex-husband, his body was tied to a large buoy in the bay. Can you tell me if he swam often?"

"He sure did. He loved the water. We went kayaking and paddleboarding a lot. And he tried to get me started on scuba diving as well."

Seeing her tears, Ray comes over to hold her.

"By any chance, Miss Cîrstea, did Carl have a special interest in birds or aircraft?"

"Lieutenant, those are definitely not hobbies that I know of. Why do you ask?"

"A lapel pin showing a black-colored bird was attached to his shirt when we found him. It is still a mystery."

"Sorry, but I can't help you with that."

"That's fine. What can you tell me about Carl's parents?"

She asks, "What do you mean? They have always been very kind to me. When Carl, Nina, and I would visit them, both were always happy to see all of us. And when they heard of the divorce three years ago, they were taken aback."

"Can I ask why you went your separate ways?"

"Let's just say we couldn't agree on a lot of things. And he lost his temper from time to time. But he never cheated on me."

"Did he ever hurt you?"

"No, he never did, at least not physically."

"I understand. And how well do you know Carl's siblings?"

"I met them a few times, Lawrence and Debra. Carl's parents had them after Carl, whom they adopted."

"That actually leads me to my next question. Do you know why they adopted your ex-husband first, and then had children of their own afterwards?"

"As a matter of fact, I never did ask. I did not think it was a big deal."

"It probably isn't," Rhombus reassures her. "Also, Miss Cîrstea, did Carl have any enemies as far as you know? Is there anyone who would want to harm him?"

"No one comes to mind, but I must ask you: Will you eventually find his killer?"

"I am certain that we will, miss."

"Well, I really hope you do. Who would tie my ex-husband onto a buoy? Is there anything else, Lieutenant?"

"Yes, there is. Your daughter is listed in the records as Nina Cîrstea, not Zimmerman. Why is that?"

"When Carl and I divorced, Nina was only one. Eventually, I was granted custody, with Carl having visitation rights. It was my idea to change her last name, and the judge approved it."

"Thank you for that explanation."

"Will that be all, sir?"

"It's no big deal, Miss Cîrstea, but I was just curious about one other thing. You have a distinctive last name. By any chance, do you have Romanian ancestry?"

"I am impressed, Lt. Rhombus. My parents are from Bucharest."

"Well, thank you, miss. I am grateful for your time. We will keep you updated on our investigation."

"Please do. Good luck, Lieutenant."

20

An hour later, Lt. Rhombus receives an update from Dr. Paris.

"Hi Rex. Those alveolar fluid tests came back on Carl Zimmerman. He is now officially our third fatality due to forced nitrogen gas inhalation."

"Are you saying that he was killed before his body was submerged?"

"Yes, I am almost 100% sure. These test results can only be reasonably explained by that sequence of events. It is much less likely that he was moved to the navigation buoy first and then suffocated at the buoy."

"I am in agreement there, Doctor."

"Rex, last time we talked, you were going to ask Detective Novo to survey those local stores about sales of nitrogen gas. Did he come up with anything?"

"Danica, Reynold checked various local businesses for nitrogen gas purchases, and the buyers in the last several months have clean rap sheets. But I know you said to me earlier that almost anyone can get this gas over the internet."

"I did say that, and in reality it's not that difficult. Many companies can ship pure nitrogen gas to any potential buyer. For example, I saw one site where you can purchase 17 liters of pure nitrogen gas for under $50."

"In other words, if you have a credit card, you can acquire it."

"That's right. But let's also consider the possibility that one of those local buyers of nitrogen gas may be a first-time criminal with no past police record. Also, if the killer paid cash to purchase it locally, his name would not be recorded by the stores."

"You have good points there, Danica. We will keep those buyers in mind for now. But let's say someone is able to get the pure nitrogen gas. How can he administer it with the purpose of murder?"

"The perpetrator would have to expose the victim to the gas using a face mask with a good seal around the nose and mouth."

The lieutenant asks, "But wouldn't the victim be resisting the whole time the mask was being forced upon him?"

"That's true, so the killer would first need to incapacitate or strongly hold down the victim."

"I see what you mean."

"But Rex, as we discussed before, if each victim was knocked out from a blow to the head, he would not be resisting the forced inhalation of pure nitrogen gas. In that scenario, the victim would then calmly breathe in the pure nitrogen and exhale carbon dioxide as usual. Meanwhile, their oxygen levels would rapidly drop, leading to death."

"Danica, are you suggesting that each murder victim may have experienced a relatively painless death?"

"I am, other than the head trauma. For this reason, pure nitrogen gas asphyxiation is being considered in some states for euthanasia and the death penalty. As I have said, there have already been suicides using the method."

"Now, if someone wanted to use pure nitrogen gas for a homicide, what kinds of masks would have good seals around the nose and mouth?"

Paris responds, "I would say non-rebreather oxygen masks and scuba diving masks."

"Doctor, I think that's our next step. We will check local stores, including hospital supply businesses and scuba diving shops, for recent purchasers of those types of masks. In addition, we'll ask hospitals about any recent thefts of these masks."

"Great idea, Rex. If we come across an individual who bought both pure nitrogen gas canisters and non-rebreather/scuba masks in the recent past, such a person would clearly have the means to commit the recent murders."

"My sentiments exactly. I will look into it immediately."

After getting off the phone with Dr. Paris, the lieutenant gives Detective Novo his new assignment.

Lt. Rhombus then calls Maya Pitcairn, the second victim's widow. He is aware that Detective Stiles has already interviewed her. But he sets up another meeting with her to pursue any possible ties between her husband and the other two murder victims.

He drives to her apartment in the suburb of Pamplona, just outside Quai Natia. Rhombus knocks three times and identifies himself. After he displays his badge in front of the peephole, she opens the door, forcing a smile. Her dirty blonde hair is swept back in a ponytail.

"Hello, Mrs. Pitcairn. You have met Detective Stiles. Do you remember him?"

"Why yes, sir. And you are his boss?"

"That's right. I am Lt. Rhombus, in charge of the homicide unit. I just want to follow up on some details regarding your late husband."

"Of course," she says, using a small handkerchief to dry her nose. "Please, call me Maya. A cup of tea?"

"No thank you. Do I detect some Czech as well as English in your accent?"

"Very good, Lieutenant. You are quite astute. I was born in Zdiby, just outside of Prague. My parents and I moved to London when I was very young, and then to Quai Natia about five years ago."

"Did you meet your husband Matt in London?"

"Sir, we met here in Quai Natia during a promotional event for the Penalty Kicks soccer team. Matt ran the event and gave two friends and me tickets to a game. He was so thoughtful."

"I am deeply sorry for your loss, Maya. But I come to you today to seek any potential links between your husband and the other two recent murder victims, Mr. Jackson Moreau and Mr. Carl Zimmerman."

"I have read the papers and seen the news. Who could be behind all of this? Do you have any suspects?"

"We are working on various leads at this time, ma'am. Detective Stiles told me your husband had a brother and that his mother is still alive."

"That is correct. Matt's brother Murray lives in Washington, D.C. And his mother Alicia is a sprightly lady who resides just outside of Phoenix. I believe his father Samuel was killed in a car accident two years ago because of a drunk driver."

Lt. Rhombus questions her further.

"Do you know any details about that accident? Was there any investigation into the driver who hit your father-in-law?"

"Not that Matt was aware of. He just said it was a tragic event."

"Where did it happen?"

"Somewhere in Dallas, Texas, as I recall. The supposedly drunk driver hit Mr. Pitcairn as he was crossing the street."

"Do you know if your husband's father had any medical conditions that could have contributed to his death?"

Mrs. Pitcairn reflects for a few seconds.

"Other than having mildly high blood pressure and being a little overweight, he was as healthy as a proverbial horse as far as I know."

"And is Matt's mother in good health?"

"Yes, I spoke with her by phone a week ago."

The lieutenant now asks her to think about her deceased spouse.

"I have been told that your husband was an excellent billiards player. But are you aware of any interest he had in birds or birdwatching?"

"As I told Detective Stiles, I know nothing about that. Is this about the lapel pin?"

"That's right, ma'am. We have found one with the image of a black bird on all three recent murder victims. And it remains a conundrum."

She is also clearly perturbed by the mystery.

"Maya, by any chance, was your husband interested in planes or aircraft to any extent?"

"On the contrary. He felt uncomfortable on airplanes, and he avoided flying when he could."

"I hear you. By the way, do you know about a company called the Constellation Fertility Center?"

"Are you asking if I have ever been a client there?" she asks, guessing. "No, I have never been in contact with that facility, Lt. Rhombus."

"And one last thing, Mrs. Pitcairn. Did your husband ever mention the names of Jackson Moreau or Carl Zimmerman in the past? Or have you seen these men before?"

He shows her digital images of the two men.

She carefully looks at the photos. Finally, she responds, "No, sir, I do not recollect either of these men, and Matt never mentioned them."

"All right, Mrs. Pitcairn. I want to thank you for your help in this difficult time. Here is my card. You can call me anytime, day or night."

"Lieutenant, can you tell me if these murders are going to stop any time soon?"

"Ma'am, I am confident that we will catch the one or ones responsible -- that you can bet on. But I just can't tell you when."

Disappointed, she states, "I appreciate your efforts, Lt. Rhombus. Please call me once you find anything about Matt's killer. He can not get away with this!"

"You have my word on that. Have a good day, Maya."

21

"This is Tannenbaum Enterprises. How can I be of service?" says a friendly voice.

"Good morning. This is Detective Stiles of the Quai Natia Police Department. May I speak with Mr. Winston Banks please?"

"Sir, Mr. Banks no longer works here. He was transferred to the San Jose office several months ago."

The detective is connected to the other office and is told that Banks just went on holiday and should return in a week. The secretary gives him Winston Banks' home and cell phones. But Stiles finds that he is not reachable at these numbers.

Thinking about his options, Detective Stiles decides to check with the local airports. After several calls, he finds that Mr. Banks took a flight to Nassau in the Bahamas two days ago and is scheduled to return in about five days.

Not wanting to wait until his return, the detective calls the San Jose office again and asks for emergency contact information on Banks. Accordingly, the administrative staff gives him the telephone of Mr. Banks' sister Kiki.

"Good afternoon, is this Kiki Banks?"

"Yes, this is she."

"Hello. I am Detective Stiles of the Quai Natia Police Department. You may have heard about some recent unwonted homicides in the area."

"I have been really busy recently, so just vaguely. What does that have to do with me?"

"Miss, I have some questions regarding your brother, Winston Banks. Can we meet briefly to discuss?"

"Oh, wow. Is Winston a suspect in the murders?"

"It might be better if we talk in person. Can we meet today or tomorrow?"

"I suppose so," she says with some reluctance.

"Would you rather come to the police precinct or meet near your work or home?"

"Let me think. How about 5 p.m. today, at Mayberry Square in Cordoba?"

"I know the place, miss. Thank you for your cooperation. See you then and there."

Several hours later, the detective arrives in Cordoba, a town less than an hour from Quai Natia. He sees a lush park and drives along tree-lined streets, passing two traffic circles on the way to Mayberry Square.

Once at the plaza, he spots Miss Banks at the southern entrance. She has shoulder-length red hair and is wearing an amber dress and light orange sweater.

Detective Stiles shows his shield.

"It is very nice of you to meet me, Miss Banks. Where is a good place to chat?"

"Good afternoon, Detective. There is a green wooden bench in a quiet area over there."

"Please lead the way."

She reaches the bench and sits down first. As she shifts in her seat, the detective glimpses her smooth legs and a small tattoo of a dove on her ankle.

"Now, what is this about my brother being involved in some crime? You seemed very eager to see me when you called."

Stiles sits next to her.

"Miss Banks, one of the recent murder victims in Quai Natia was Jackson Moreau. Our investigation has determined that your brother Winston is the sperm donor who helped a lady give birth to Mr. Moreau."

"So are you saying that Winston slept with this lady?" Kiki asks.

"Actually, no. He donated to a fertility center in 1994 and his sperm was selected by the woman wanting to become pregnant."

"Detective, when did sperm donation become a crime?" she asks.

"It is not, miss. But Jackson Moreau was murdered over two weeks ago, and there have been two more murders since then. We would like to interview your brother to see if he has any other connection to Mr. Moreau."

"Do you think Winston is involved in the killings? I thought he just donated sperm."

"Maybe not. But we need to ask him if he has been in contact with the murder victim in any way."

"I still don't see how Winston could even know the donor offspring."

"Have you spoken to or seen your brother recently?"

"Winston is really my half-brother. His father was some loser who had a fling with my mother years ago."

"I totally get it. When did you last see your half-brother?"

"That would have been several months ago, before he decided to leave Monterey and transfer to his company's San Jose office."

"And why was that?"

"He told me his girlfriend was crazy and that he had to get away from her at all costs."

"Did he say why he thought she was crazy? And can you give me her name?"

"He never told me her name. But he said she was unstable and overly possessive. Once, she released the air from his car's tires when she saw him looking at another woman."

"She does sound disturbed," says Detective Stiles with his eyebrows uplifted.

Miss Banks adds, "On top of that, I was told that her brother was pretty mad after Winston broke up with her."

"Do you know if he threatened your half-brother?"

"Not in so many words, but I don't believe Winston wanted to take any chances."

"Miss, do you know how I can find your brother now? I tried his phones without success. And his workplace says he has been on vacation for a few days."

"Did you call his cell and his home phone already?"

"Yes, I have, Miss Banks. And I found that he took a flight to the Bahamas two days ago."

"Call me Kiki, Detective," she insists as she plays with her reddish mane.

"Of course. Do you have any other phone numbers for your brother? Or can I call your mother if possible?"

"In the past, on those occasions when Winston left the country on vacation, I seem to recall that his cell phone didn't receive calls from me. I think he doesn't have an international calling plan. Or he turns his phone off."

"What you say makes sense."

"But let me give you my mother's home and cell phones. I don't have more contact information for my brother. Sorry."

She writes two telephone numbers on the back of one of the detective's cards.

"I am thankful for your time, Kiki. On a separate matter, I notice you have a tattoo of a dove. Do you have a special interest in birds?"

Miss Banks blushes to some degree.

"Not really. I thought the small tattoo looked nice and would be a good symbol for peace."

"Spreading world peace is very admirable, Kiki. What about your half-brother? Is he a bird-lover?"

"Winston?" She chuckles. "He is not that type of guy, Detective. So is my brother a suspect in the murders?"

"At this point in time, he is only a person of interest. If he contacts you, please call me."

"Sure thing. And feel free to let me know if I can help further."

She winks at him as they part ways.

22

Back in his Mustang, Detective Stiles dials the phone number just given to him.

"Mrs. Kendra Banks, please."

"That is Ms. Banks. And to whom am I speaking?"

"Hello, ma'am. This is Detective Eli Stiles of the Quai Natia Police Department. I would like to ask about your son, Winston."

The 63-year-old greying brunette asks, "Why? Has he gotten himself into any trouble?"

"We are investigating some recent murders and I would like to talk to you in person about your son. Your daughter Kiki gave me your phone number."

"Are you able to tell me if either of them is a suspect? I did not raise any killers, Detective."

"Neither is a suspect at this time, Ms. Banks. Can we please meet somewhere soon?"

"That depends. Are you anywhere near Pasadena? I am here for a reunion with some of my former sorority sisters."

"Oh, okay. Let me make a call, and I will arrange for either myself or a colleague to meet you there."

"That would be fine. You can find me at the Eclipse Hotel. I will be here for several days."

"Let me make a note of that. And I will call you in the next few hours to confirm the meeting. Good day, ma'am."

Immediately after he gets off the line, Stiles calls his lieutenant and explains the situation regarding Winston Banks. Lt. Rhombus agrees that he can ask Lt. Durso to meet Ms. Banks if she is available. In addition, Rhombus tells the detective that the third victim, Carl Zimmerman, also succumbed to pure nitrogen gas.

"Our serial killer's M.O. is consistent, R-double. And it's very clear that we need to put a stop to this murder spree soon. I'll call Lt. Durso right away."

"Carry on, Eli."

The detective now calls the Esplanade lieutenant for her help.

"Eli, how good to hear from you. How was your visit to the Constellation Fertility Center?"

"Somewhat helpful, Bianca. I am now trying to get hold of Winston Banks. He donated the sperm leading to donor offspring Jackson Moreau, our first murder victim."

"Any luck so far?"

"I still haven't been able to reach him. But Kendra Banks, Winston's mother, is in Pasadena for an event the next few days. Would you mind meeting her there to seek any clues regarding our case?"

"I am busy at my precinct today, but I can drive there tomorrow."

"That would be fantastic, Bianca. Thank you. I am not yet sure how she can help us find the Black Bird Killer, but Rex is more hopeful than me."

"If Rex is optimistic, you know that is a good sign. He has a sixth sense about these things."

"I can't argue there. Also, the cybercrime on the fertility center's computer network a few months ago was quickly quashed by the technical staff. And there have been no further breaches."

"That is great news. But I have a feeling you have more information for me."

"How did you know? You seem to have a sixth sense of your own."

"If you say so, Eli. So what else do you have in store for me?"

"Bianca, were you told of the third murder victim discovered just outside Quai Natia?"

"I have been swamped at work this last week, so no. When did this happen?"

"About five days ago. A body was found tied to a navigation buoy in Biscay Bay. And a black bird lapel pin was attached to the male corpse's shirt."

"Wow. That's three homicides now. Has the cause of death been determined?"

"Actually, I just got off the phone with Lt. Rhombus, who says nitrogen gas asphyxiation was confirmed once again."

"Did you get any clues at the crime scene that point to a specific perpetrator?"

"I regret to say that we didn't. No DNA or fingerprints or murder weapon. And no witnesses."

"Well, I hope my upcoming visit with Ms. Banks will be helpful in the investigation. I have to go now, but send me anything you have on her and her son."

"I'm more than happy to. And I'll tell Ms. Banks to expect you tomorrow. Bianca, thanks again."

23

The 90-minute drive to Pasadena is uneventful as Lt. Durso listens to an audiobook in her SUV. Once in the city, she finds the Eclipse Hotel and pushes through the revolving doors in her sienna-colored pantsuit and black Nine West pumps.

Showing her shield to the front desk staff, she asks where she can find Ms. Kendra Banks. The perky dark-haired brown-eyed concierge makes a call.

"Yes. A lieutenant. She has a police badge, yes. Okay, sounds good."

The concierge smiles at Durso as she hangs up.

"Ms. Banks can meet you in our Skylight restaurant in about 10 minutes. Let me take you there."

Arriving at the restaurant, the lieutenant notices a Rubenesque lady in her 60's. She is wearing a periwinkle dress.

"Ms. Kendra Banks?"

"Lt. Durso. Thank you for meeting me here. You can call me Kendra."

"Let's get a table. You know, my husband and I stayed at a fancy hotel like this in Santa Barbara several years ago."

The ladies sit down and are served some cold water by the waitress. Ms. Banks, 5-foot-8 with high cheekbones, swallows a mint.

"Lieutenant, how have you managed to stay together with your husband, if I may ask? I have been divorced for about six years now. We started growing apart about 10 years ago."

"Let's see. I have been married for over nine years now. The secret as I see it is taking turns making the decisions. And giving in when it is not that important to you."

"I wish it was that easy. And having children from different men does not help."

"Kendra, speaking of children, I wonder if you can tell me a little about your son Winston. Have you talked recently?"

"How do you know about him? Has he done anything wrong?"

"Not as far as I know. My colleagues and I are searching for a serial killer, and it turns out that your son's donor sperm led to the birth of a donor offspring, who was our first murder victim."

"Yes, he told me he donated once in college. But the facility was too far away for him to do it again."

"It is my understanding that he left his job in Monterey because of a girlfriend?"

"He told me the same thing. She would always be suspicious that he was cheating on her."

"Have you talked to him since he moved to San Jose?"

"Yes, in January – but not since. He has always been pretty independent, and he often rebelled against authority as he was growing up. I also think that he has had bad luck with women."

"How do you mean?"

"It's just that he can't seem to settle down with one."

"Is that by choice, Kendra?"

"You know, I really can't tell sometimes."

"At any rate, we have been unable to contact your son using his home or cell phone. But he has apparently taken a trip to the Bahamas for vacation. Do you have any numbers other than these?"

Lt. Durso shows her the phone numbers.

"No. That is also all I have. Let me try him right now."

After calling her son's cell, she is directed to voicemail.

"Win, it's your mother. Haven't heard from you in a while. Call me real soon. Love you."

Sans souci, she now turns to Durso.

"I am not that worried, Lieutenant. He has told me many times that being on a real vacation means turning off your phone."

"That may well explain our difficulty reaching him. And what of Winston's father? Do you still keep in contact?"

"I dated Thomas Spizer, Winston's father, in about 1975. He had thick brown hair and brown eyes, with a solidly muscular body. But along with his charm came some impulsivity."

"It's hard to find the perfect man, isn't it?"

"I couldn't agree more. He was also very detail-oriented, and he obsessed over his photography. I still may have his old number, which may or may not be useful to you now."

"Anything would help, Kendra."

"He had no plans to marry me, but he at least supported me financially as I was raising Winston. Here is the last number I have for him."

"Thank you," says the lieutenant.

"Do you think my son could be involved in those serial murders?"

"At this time, he is not a suspect, ma'am. We are only trying to determine if he had contact with the first murder victim before he was killed. Also, I am curious as to why Winston's last name is listed as Banks and not Spizer."

"Oh, right. My maiden name is Banks. Once Winston found out that Thomas declined to marry me, he decided to change his last name to Banks when he turned 18."

"That makes sense. And you have a daughter as well?"

"Yes, Kiki. Her father is James Dobrev. When we divorced six years ago, she also took my last name."

"And you have had no communications with either man for at least several years now?"

"None, Lieutenant. Now, I hate to be rude, but my friends and I are supposed to meet soon. Is there anything else?"

"I have one more thing to ask of you. Do you recognize these names or the men in these photos?"

Lt. Durso shows her the names and images of the three Quai Natia area murder victims.

Ms. Banks points to the digital photo of Jackson Moreau. "This one has a resemblance to Winston and his father. I don't recognize the other two."

"Kendra, that is the donor offspring of your son. He was murdered almost three weeks ago."

"I guess that explains the likeness."

"Well, I enjoyed meeting with you, Kendra. You have been very nice. Please call me if you reach your son. And I will do the same."

Now feeling a little unsettled, Ms. Banks gives the lieutenant a polite smile and bids her farewell.

As she exits the hotel and walks toward her silver Ford Explorer, Durso dials the phone number of Thomas Spizer. A woman with a mildly coarse voice answers.

"This is Melina. Can I help you?"

"Oh. Good day, ma'am. I am Lt. Durso of the Esplanade Police Department. I am trying to reach Thomas Spizer."

"You've reached his phone. Mr. Spizer was my husband, but he died about 10 years ago. What is this all about?"

"I think it is better if we discuss the matter in person, Mrs. Spizer."

"How did you get this number?"

"I can't tell you over the phone, but I will be happy to do so when I see you. Do you know of a place we can meet soon?"

"I live about an hour from Esplanade, in the small town of Blackstone."

"Blackstone -- I know where that is. Can you give me a place where we can get together soon? Would that be all right?"

With hesitation, Mrs. Spizer agrees and suggests the local delicatessen at 6 p.m.

24

The lieutenant arrives in the town of Blackstone approximately 10 minutes before 6. After parking near the Continental Delicatessen, she walks into the restaurant to find a lively crowd on this early Thursday evening. Framed posters of vintage Americana are scattered throughout. In one booth, she spots a skinny lady with greying brown hair.

"Excuse me, but I am looking for Mrs. Spizer."

"I'm Melina Spizer. You must be the police lieutenant. Can I see some ID?" she asks, taking a puff from her cigarette.

After she shows her badge, Lt. Durso joins the widow at her table.

A bitter Mrs. Spizer then utters, "Haven't you put my husband through enough? You know it was never proven that he hurt those girls."

Caught off-guard, the lieutenant responds, "I'm sorry, ma'am. What girls?"

"You know, the young ladies they said my husband killed, when he was living in Nebraska in the 1970's. Thomas was questioned by the police on many occasions about these serial killings in the Mycenae area. But they never had the evidence."

"Excuse me, but I was not aware. I was given his -- or now your -- phone number by an old friend of your husband."

In her head, Lt. Durso realizes that there is no good reason to reveal to Mrs. Spizer who Kendra Banks and her illegitimate son Winston are. This information would only further upset her.

"Where were those serial murders again?"

"In the area of Mycenae, Nebraska. All college coeds. I don't think they ever caught the killer."

"And why did they suspect your husband?"

"I believe some eyewitness described a person who looked a little like my husband, but Thomas had a good alibi and I know he couldn't have done such dreadful things."

"Based on what you just said, it looks like he was innocent, Mrs. Spizer. If I may ask, how did you meet your husband?"

"In late 1976, I attended a wedding in Topeka, Kansas, and he was the photographer. He approached me and we started dating. Less than a year later, we got married."

"And when did you move to California?"

She looks like she is about to cry.

"After he was murdered."

The lieutenant is again bowled over.

"I try not to think about it, but it happened in Kansas City in 2009, on a Saturday night. Outside some bar, someone, who may have been drunk, stabbed my husband, and he didn't make it."

"I am so sorry, Mrs. Spizer. Was the killer ever put in jail?"

"Actually, the police never caught him – he reportedly ran into the night and vanished."

Lt. Durso tries to lighten up the widow's mood.

"And how did you decide on Blackstone?"

"You see, I wanted to move to a small town with a warmer climate. Plus I have some friends in Bakersfield nearby."

"Okay."

"And I kept Thomas' phone and his phone number as a sort of way to remember him. I used to get calls from his old friends, but not anymore."

"That's very sweet. Was your husband always a photographer, Mrs. Spizer?"

Taking a drag on her cigarette, she answers, "He did what he loved, and that was photography. Weddings, baby pictures, even some sports photos for magazines."

The waitress arrives and asks the ladies for their orders.

"Some pumpkin pie and iced tea, please. And what will you have, Lieutenant?"

"Miss, I will have a blueberry muffin and coffee. Thank you."

The waitress scribbles some notes and says she will return.

"Ma'am, did you and your husband have any children?"

"One -- Sammy. My angel."

Mrs. Spizer takes out a photo of a young man from her purse. He has thick light brown hair and an aquiline nose, and he is dressed in a charcoal grey blazer."

"He looks like a fine man. When was this photo taken?"

"About two years ago. A few months before --."

She chokes up as she painfully expresses the words.

"—he was killed in a car accident."

Lt. Durso is notably saddened by the two personal losses haunting the widow.

"You have my deepest sympathy, Mrs. Spizer. Did the accident occur locally?"

"No, he was living in Dallas, and someone hit him and just drove off. They never found out who."

The server returns with their orders, then the two eat in silence for a minute.

"I want to thank you for speaking with me today, ma'am. And I regret having to bring up these memories."

After wiping away her tears, the small-boned senior says, "Lieutenant, I know one of Thomas' old friends gave you this phone number. But can I ask what you are really investigating at this time?"

"As it happens, I am working with the Quai Natia police as they look into a recent string of murders in that area."

"And how does that relate to my husband?"

"The person who gave me his/your phone number is related to a person of interest in the case. But after talking to you, I see no obvious connection between your husband and the murders in the Quai Natia area."

"I am happy to hear that, Lieutenant. The last thing I need is more bad news in my life."

"That's for sure. Mrs. Spizer, I am very glad to have gotten to know you for this brief time. In fact, I will look into your husband's and son's deaths and call you if I find something important."

"Bless you, Lieutenant."

"Thank you again, ma'am. Here's my card. Be sure to call me if I can be of any help in the future."

25

"Help! Somebody help!"

Charlee has just found her friend Billy barely breathing and unconscious on the grass at Franklin Delano Roosevelt Elementary School. His face is expressionless and ashen. Seeing no one around, she runs to the school nurse's office.

Nurse Frost immediately follows her to the scene and takes Billy's vital signs.

"Thank goodness," says the nurse, letting out a sigh of relief.

The boy is now breathing more easily with only a mildly high blood pressure and mildly rapid pulse.

"Is he going to be okay?" asks a fearful Charlee.

"I believe so. Did you find him like this?"

"Well, I was leaving school after I stayed late for art class. Then I saw Billy on the grass. He was not moving. And I think I saw someone running toward those trees."

"Did you recognize who it was, Charlee?"

"No, not really."

"That's okay. I will call 911 now."

After several minutes, Billy is able to talk. The ambulance arrives in less than 10 minutes, and two paramedics place him on a stretcher. Supplemental oxygen and a heart monitor are hooked up.

Upon arriving in the emergency room, the boy is still woozy. Blood samples are taken as the doctor on duty evaluates the child. Soon after, the frenzied mother Hanna Moreau is on the scene and hugs her son tightly.

"How are you feeling, Honey?" Are you hurt?"

Billy, oblivious to the events of the last hour, says, "I have a headache and I'm a little sleepy, Mom. Where are we?"

"In the hospital. You're safe with me. Just rest now."

She stays with her son as nurses frequently check his vital signs.

Dr. Graf introduces himself 15 minutes later and reports that all preliminary tests look good.

"What could have happened, Doctor?" asks a frantic Mrs. Moreau.

"All the blood tests are normal so far, but something dull hit him in the back of the head. Did he fall on his head?"

"The school nurse told me that no one saw him fall. But she said his friend Charlee saw a person running away when she came upon Billy."

"That person may have hit Billy on the head and then fled the scene. Also, we are waiting for results of his head CT scan."

"My God! Do you suspect he has a brain injury?"

"I hope not, Mrs. Moreau. But the suspicion is high enough to justify the test."

"All right. I have confidence in you, Doctor."

Mrs. Moreau then remembers a card she was recently given. She proceeds to call Lt. Rhombus using her shaky hands. Half an hour later, Rhombus meets her at Billy's bedside. She is clearly a bundle of nerves, so he tries to calm her.

"I am so happy to see you, Lieutenant! I didn't know who else to call. Who would want to hurt my little Billy? He has lots of friends at school."

"The important thing, Mrs. Moreau, is that your son is safe and alive. Now, do you know what happened?"

"Let me think. His friend Charlee found him unconscious at his school and also may have seen someone running away."

"Did she get a good look?"

"I'm not sure. That's all I remember the nurse telling me."

"Thank you, Mrs. Moreau. I will now talk to Billy briefly. Tomorrow, Dr. Paris will interview Charlee and see your son for some additional tests. Do you still have family in town?"

"My sister and her husband had to leave about two weeks ago. But I'll call my mother-in-law to see if she can come up from Green Springs again."

"That's a good idea. For now, my priority is to keep you and your son out of harm's way, so I will assign a police officer to your home. And let's arrange for your son's schoolwork to be done at home for now."

"Lt. Rhombus, could my husband's murderer have been involved in today's attack on my son?"

"We have to assume that until proven otherwise, ma'am. For everyone's safety."

The lieutenant again tries to console the jittery mother.

"I will be back soon, Mrs. Moreau. Do not leave the area."

Rhombus exits the room and calls for police protection at the Moreau residence. He also informs Dr. Paris about the assault and asks her to see Billy and Charlee the next day.

"Doctor, please try to jog the boy's and his friend's memories tomorrow about today's event."

"Will do. Also, I will run some other specific tests."

"Do you have any thoughts about the incident, Danica?"

"A few. Was a black bird pin seen on Billy's shirt?"

"Not this time, Doctor."

"That's somewhat reassuring. But I think it would be prudent to make sure that all the children of our victims are safe. I seem to recall that our third victim had a daughter in Utah. And our second victim had no children."

"Good idea -- I will arrange it."

"And Rex, could you think of a reason why Mrs. Moreau wasn't attacked instead of Billy?"

"Good question. The culprit is maybe just targeting males. But why?"

"My opinion is we should err on the side of caution and arrange for protection for all the victims' local family members. That would include their spouses and possibly parents."

"Your recommendation makes sense, Danica. I will take care of it. And what of the boy in the emergency room now?"

"Rex, if the initial tests look good there, I would conclude that the assailant hit Billy in the head but did not get the chance to kidnap him or harm him further."

"That is a sensible idea. However, I believe there is another possibility for why he didn't go further today in the crime."

"And what would that be?"

"It is my suspicion that the attacker, at the moment he was about to inflict permanent harm on Billy, considered the youth and innocence of the victim."

"Why do you think he had a change of heart, Rex?"

"I am not sure. But because he has been meticulous in planning and committing all the other murders, why should this attack have been any different?"

"So you're suggesting he has at least some sense of morality?"

"That is my gut feeling, Danica. But his cruel actions are not forgivable by any means."

"Whatever the reason the assailant didn't go through with the kidnapping or worse today, Billy can count his lucky stars that he is mostly unscathed."

"You can say that again. But the next victim may not be as fortunate. I will see you at your office tomorrow morning, Doctor."

26

The following day, Dr. Paris prepares to question Charlee about the unknown person fleeing the scene where Billy was attacked. Her mother is also present.

"Good morning, Charlee. I am Dr. Paris, but you can call me Danica. I just want to ask you a few questions about the person you saw running away from Billy. Would that be okay?"

"Sure."

"Great! First of all, can you tell me if the person was tall or short?"

The grade-schooler says, "I would say tallish."

"Okay. What about the person's body? Was it thin, chubby, or in the middle?"

"The person looked thin or normal."

"Got it. Could you recall if it was a man or woman? Did you manage to see his or her face?"

"The person was running away, so I really can't say. But he sort of ran like a man."

"I see. Charlee, do you know if he was an older man?"

"I couldn't tell, but he moved pretty fast."

"That's great, Charlee. Now, did you notice anything funny about how the person moved?"

"No, nothing funny. Like I said, he ran pretty fast."

"And did you see him carrying anything?"

"No, I don't think so, but I can't be sure."

"We're almost done, Charlee. Are you able to tell me what the person was wearing?"

"I remember blue jeans and a dark hoodie. It could have been dark blue or black."

"Was there a special design on the hoodie?"

"Not that I can tell. I believe it was just dark blue or black."

"Finally, Charlee, please think hard. Can you remember anything else about the person running away yesterday?"

After several seconds of thought, she shakes her head.

"Thank you, Charlee. I appreciate you coming in today. And you were very brave yesterday. As a special treat, I will walk you and your mother to the cafeteria now and both of you can have anything you want there."

"Do they have pizza?"

"They sure do! And if you remember anything else about the person who hurt Billy, make sure to tell your mom to call me."

"I sure will, Doctor – I mean Danica."

Dr. Paris walks both of them to the cafeteria and gives them a voucher before saying farewell.

Meanwhile, blood, urine, and hair samples are collected from Billy Moreau at the laboratory. He is then directed to Dr. Paris' office, where Mrs. Moreau and Lt. Rhombus have joined the doctor.

"How are you doing, Billy? I am Dr. Paris. You can call me Danica."

"Fine, I guess. That's a cool name. Are you a real doctor?"

"I am a doctor who works with Lt. Rhombus here. Do you remember him?"

"Yes, I saw him at the hospital, at the emergency room."

"Good memory, Billy. Are you having any problems now?"

"I still have a headache from yesterday. Do you know what happened to me at school? I felt this pain in my head before I passed out."

"Do you recall seeing someone before you felt the headache and got very dizzy?"

Billy, looking weary from not sleeping well, is struggling to keep his brown eyes open.

"Not really. It was about 5 o'clock and baseball practice just finished. I was walking, then all of a sudden my head hurt and I found myself on the ground. Nurse Frost and Charlee were looking over me. Then they started shaking me and shouting at me."

"They were simply trying to see if you were all right, Honey," says Mrs. Moreau as she gets a little teary-eyed.

"Now, this is important, Billy. Did you have any headache at baseball practice?"

"Not that I remember. But my head hurt a lot for a few hours after I woke up on the grass. There is only a little pain now."

"You are doing really well, Billy. Do you have any questions for me?"

"Yeah. My mom says I have to stay away from school for a while. Is that right?"

"That is correct, but just for a short while, so you can get all better."

"Well, if I have to," he says dejectedly.

Lt. Rhombus intervenes and Officer O'Neill quietly walks into the room.

"Billy, Danica and I have to talk to your mom for a little while. Maybe Officer O'Neill can interest you in some ice cream at the cafeteria. Would you like that?"

The grade-schooler responds, "Okay, but what happened to me at my school? And what about all those tests they did on me?"

"Someone tried to hurt you but we are looking for this person. That's why you will have to study at home for now. But your friends can visit when they like."

"Oh, they can?"

"Sure. And I can tell you that we will be working on those tests as soon as possible."

"That sounds good."

"Now, let's get that ice cream," says the officer with a smile as she leads Billy out of the room.

Rhombus then turns toward Mrs. Moreau.

"Some bad news and some good news, ma'am. I have been informed by Dr. Paris that your son was hit in the head with a blunt object yesterday, but there are no problems on the Head CT scan or blood tests."

Trying to stop crying, she asks, "Detective, what does that mean? Will my son be okay? Is there any permanent brain damage?"

The doctor answers.

"Ma'am, I think he will be fine. The relatively mild head injury should have no long-lasting effects on him. But it is our belief that the assailant was trying to subdue your son and then kidnap him."

Mrs. Moreau is beside herself in rage and fear.

"First my husband and now my son! Who is this monster? Is he coming after me soon?"

The lieutenant says, "An officer has been posted outside your home for protection, and we have arranged for Billy to study at home indefinitely for now – at least until we are sure you are both out of danger."

"But Lieutenant, will we ever be able to live our lives normally again?"

"Yes. On that you have my promise. I just can't tell you when quite yet, Mrs. Moreau."

"Why is my family being targeted? Can you tell me that?"

"We are getting closer to finding that out, ma'am. Someone of interest is the sperm donor used by your mother-in-law to get pregnant with Jackson."

"What are you saying? Do you mean Jackson's real father is not Cliff?" she asks incredulously.

Rhombus replies, "According to your mother-in-law, your late father-in-law became infertile, so they went to the Constellation Fertility Center in Cinnamon Meadows. She was implanted with donor sperm, and your husband was born nine months later."

"I don't remember Jackson ever telling me that."

"Actually, his mother told us she meant to tell him but never got around to it. But rest assured that for all intents and purposes, Cliff

Moreau was your husband's true and legal father," says the lieutenant.

"This is all news to me. Do you have any more surprises for me today?"

"Not at this time, Mrs. Moreau."

"Well, I feel that I need to do something. I would like to offer a reward for information leading to the arrest and conviction of my husband's killer and son's attacker."

"That would be fine. I will call the clerk in our precinct who is handling those matters. He can fill you in on the details."

After taking a deep breath, Mrs. Moreau stands up and shakes hands with Lt. Rhombus and then briefly hugs Dr. Paris.

"I have faith in both of you, but please find the culprit as soon as possible. Billy and I can't get on with our lives until that happens."

"Try to remain patient if you can, ma'am. As soon as we know more, so will you," says Rhombus, trying to comfort the distraught mother.

27

"They may see us, Rafa," she whispers.

"So what if they do? You feel great right now, don't you?"

"Yes, but we might both get fired," she says in a semiserious tone.

"Well, I guess that would not be good."

He continues to caress her lower back. They kiss some more before finally embracing one last time. Soon, both leave the snack lounge, separately.

Detective Stiles is on his way to get a bottled water when he runs into Dr. Paris.

"Hey there, Danica. Are you okay?"

"What do you mean, Eli?"

"Well, your face is a little red and you seem a little jumpy."

Trying to think of something plausible, she answers, "I was trying to get a candy bar from the vending machine. But the bar wouldn't fall down, so I had to shake the machine a little."

"Did you eventually get it down? Where's the candy?"

"Yeah, I already ate it -- a delicious 3 Musketeers bar."

"Glad you enjoyed it. What brings you to the precinct today?"

"Oh, I just had to drop off some papers at Rex's office. What's up?"

"Listen, since I caught you, you should know that Lt. Durso and I have recently interviewed some people of interest in the case of the Black Bird Murders."

"Tell me all about it," she expresses with keen interest.

"First of all, I found out that our first victim, Jackson Moreau, was born when his mother was implanted with donor sperm from a Winston Banks."

"I am somewhat aware of that, Eli -- Rex briefly mentioned it."

"Good to know. As you would expect, I have been trying to get hold of Mr. Banks. Meanwhile, Lt. Durso discovered that Banks' father was Thomas Spizer. Of note, Spizer was a suspect in various serial killings in Nebraska in the 1970's!"

"Let me get this straight. Thomas Spizer's son is Winston Banks, and Banks donated sperm that led to the birth of Jackson Moreau. That means that Spizer was technically the grandfather of our first victim. And he was accused in the past of being a serial murderer."

"You get the idea, Danica."

"It sounds like more than a coincidence to me. Was Mr. Spizer ever convicted?"

"According to his widow, there was insufficient evidence to do so."

"And who were the victims of the murders?"

"All coeds in the area of Mycenae, Nebraska."

"So Eli, do you think Winston Banks is involved in the Black Bird Murders?"

"I really can't say at this time. I still only see him as a person of interest. And he is even more interesting since he has been unreachable for the last week. Mr. Banks was supposed to be on vacation in the Bahamas, but he should have returned two days ago."

"Quite a story! By the way, I notice you have used the past tense when referring to Thomas Spizer."

"Good pick up, Danica. Mr. Spizer was stabbed to death in Kansas City in 2009. And listen to this: He and his wife Melina had a son Sammy, who was killed in a car accident in Dallas about two years ago."

Detective Stiles is silent for a few seconds.

"I just thought of something: The widow of Matt Pitcairn, our second victim, told me that his father, Samuel Pitcairn, also died in a car accident in Dallas in 2017. And it may well have been a hit-and-run situation."

"What are the odds of those two people, Sammy Spizer and Samuel Pitcairn, being victims of a car accident in the same year and same city?" asks Dr. Paris. "Could those two men have been in the same accident? Or could there be another possibility?"

"What are you contemplating, Danica?"

"Could Sammy Spizer and Samuel Pitcairn have been one in the same person?"

"Wow! That is definitely plausible."

"Eli, let me look into Samuel and Sammy, and I'll call Reynold to help. Meanwhile, can you call the Mycenae Police Department and get more details on the serial murders in the 1970's?"

"Your wish is my command. Incidently, Rex told me he wants to meet with the whole team, so we will let him know when we finish our tasks, okay?"

"You have a deal."

28

In her modest office at the Esplanade police station, Lt. Durso is all business in her xanadu grey pant suit, reviewing various reports and delegating some assignments to her detectives. No significant violent crimes have occurred in her town for some time now.

As it buzzes, she sees "Unknown Caller ID" on her phone.

"This is Lt. Durso."

"Lieutenant! This is Kendra, Kendra Banks! It's about Winston!"

"Slow down, Ms. Banks. What about your son Winston?"

"The San Jose police just called me! They told me he's dead!"

"I'm sorry. Did you say he is dead?"

Weeping, she is unable to speak coherently for several seconds.

"Some students stumbled upon his lifeless body in his former high school. He was found face-up at the middle of the football field's 50-yard line."

"Good heavens! Did the police say how long his body had been there?"

"They said maybe two or three days."

"You have my deepest condolences, Kendra. Do you know why no one saw your son's body earlier?"

"Well, the school had been closed for spring break until today."

"Oh, I see. Ms. Banks, let me call the San Jose Police Department and try to get more details for you."

"Please do, Lieutenant! I can't think right now!"

"That is totally understandable. I will ring you once I know more."

"Thank you."

After hanging up, Lt. Durso first contacts Detective Stiles.

"Hello, Eli. A minute ago, Ms. Kendra Banks informed me that some students discovered the body of her son Winston Banks. Didn't you tell me he was returning from the Bahamas last Friday?"

"That's right, Bianca. His flight touched down at 5 p.m. in San Jose International Airport three days ago. I have been attempting to reach him since then."

"Well, your search is over. Banks' dead body turned up at his former high school in San Jose. I will call the San Jose police and get more information."

"By any chance, was a lapel pin seen on the corpse?"

"I don't know yet, Eli. I'll be in touch."

She gets off the phone and calls the homicide lieutenant at the San Jose Police Department. He informs her that Winston Banks' body showed mild head trauma but no clear cause of death. And a black bird pin was in fact attached to his shirt.

Lt. Durso soon notifies Lt. Rhombus about the latest victim of the Black Bird Killer.

"That's Thomas Spizer, S-P-I-Z-E-R. He was a suspect in the 1970's for the murders of a number of college coeds."

Detective Stiles is on the line with Mycenae's finest to clarify why Mr. Spizer was not arrested for the heinous crimes.

"Here it is," says Detective Pippen. "Seventeen victims, all college girls, kidnapped while walking alone on or around campus. All their bodies eventually turned up in the local parks."

"Do your records say how they died?"

"Yes. It was pretty gruesome. All of them were strangled with nylon rope. But only after they were raped as well."

"That perpetrator was one despicable human being. Were there many suspects?"

"Well, Detective, there were several. But a witness saw one of the kidnappings and our sketch artist drew an image that we posted throughout the area. Spizer resembled the person seen by the witness, but it says here there wasn't enough evidence to keep him in custody."

"Did any of these suspects have a criminal record?"

"Let's see. My computer says that Thomas Spizer was our best bet, because he had been accused of assault by an ex-girlfriend. But she later dropped the charges."

"Are you saying that all the slayings remain in your cold case files?"

"Affirmative. There was no other lead or piece of evidence to pursue."

"All right. Did the murders and rapes stop in 1974, just like that?"

"That is what it looks like. Detective Stiles, what is your interest in these crimes?"

"We are currently searching for a serial murderer in Quai Natia, California, and the name Thomas Spizer came up in our investigation. Incidently, are you aware that he was stabbed to death in 2009, according to his widow?"

"Yes, I already have that documented in his file, Detective."

"Okay. I was simply checking to make sure."

"Do you need anything else?"

"Actually, I was also thinking that all those records on the Mycenae serial murders might possibly help in our investigation in Quai Natia. Would you mind giving me access to all those files?"

"That should not be a problem, once I clear it with my captain."

"Thank you, Detective Pippen. If we find out more on Mr. Spizer or the Mycenae murders, I will be sure to call."

"Good hunting, Detective."

Dr. Paris looks into her suspicions regarding Sammy Spizer and Samuel Pitcairn. She calls Melina Spizer and asks her to text a photograph of her son Sammy. Soon after, Paris gets hold of Maya

Pitcairn, who is instructed to send a picture of her father-in-law Samuel.

Once the doctor receives these images, she compares them and sees a definite resemblance. She is almost certain that Sammy Spizer is the same person as Samuel Pitcairn, or they are twins. On the off-chance, Dr. Paris phones Alicia Pitcairn, the widow of Samuel, who lives in Arizona. She reassures the doctor that her husband had no twin brother.

Next, Paris recalls that Sammy Spizer was born in Topeka, Kansas, and that Samuel Pitcairn was killed in Dallas. She asks Detective Novo to call the district court of Shawnee County, which includes Topeka. She contacts the district clerk's office of Dallas County. An hour later, Novo verifies that Sammy Spizer officially changed his name to Samuel Pitcairn in 1995 before he got married. He moved with his family to Dallas in 1997.

Finally, with the help of Detective Novo, Dr. Paris checks the police records of Sammy Spizer/Samuel Pitcairn. It turns out that Samuel Pitcairn was charged with domestic assault and battery on three occasions – in 2004, 2007, and 2011. He was found guilty twice for a Class A misdemeanor, serving jail time for six months both times.

The doctor calls Detective Stiles to make sure he is ready. Then she arranges a team meeting at Lt. Rhombus' office for the next morning.

29

On the very next day, before Lt. Rhombus arrives,
Detective Stiles, Dr. Paris, and Detective Novo compare notes on
what they know about the Black Bird Murders. Patiently, they sit as
the lieutenant enters his office.

"Good morning, Danica, Eli, and Reynold. I am sure you already
know that our murder count has increased to four."

"We do, R-double. I got word from Lt. Durso yesterday."

Rhombus reports, "Bianca informed me that Winston Banks
was found murdered at his former high school in San Jose. As you
all know, he was the sperm donor associated with donor offspring
Jackson Moreau."

Stiles says, "He returned from his Bahamas trip a few days ago,
and I had been trying to reach him before I received the news."

Her straight chestnut hair flowing onto her teal jacket, Paris
asks, "But San Jose? That is almost two hours from here by car."

"Evidently, the Black Bird Killer is not limiting his activities to
the immediate area of Quai Natia any longer."

"That's what it looks like, Rex."

"And you should all be aware that Mr. Banks' body was also
sporting a certain lapel pin."

"I presume bearing the image of a black bird?" asks Novo.

"None other," says Lt. Rhombus. "And blunt head trauma was
detected as well."

Dr. Paris comments, "I was just going to ask about that. And how was the body discovered? Has a cause of death been determined?"

"No C.O.D. so far, Danica. The corpse was lying face-up at the center of the football field's 50-yard line no less. Apparently, he had been dead for two to three days."

"Once again, another curious crime scene, at a location the murder victim appreciated while alive. He played quarterback for the football team in high school."

"That is right on the money, Doctor," says the lieutenant.

"Was anything stolen from the victim?" asks Detective Novo.

"Negative, Reynold. His watch and wallet were not taken," answers Rhombus.

"What about Banks' former girlfriend in Monterey? She was very bitter about their recent breakup. And her brother was apparently angered by the whole matter. Might they be involved?"

"Good idea, Eli. Do we have their names?"

"Mr. Banks' sister Kiki could not give those to me. But maybe we can ask Banks' former workmates and friends."

Lt. Rhombus says, "Let's keep them in mind for now – we may pursue that avenue soon."

Dr. Paris then asks, "By the way, Reynold, in your recent search, did you happen to find anyone who bought both pure nitrogen gas and scuba or non-rebreather masks from local stores?"

"I came up empty in that pursuit, Danica. Records show that 149 persons locally purchased either nitrogen gas or a special mask in the last four months. But no one purchased both. And overall, I only came across one buyer of either item with a criminal history. She was convicted of a tax fraud misdemeanor two years ago."

"What does that person do? Is she possibly our murderer?"

"She is a 42-year-old massage therapist, who is right-handed."

"That person doesn't exactly fit our killer's profile," says Paris.

"No, she does not. I have a feeling that the assailant purchased the items online or outside the Quai Natia region. Or he paid cash locally so the stores would have no record."

"R-double, there is also the possibility that he bought these items more than a few months ago. He may have been planning these murders for longer than we think."

"That is definitely a consideration, Eli. Now, what new information do you all have for me today?"

"Rex, it has come to our attention that there were 17 serial rapes-murders in the area of Mycenae, Nebraska, between 1970 and 1974. Thomas Spizer was a leading suspect who was arrested but later released. In 2009, he was fatally stabbed by an unknown assailant."

"Detective, how did you come across these facts?"

"Spizer's widow revealed them to Lt. Durso, and I called the Mycenae Police Department to confirm."

"And how is Thomas Spizer related to our recent series of murders?"

Dr. Paris answers, "Well, Spizer had a son Sammy, who later changed his name to Samuel Pitcairn. As you know, Samuel Pitcairn was the father of our second victim."

"Wasn't our second victim's father killed two years ago in a hit-and-run event?"

"Rex, that's exactly right."

"So Thomas Spizer, a serial murder suspect, and his son Sammy were both killed. As was Sammy's or Samuel's son, Matt Pitcairn, our second local victim. Do you know what all of this means?"

The room becomes silent.

But a few seconds later, Detective Stiles exclaims, "Yes! Those three men --Thomas and Sammy Spizer, Matt Pitcairn -- are part of a lineage or family tree."

"You hit the nail on the head, Eli. And in my opinion, their murders were not coincidental."

"I can't help but agree, Rex," says Paris.

"Now, let's say that consanguinity is the basis of the recent murder spree. Then why hasn't Murray Pitcairn, Matt's brother in Washington, D.C., been harmed?"

"He may be the next victim. We need to check on him as soon as possible," answers Detective Novo.

"Please take care of that, Reynold. Another question is why Sammy Spizer changed his name to Pitcairn?"

"Rex, I have a theory on that."

"Let's hear it, Danica."

"I believe Sammy found out that his father, even if not convicted, was a leading suspect in the Mycenae murders. And to avoid any possible connection to the serial killings, Sammy decided to change his last name to Pitcairn."

"That's a good idea," says Rhombus.

"And that may also be the reason Sammy/Samuel moved from Kansas to Texas, which is farther from Nebraska, where the Mycenae murders occurred."

The lieutenant says, "Definitely possible, Reynold. Now, looking at the bigger picture, can we show that the other Black Bird Murder victims were linked to Mr. Matt Pitcairn?"

"I guess we would need to check if they are also part of that family tree," suggests Dr. Paris.

"Exactly what I'm considering, Doctor. What do we know about Jackson Moreau, victim number one? Is he related in any way to the Spizer-Pitcairn line of descent?"

"Well, the Constellation Fertility Center records indicate that Jackson Moreau was the biological son of Winston Banks. And both are now dead," says Detective Stiles.

"So our fourth local victim, Winston Banks, and our first victim, Jackson Moreau, are first-degree relatives. Now, is either one related to Thomas Spizer?" asks Lt. Rhombus.

"In fact, they both are!" answers Stiles. "Lt. Durso told me that Spizer was the father of Banks. That puts Spizer, Banks, and Moreau in a direct line of descent. Thus, we now we have a genetic link among three of the four victims of the Black Bird Killer!"

"That's correct, Detective. Our family tree now includes Thomas and Sammy Spizer, Matt Pitcairn, Winston Banks, and Jackson

Moreau. Equally significant is the fact that Thomas Spizer is the common ancestor."

Dr. Paris adds, "Our line of reasoning would also explain why Jackson Moreau's son Billy was assaulted. Fortunately, he was not killed. But what about Jackson's sister Emma?"

"She and Murray Pitcairn may well be in jeopardy as we speak. I suggest we look into both of them now," says Novo.

Lt. Rhombus agrees.

Detective Novo contacts Murray Pitcairn, who confirms that he is the half-brother of Matt Pitcairn, with a different father. Murray recalls no recent problems, and he was told of his brother's death by his sister-in-law Maya.

Detective Stiles then calls Emma Lane, the sister of Jackson Moreau. She reports no recent events out of the ordinary. She also says that Jackson's widow Hanna recently informed her of her brother's death.

Rhombus is reassured. But the lieutenant surprises everyone by saying, "I am not too concerned with Murray Pitcairn or Emma Lane becoming a potential victim, however."

"Why is that, Rex?" asks the perplexed doctor.

"Let's first consider Murray Pitcairn. He is the half-brother of Matt Pitcairn, with a different father. Therefore, Murray Pitcairn is not part of the family tree of interest."

"You are right!" says Stiles.

"Regarding Emma Lane, she was born to Cliff Moreau and Astrid Moreau, with no sperm donor involved. As a result, she is not genetically related to Thomas Spizer either."

"Once again, that makes good sense," remarks Novo.

His reasoning is impeccable, but the lieutenant concludes, "Nonetheless, let us arrange police protection for both, to be on the safe side. Make it so, Eli."

30

Attention now turns to the third Quai Natia murder victim, Carl Zimmerman.

Dr. Paris points out, "Zimmerman's parents have yet to respond to my phone calls regarding their adoption of Carl. But at the moment, there is no known biological connection between our third murder victim and the Spizer-Pitcairn-Banks-Moreau family tree."

"R-double, even if we can verify this relationship between Thomas Spizer and all the recent murder victims, we still have no good suspects for the Black Bird Murders."

"I am aware and equally concerned, Eli. For now, please review the files on the Mycenae serial murders in more detail. Danica, let me know when the Zimmermans call you back. And Reynold, make sure to contact former workmates and friends of the now deceased Winston Banks – see if you can get the names of Banks' former girlfriend and her brother."

Everyone acknowledges his/her assignment and the meeting is adjourned.

Less than an hour later, Dr. Paris receives a call back from the Zimmermans, who were visiting family in Vancouver to spread the word of their son's death. They had turned off their cell phones for about a week. At the doctor's request, both agree to fly to Quai Natia before returning to their home in Missouri.

Meanwhile, Detective Novo calls the Monterey office of Tannenbaum Enterprises and speaks to a couple of former colleagues of Winston Banks. One of them identifies Banks' recent girlfriend as Chloe Davis. Police records demonstrate two arrests for theft of women's clothing. Her only brother is named Julian, who has received several speeding tickets.

Warrants are obtained for the Davis siblings' credit card and phone records. Surprisingly, these records show purchases and calls in the last two months in the state of Florida. Novo visits their last known places of work and finds out that both moved to the Sunshine State in late January. Hence, they can not be responsible for the Black Bird Murders.

In the late afternoon, Tammy and Randy Zimmerman see Dr. Paris at her office.

"Thank you for changing your itinerary and agreeing to meet with me again. I am sure you are still grieving over the death of your son."

"You're welcome, Doctor. We thought a trip to see some relatives would help us better deal with the devastating news."

"I can only imagine what you have been going through. And please forgive me for asking you a sensitive question before I update you on our investigation."

"What is it, Dr. Paris?"

"You told me earlier that you adopted Carl, then you later had two more children of your own."

"Yes, that's right," says Mrs. Zimmerman with some hesitation.

"But why would you adopt first, knowing that you would be able to give birth and have Debra and Lawrence afterwards?"

The Zimmermans look at each other, realizing their white lie has been discovered.

"I'll be forthright with you, Doctor. I lied about the adoption because I did not want to relive the terrible incident that happened in 1975."

"What occurrence was that, ma'am?"

"I was working in Omaha, Nebraska, at a bookstore, and I met a man named Thomas Spizer."

"Did you say Thomas Spizer?" Paris asks.

"Yes, do you know of him?"

"Sorry. Please continue, Mrs. Zimmerman."

"As I was saying, he seemed nice and ended up asking me out. But our first date did not go very well – he just kept talking about his job, in photography, the whole time. In fact, he caught a bad flu after that date, and he didn't call me back for over a month."

She is noticeably becoming more anxious as her husband holds her.

"I was reluctant to meet for a second date, but he was persistent, so I agreed. He seemed more pleasant, but I knew he was not the one. When I told him I didn't want to see him again, he became irate."

"Angry enough to hurt you?"

"He started kissing me and touching me while I resisted."

"Mrs. Zimmerman, did he sexually assault you?"

Now tearful, she finally admits, "Yes! He violated me! That monster! And it took all the courage I had to eventually put the whole matter behind me."

"I am extremely sorry to hear that, ma'am. Did you formally file charges against him?"

"I really thought about it but then read about the poor conviction rate for accused rapists. And I would have had to go public about everything."

"Are you saying that you opted not to file charges?"

"That's right. I decided that the ordeal of having my private life scrutinized and having to testify in court would not be worth it. Basically, I realized that there was no guarantee that the evil man would be convicted."

"It is unfortunate that so many rapists aren't convicted for their crimes, and I can understand your difficult decision. Did anyone else know of the assault, Mrs. Zimmerman?"

"Only one other person at the time, and that was my brother Dominic. He was my bedrock as I slowly recovered from the nightmare."

"Ma'am, how did your brother take it?"

"Oh, Dominic was furious. He wanted to track down Spizer and probably hurt him. But I convinced him that if he went through with it, he would go to jail or worse and I would never see him again."

"Did your brother agree to stay away from Mr. Spizer, just like that?"

"It took some convincing, but I believe he did."

"Ma'am, would you mind if I speak with your brother Dominic? Where does he live?"

"If you must. His name is Dominic Vikander, in Lincoln, Nebraska. Here is his number."

"Thank you. And Mrs. Zimmerman, you mentioned that you lied about Carl's adoption?"

"Doctor, let me be clear. I never adopted Carl. Carl was the result of my rape!"

Dr. Paris is stunned by the revelation, and she is silent for a few seconds.

"Now I understand. What you went through must have been quite a harrowing experience!"

"I would not wish it upon anyone."

"And I am sure keeping Carl was not an easy choice for you. Statistically, only about a third of the children born due to a rape are raised by the biological mother."

"Carl turned out to be a fine man, so I have no regrets."

"By the way, ma'am, can you tell me why Carl's last name is Zimmerman, not Spizer or Vikander?"

"That was my idea. When he was born, I gave him my maiden name, Vikander. But after I met and married Randy two years later, I changed Carl's last name to Zimmerman."

"Well, that explains it. Again, I admire you for your tremendous courage. What's more, I actually have some information for you about Thomas Spizer."

"Really? Is it good or bad?"

"I would say some of both, but overall good."

Trying to compose herself, the distraught lady says, "Okay, Doctor. Go ahead."

"I want you to know that Thomas Spizer was suspected of being a serial rapist-killer in Mycenae, Nebraska, from 1970 to 1974."

Mr. and Mrs. Zimmerman are flabbergasted.

"You mean I was raped by a serial killer? Of how many people?"

"He was only a suspect. We are still trying to verify that he was the serial murderer of 17 college girls."

"Dr. Paris, if the last murder happened in 1974, that would mean he raped me less than a year later. I guess I'm lucky to be alive!"

"I would agree. We can also be sure he will never hurt anyone again – he was stabbed to death in 2009, in Kansas City."

"Serves him right! There is some justice in the world! But Doctor, could my brother have killed him?"

"Mr. Spizer's murderer was never found. So we will look into your brother, as is protocol."

"I hate to ask, but if Spizer was the Mycenae murderer, why do you think he spared my life?"

"The answer to that is not evident at this time, Mrs. Zimmerman, but I have an idea."

"Please tell me, Dr. Paris."

"All right. You said he had some flu virus after your first date. I speculate that this virus may have spread to his brain and altered his behavior."

"Can that happen, Doctor?"

"It is not common, but many viruses can travel to and infect the brain in the right circumstances. And the resulting encephalitis could change one's personality and actions."

"I was not aware. Apparently, I was also fortunate that I didn't get the same virus. At any rate, thank you for giving me closure on that terrible man."

"I am happy to do so, Mrs. Zimmerman. Now, I would like to update you on our investigation of your son's murder."

"What can you tell us?" asks Mr. Zimmerman.

"We now know that Carl was the third of now four recent murder victims in the Quai Natia area. And he either died by being drowned or he was killed before being submerged."

The doctor purposely doesn't reveal the true cause of death, which is being kept from the public by court order.

"Other than drowning, what else could have killed him?"

"That is a difficult question to answer now, and we are still getting all the facts straight."

"Do you have any good suspects at this time?"

"We are continuing to look into some possible culprits, but no arrest has been made yet."

Mr. and Mrs. Zimmerman are noticeably disappointed.

"I need to ask you, Dr. Paris. Do you believe Carl suffered in his death?"

"We can't be sure, but based on my findings so far, I do not think he was in much distress when he died. There were no stab wounds or bullet wounds seen on his body."

Mr. Zimmerman says, "Well, if you're right, that gives us some consolation in knowing he didn't experience a lot of pain in his last hours. Doctor, my wife and I have had a long day. If there is nothing else, may we go now?"

"Of course. Also, please note that as a precaution, we have arranged for police to watch your son's ex-wife and daughter in Utah, in the event the assailant targets them."

"Thank you for everything, Dr. Paris."

"You're very welcome. We will keep you informed about any progress we make."

Paris shakes their hands and wishes them a safe trip home.

31

As the sun sets and dusk closes in, Lt. Rhombus is called by his fidus Achates from Esplanade.

"Bianca, when did you become aware of this?"

"About 30 minutes ago, Rex, after Officer Edmondson called me from Blackstone, California. He saw my card near Melina Spizer's phone at her home."

"Isn't Melina Spizer the widow of Thomas Spizer?"

"She is. I met with her last week."

"And why was this officer at her place?"

"A friend of Mrs. Spizer was concerned when she didn't answer her door. So she contacted the police, who broke into her apartment and discovered her unconscious on the floor. She was taken to the hospital due to an apparent overdose of Valium."

"Poor Melina Spizer. Did she appear suicidal when you met with her recently?"

"Maybe a little gloomy, but not suicidal. I realize she has lost her husband and her only son, but something else must have triggered this unfortunate act."

"Would you mind paying a visit --."

"I am way ahead of you, Rex. I called her main doctor at the hospital, and she says Mrs. Spizer is now in stable condition. I will go to Blackstone first thing in the morning."

"That is great news that she is at least stable. And I can't thank you enough for helping us out."

"I have no doubt you will make it up to me someday, Rex. "

"Speaking of which, I recently suggested a nice dinner, compliments of yours truly. Let's make it two!"

"I very much like that idea."

"I had a feeling you would. We'll talk again soon, Bianca."

"Arrivederci."

As she drives into the small town of Blackstone the next morning, Lt. Durso calls the police station and arranges a meeting with Officer Edmondson at the precinct.

"Good day, Officer. I am Lt. Durso of the Esplanade Police Department."

"Glad to meet you, Lieutenant. I believe we spoke briefly yesterday evening about Mrs. Melina Spizer."

"Yes, that was me on the phone."

"Well, let me fill you in. We received a call last night that a neighbor of Mrs. Spizer came by to borrow some milk, only to get no answer at the door. The lights were on, and she tried her phone, but there was no response. So this friend decided to call the police."

The officer continues.

"After we showed up at Mrs. Spizer's door, we knocked but no one answered. Consequently, we forced the front door open. Inside, we found Mrs. Spizer unresponsive on the living room floor, with an almost empty bottle of Valium nearby. I started chest compressions with rescue breaths before the paramedics arrived. Then she was rushed to Blackstone Hospital."

"How did she look before the paramedics took her?"

"She was barely breathing, but the paramedics at least stabilized her before transport. It appeared she was trying to or intending to call you, as we saw your business card on the nearby coffee table."

"I actually just met with her less than a week ago at the Continental Delicatessen."

"What do you remember discussing with her that day, if I may ask?"

"Melina is the widow of Thomas Spizer, who was once suspected to be a serial killer. His former girlfriend Kendra Banks led me to Mrs. Spizer. The details aren't important, but this girlfriend gave birth to the sperm donor of a recent murder victim in Quai Natia. This sperm donor was also discovered dead two days ago."

"Are you referring to those recent homicides with extraordinary crime scenes?"

"Yes, I am. There are currently four unsolved murders in the Quai Natia area, several hours from here."

"I read that one of the victims was tied down to a navigation buoy. And another was buried in a golf course bunker!"

"All of that is accurate, Officer. So after I met Mrs. Spizer, she told me that her late husband was suspected of serial murders in Nebraska in the 1970's. He was fatally stabbed sometime in 2009. What I can say is that she truly believes that he was innocent of any crimes."

Officer Edmondson adds, "I did not live or work here when Melina Spizer arrived about 10 years ago. But rumors suggest that she was initially ostracized when word got around of her late husband being a possible killer in the past. Over time, though, the people of the town have accepted her with warmth."

"Does she have a history of suspicious or malicious activity here?"

"On the contrary. She is squeaky clean in the police files."

"If you have no objections, Officer, I would like to look around Mrs. Spizer's apartment for a brief time."

"That is fine with me. The front door is closed, but a little push will get you in. Remember, we had to break it in last night."

"Farewell, Officer Edmondson. You've done good work. Have a great day."

32

Not more than 20 minutes later, the lieutenant parks her car near Mrs. Spizer's apartment. She gets past the yellow police tape and pushes the front door open. In the living room, she sees an almost empty Valium pill bottle with some tablets spilled on the carpet. Nothing remarkable is noted in the kitchen.

Lt. Durso climbs up the wooden stairs to the main bedroom. Everything initially looks in order, but a half-open ivory-colored clothes closet catches her eye. Inside, she notices a locked safe.

As she is about to check the rest of the room, she glimpses the white edge of some paper peeking from under the safe. Carefully, she pulls out an 8 x 11 inch photograph. It shows a fair-skinned young woman, maybe in her early 20's, walking with a backpack in the distance. Looking all around the safe, the lieutenant sees no other photographs on the floor.

She then briefly inspects the guest bedroom and bathroom on the second floor. Once she is done with her search, Lt. Durso uses her smartphone to get directions to Blackstone Hospital.

The modern community hospital is only a short distance from Mrs. Spizer's residence, and the lieutenant pushes her wind-blown dark hair to the side as she talks to the receptionist. She flashes her badge and is led to the intensive care unit, where Melina Spizer is about to be taken off the ventilator.

"Hello. I am Lt. Durso. Would it be all right if I talk to Mrs. Spizer now?"

"She has been very lucky, Lieutenant," says the charge nurse in blue scrubs. "Let us do our job and please come back in about 30 minutes. She should be able to talk then."

A half hour later, after snacking on a Clif bar, the lieutenant appears at the bedside of Mrs. Spizer. She is told by the nurse to limit her time with the patient to a few minutes.

"Hello, Melina. Do you remember me?"

Connected to supplemental oxygen by nasal cannula, the patient perks up somewhat, saying, "Lt. Durso? I almost called you."

She has to stop talking briefly to catch her breath.

"After we talked several days ago about my husband, I became curious. Then I recalled a safe that Thomas used when he was alive. Only I did not have the combination – he never gave it to me."

"Slow down, Melina. Take your time."

"As I was saying, I looked for the combination in my apartment for almost a day. Eventually, I discovered an old address book of Thomas."

"Oh, did you see the safe combination in the book?"

"When I looked through it, all I remember seeing were addresses and phone numbers of people we knew."

The lieutenant listens intently as Spizer speaks at a slow pace.

"But there was one person in the book whom I did not recognize, listed only as Winston. I called the phone number, but it was disconnected."

"So what did you do?"

"Well, I came up with this notion that the phone number may be a code for the combination of the safe."

She breathes a few times before continuing.

"After trying a few permutations of the numbers, I was able to open the safe."

"Wow! I am impressed, Melina. You should be a police detective!"

The patient is flattered. "You know that I taught mathematics in high school, don't you?"

"We did not discuss that, but I know now."

"Anyway, in the safe, I came upon many black and white photos of more than a dozen young women -- women I didn't recognize."

"What did you do next?"

"I did not know what to think, so I took a few old Valium pills to relax."

"Melina, you probably took more than a few, since the police found you unconscious in your apartment."

"Oh dear. That explains why I am in the hospital, doesn't it?"

"I am afraid so. And the paramedics only reached you in time because your neighbor saw your lights on and you weren't answering your phone or the door. So she became worried and ended up calling the police."

"Are there people at my home now?"

"Not at this time. But when I looked over your place for evidence of a crime, I saw a locked safe in the main bedroom closet. And on the carpet under the safe, there was a black and white photograph of a woman in her early 20's. What did you do with the other pictures?"

"I must have dropped that one. I put all the other photos back into the safe."

Lt. Durso asks, "Do you remember the safe combination, Melina?"

"Not exactly, but I can figure it out if you give me Thomas' address book. I may have shoved it into my handbag."

Suddenly, alarms sound as two nurses enter the room.

33

"Sorry, but we need to ask you to leave, Lieutenant.
Mrs. Spizer's pulse and blood pressure are spiking and we need to assess her. Probably just the stress of your interview."

"I understand. I will step out soon, but can you first show me the personal belongings that came with her to the hospital?"

One of the nurses points to a personal storage area in the room.

Lt. Durso finds Mrs. Spizer's handbag, with an address book inside. She looks up the name Winston and sees a phone number. After writing down the number, she exits the room as the patient is attended to.

Almost 30 minutes later, Lt. Durso returns to Melina Spizer's bedside once she is again deemed medically stable by the nursing staff.

"What happened, Lieutenant?"

"You just fell asleep for a while there. Do you feel okay?"

"Kind of. I am a little woozy."

"Okay, Melina. I will leave you to rest, but I only have one or two more brief questions for you. Are you up for it?"

The patient nods.

"While you were sleeping, I saw this address book near your possessions. Inside it, this is the phone number for Winston. Can you tell me how you deciphered it to get the safe combination?"

"Let me think. I ignored the area code. Then I used the first two digits as the first number of the combination, the second two as the second number, and the third two as the third number."

"Well, using your method, that would make the combination 25-20-12. Does that sound familiar?"

She ponders for a while then carefully answers, "Yes, I believe that is right."

"Excellent, Melina. Now, would it be okay if I opened the safe to get a look at all those photographs you saw?"

"You have been very nice, Lieutenant. So yes, I trust you. But who are those women in the photos?"

"I really can't say until I see the pictures, Mrs. Spizer. But after I get into the safe and collect the photos, I will come back here to check on you. Don't worry about anything."

The patient whispers, "See you then," before drifting into sleep.

Lt. Durso leaves the hospital and makes a beeline to Mrs. Spizer's flat. She gets past the familiar yellow police tape and slowly pushes the front door open.

Once inside, she goes to the main bedroom upstairs and specifically to the safe in the closet. While crossing her fingers, she dials the three numbers of the combination. What follows is a feeling of invigoration as she successfully opens the safe. Three large envelopes are removed, each containing about 20 photographs. In total, about 17 different young women are pictured.

Durso then drives to the local police precinct and presents all the photos to Officer Edmondson and his captain. They agree that she can take possession of all the photographs for the purpose of finding the perpetrators in the Mycenae and Quai Natia serial murders.

"Good luck, Lieutenant," says Officer Edmondson. "Let me know how it turns out."

"Thank you, Officer. I appreciate all your efforts. It was very good to meet you."

"Likewise."

As promised, Lt. Durso returns to Blackstone Hospital to see Mrs. Spizer. She shows her the different photographs, and Spizer asks who the young ladies could be. The lieutenant, not wanting to upset the hospital patient, tells her she will meet with her police confreres to figure it out.

The sun is barely visible behind the clouds on this overcast day as Durso starts her drive back to Esplanade. An hour later at her police precinct, she calls Lt. Rhombus before sending him digital photos of the dozens of black and whites found in Thomas Spizer's safe.

"I hope you received all the pictures, Rex. They were kept in a safe that Thomas Spizer used when he was alive. As for Melina Spizer, she is slowly improving after her accidental overdose of Valium."

"It is a relief that she is fine. You are certain that no one tried to harm her?"

"Very much so. Rex, what do you make of the images?"

"The photos appear to be those of college age women."

"Hmm. Might they be the victims of the Mycenae serial murders in the 1970's?"

"That's exactly what I'm suspecting. It sounds like you may have hit a home run here, Bianca."

"Thank you. A little detective work never hurts."

"Eli has been reviewing the files of those killings. I will have him look at these photos as well."

"If the information matches, we should have ironclad evidence that Thomas Spizer was in fact the Mycenae serial killer."

"Indeed. And the Mycenae Police Department, as well as families of the murder victims, will be relieved to know that. The question would then be how all of this relates to the Black Bird Murders."

"Rex, I am sure you already have some ideas on that. Be sure to give me updates on your progress."

"That I can promise you. Have a wonderful evening, my good friend."

34

Detective Stiles has spent the better part of the last 24 hours poring over the cold case files of the Mycenae serial murders. In addition, he also has looked at the photographs recovered by Lt. Durso.

"Eli, have you had ample time to review all the police records on the Mycenae murders, as well as the photos from Thomas Spizer's safe?"

"Affirmative, R-double. I believe some suspects have come to the fore."

"Outstanding. Meet me at the police station within the hour please. And ask Dr. Paris and Detective Novo to join us."

"Rex, if you don't mind, Reynold will not be able to come in today – he says his knee has really been acting up."

"That will be fine. I'll see you and Danica soon."

"We'll be there."

An hour later, at 10 a.m., most of Lt. Rhombus' team is present near the whiteboard at the precinct.

Before they talk about the findings of Detective Stiles, Rhombus brings up the cause of death of the Black Bird Killer's fourth victim.

"Doctor, has the San Jose medical examiner drawn any conclusions about what caused Winston Banks' death?"

"He did. Blood tests showed lactic acidosis, and signs of definite asphyxiation were discovered on examination of the internal organs. He agreed to check for pure nitrogen gas as the cause of the asphyxiation, and those special tests will be back in a couple of days."

"Thank you for the update. On another front, I was told that you met with the Zimmermans late yesterday."

"Yes, finally. They had been in Vancouver grieving with family for over a week, with their cell phones turned off."

"That accounts for our recent difficulty contacting them. So, did they clarify why Carl was adopted before they had more children later on?"

"They sure did. Mrs. Zimmerman lied to us about the adoption. There was never any adoption. Carl was born when Mrs. Zimmerman -- or Miss Vikander at the time -- was raped by Thomas Spizer in 1975!"

Lt. Rhombus and Detective Stiles are stunned.

"That is startling. Why did she lie to us?" asks the lieutenant.

"The main reason is she did not want to discuss the sexual assault again. She was probably also somewhat embarrassed."

"Was Spizer convicted of the rape?"

"It was a tough decision, but she ended up not formally accusing him."

Rhombus reflects for a moment and says, "If Carl was born due to the past rape of Tammy Vikander/Zimmerman by Mr. Spizer, do you both know what that indicates?"

There is a brief quiet in the room before Stiles exclaims, "Actually yes, I do! Carl Zimmerman can now be considered a direct descendant of Thomas Spizer, just like the other recent victims."

"We are on the same wavelength, Eli," says Lt. Rhombus. "In this situation, Spizer's genes were literally forced upon our unfortunate third victim."

"That makes perfect sense, Rex," says Dr. Paris.

"Thank you. So now, we have established an extensive family tree that runs from Thomas Spizer to all the recent murder victims. But how can this information lead us to the Black Bird Killer? Eli, what more have you learned about the Mycenae area serial murders?"

"I am glad you asked."

On the large whiteboard, the detective writes down the names of all 17 victims at Mycenae, Nebraska, between 1970 and 1974. Their pictures from the police records are also displayed.

"These young women were all the known rape-murder victims based on the Mycenae police files. They were all single female college students in their early 20's, but with different hair colors, body types, nationalities, and college majors."

"Did the assailant have a modus operandi in the different crimes, Detective?"

"Yes. The pattern involved abducting the young woman when she was walking alone on or near her college campus, holding her hostage for up to a week, raping her an undetermined number of times, and finally killing her by strangulation."

"What a wicked man! Were there any distinctive marks on the victims' bodies? And where were the corpses discovered by the police?" asks the doctor.

"The dead victims were all found fully clothed in the local parks. Different types of bruises were seen on them, including ligature marks in the neck. And for your information, no black bird lapel pins were seen on any of them."

"And have we identified the killer, Eli?"

"R-double, I think so. Last time we noted that Thomas Spizer was the leading suspect, but evidence was insufficient to convict him. But earlier today, you gave me these photos of 17 young women. They were recovered by Lt. Durso in a safe Thomas Spizer kept when he was alive."

Detective Stiles lays out these photos on the computer screen. After looking at these pictures, everyone realizes they show the same 17 women seen in the Mycenae police records for the victims in the 1970's.

Stiles declares, "Based on these new findings, we can now close the cold case files on the Mycenae serial murders. Thomas Spizer was undoubtedly the serial killer."

Lt. Rhombus says, "Good work, Eli. And kudos to Lt. Durso as well. Please inform Lt. Durso, who must decide how to break the news (or not) to Mrs. Melina Spizer. And also relay our conclusions to the Mycenae Police Department when you can."

"Consider it done," replies the detective.

"However, I am bothered by one detail," says the lieutenant. "Why did Thomas Spizer stop killing after 1974? He raped Miss Vikander in 1975 but did not murder her. And we know of no killings by him between 1974 and when he died in 2009."

At that point, Detective Stiles states, "Well, we know that serial killers often go through so-called 'cooling-off periods,' during which there is a significant break between murders."

"That is true, Eli. But it seems he took a permanent break from killing for 35 years before he himself was slain."

"I agree, Rex. Mrs. Zimmerman also asked me about the cessation of the serial murders. I think there may well be an explanation," says Dr. Paris.

Rhombus and Stiles wait with anticipation.

"Mrs. Zimmerman, who dated Spizer in early 1975, told me he contracted a bad flu after their first date and didn't see her for over a month before their second date. My suspicion is that this flu virus caused a mild encephalitis that altered Spizer's personality and psychopathic behavior."

"What is encephalitis, Doctor?"

"An inflammation of the brain substance, usually but not always caused by a virus."

"So you feel this brain inflammation or infection could have been enough to stop him from killing any longer?"

"Yes, I do. It is medically known that encephalitis can affect practically any part of the brain. I believe that Spizer's flu virus attacked a certain region, such as the area between the prefrontal cortex and amygdala."

"How could a virus there inhibit his violent tendencies, Danica?"

"Well, this brain location is often associated with psychopathic behavior and loss of a sense of guilt over one's actions. Consequently, a virus affecting that brain region could suppress or alter Mr. Spizer's criminal behavior."

"Doctor, as usual, your insight is very illuminating and much appreciated. Thanks to this probable virus, Mrs. Zimmerman and probably other women are fortunate to be alive."

"I am with you there, Rex," says Dr. Paris.

As her phone buzzes, she glances at the display.

"Gentlemen, please give me a few minutes -- I need to take care of this call from the hospital."

"Of course."

"When I get back, I will present a theory of mine regarding the Black Bird Killer."

"We'll be here waiting."

35

A little over five minutes later, Dr. Paris returns and proposes her new theory on the serial murderer still at large.

"I have reviewed several studies strongly suggesting a genetic predisposition in most serial killers. However, they also require an environment that promotes this disregard for human life."

"Do you believe Mr. Spizer or the Black Bird Killer grew up in such an environment?" asks Lt. Rhombus.

"We may never know for sure, but we have proof of significant violence committed by at least two of Thomas Spizer's first-degree relatives. A few days ago, Reynold and I found that Spizer's son Sammy or Samuel was charged with domestic abuse on three occasions. He was sentenced to some jail time for two of those accusations that led to convictions."

"Go on, Doctor."

"And we looked further into Spizer's relatives and discovered that his brother Jeremy was killed by the police in 2002. He was in the process of being arrested for viciously slaying his girlfriend."

"Very compelling, Danica."

"So based on the facts we have to date, Thomas Spizer and at least two of his close relatives have carried out violent or very violent acts. We also now know that all the recent murder victims were direct or lineal descendants of Spizer. Therefore, I posit that the Black Bird Killer wants to knock off all the progeny of Thomas Spizer, in order to prevent this 'violence gene' from propagating further."

Lt. Rhombus and Detective Stiles nod their heads while pondering her thesis.

"On top of that, I must say that there is some evidence of impulsive and/or destructive behavior in at least some of the recent murder victims."

Stiles states, "I think you are right, Danica. His mother told me that Jackson Moreau was an unruly child until high school, and Matt Pitcairn's widow conveyed his gambling problems and occasional mild assaults on her."

"Carl Zimmerman's ex-wife said he was involved in some bar fights and had a temper at times. Those were probably factors in their divorce," says Rhombus.

"What do we know about the demeanor of our fourth victim, Winston Banks?" asks the doctor.

"Lt. Durso told me he was very independent growing up, and he had a problem dealing with authority. Also, he had been unable to settle down with one woman, but I am not sure if that was by choice," says Detective Stiles.

Dr. Paris adds, "Hence, it seems that we now have clear proof of violent behavior or undesirable character traits or both throughout much of Thomas Spizer's family tree. Accordingly, it does makes sense that the Black Bird Killer believes all of Mr. Spizer's descendants must be eliminated."

The lieutenant asks, "If what you say is true, why has Carl Zimmerman's daughter in Utah not been harmed? Billy Moreau, our first victim's son, has already been attacked."

"We set up police protection for her after the assault on Billy, but she may be a future target," says Paris.

"Good point. And what about all the siblings of our recent murder victims?" asks Stiles. "Aren't they all descendants of Mr. Spizer as well?"

The doctor states, "Let's go over each of them. First, we have discussed that Emma, our first victim's half-sister essentially, and Murray, the second victim's half-brother, are not genetically related to Thomas Spizer."

"Agreed."

"Carl Zimmerman, our third victim, only has half-siblings, Lawrence and Debra, who are not related to Mr. Spizer. And our most recent murder victim, Winston Banks, only has a half-sister Kiki, who is not biologically related to Spizer either."

"Very good analysis, Doctor. So it appears that the potential future victims of the Black Bird Killer are Thomas Spizer's only known living descendants, namely Billy Moreau and Nina Cîrstea. And both are now under police watch."

"That is what it sounds like, R-double."

"Well, that takes care of our local killer's probable motive, that of doing away with serial killer Thomas Spizer and his progeny. But do we have any good suspects?"

Dr. Paris answers, "I vote for Dominic Vikander, the brother of Tammy Zimmerman. She confided in him about her rape, and he voiced to her an intent to harm her rapist. Mrs. Zimmerman told me she convinced him not to, but he would have more than enough motive to do away with Mr. Spizer."

Lt. Rhombus reminds everyone, "We're forgetting one thing, though. Was Dominic aware that Thomas Spizer was a potential serial killer?"

The doctor says, "Come to think of it, I don't believe so. When I spoke to Mrs. Zimmerman, she was surprised when I told her about Spizer's possible connection to the serial murders. So she could not have told her brother Dominic about the Mycenae events."

The lieutenant concludes, "Then Dominic Vikander is not likely our assailant, because even if he did kill Spizer out of revenge, he would have had no clear reason to murder his descendants."

"I agree 100%, Rex," says Detective Stiles.

"Nonetheless, let's check Dominic Vikander's criminal record, recent phone records, and also credit card purchases, and look into his employment history for completeness."

Everyone concurs.

"What about the resentful ex-girlfriend of our fourth victim, Winston Banks? Has Detective Novo been able to identify her?"

"R-double, Reynold told me she is Chloe Davis, and her brother is Julian Davis. She has been caught stealing on a few occasions, and he has a problem following the speed limit."

"Is it possible they are involved in the Black Bird Murders, Detective?"

"Unfortunately, I think not, since both have good alibis: The two moved to Florida about two months ago."

"Duly noted. We can scratch those individuals off our list. And Eli, please relay my thanks to Reynold, who is hopefully getting his knee looked at today."

"I will tell him later, Rex."

"Very good. So where does that leave us? Ah yes, you have been meticulously reviewing the police files on the Mycenae murders. What can you tell us, Detective Stiles?"

"As you both know, the 17 coeds in Mycenae were brutally raped and murdered between 1970 and 1974. What I did was focus my attention on these victims' relatives, who have every right to be bitter and vindictive."

"Please go on, Detective."

"But given their age in the present day, I have ruled out any of the parents of those victims as the local serial murderer. That being said, I propose that the Black Bird Killer is a vengeful sibling of one of the Mycenae victims."

"Eli, let's say that you are correct and a sibling of one of those victims murdered Thomas Spizer out of revenge. Would this person then want to kill the progeny of Mr. Spizer for the reasons Danica just described?"

"I believe so, R-double. As I see it, in some way, the Black Bird Killer already knows of the violent tendencies in Thomas Spizer's family tree. And he wants to eliminate any descendants of Spizer to prevent them from becoming psychopaths or serial killers themselves."

The lieutenant and doctor are silent for several seconds.

"You have definitely given us some food for thought, Eli. For now, we will go with your premise, as your line of reasoning does hold water. Now, are you able to say which siblings of the Mycenae victims are the most likely suspects for the Quai Natia area murders?"

"Yes, I think so. I would disregard those siblings who are currently 61 or older, since I can't imagine anyone of that age having the strength and endurance to murder our victims and then place them in the unusual crime scenes."

"Your supposition is sound. Please continue."

"That leaves exactly four siblings of our Mycenae victims as good suspects – all are age 60 or younger. They are a Nevada security guard (brother of victim Shelby Curry), a computer programmer in Sacramento (brother of victim Lynette Tapping), a schoolteacher in Maine (sister of victim Bridget Umenyiori), and a pharmacist in San Diego (brother of victim Leslie Park). Of course, the teacher is less likely because of her gender."

"All those suspects are well-grounded, Detective. And they are our only good leads at this time. Any comments or questions, Doctor?"

"No, Rex. They all seem very reasonable."

"Danica, I know you have hospital matters to attend to. And Reynold is stuck at home at this time. So Eli, please contact the educator in Maine, the guard in Nevada, and also Dominic Vikander. I will get hold of the San Diego pharmacist and the computer scientist who lives nearby in Sacramento."

As the meeting ends, there is a clear sense of optimism in the room as everyone realizes they may be close to apprehending the local menace.

36

"Good morning, ma'am. This is Detective Stiles from Quai Natia, California. I would like to speak with Mrs. Sara Miles, please."

"This is Sara. Can I help you?"

"Mrs. Miles, I work for the Quai Natia Police Department, and we are investigating some recent homicides."

Miles' heart stops momentarily as she is reminded of her deceased sister.

"Homicides? Do you think they have something to do with my dear sister's cruel murder in 1972?"

"We are looking into that possibility, ma'am. But I can tell you with certainty that your sister's killer was a man named Thomas Spizer. He himself was murdered in 2009."

"Oh, I am so relieved! At least my sister Bridget can finally rest in peace. But I believe you said you are investigating some recent homicides as well?"

"Yes, in and near Quai Natia, in the Central Coast of California. What is your occupation, Mrs. Miles?"

"I teach biology at a community college in Portland, Maine."

"And can you tell me if you have been to California in the last several months?"

"I would love to visit your state at some time, but I fell on a wet floor in late February and fractured my hip. Ever since surgery, I have been moving around in crutches."

"That's a shame, ma'am. Would you mind if I confirmed that with your orthopedist? And can you give me the phone number of a close friend nearby?"

"Am I a suspect, Detective? In my opinion, you are wasting your time."

"Just following procedure. The sooner we remove you from our list, the better for you."

"Well, I suppose. Here is the phone number of my orthopedist and the number of my good friend Helen who lives in Vermont."

Stiles writes down the numbers and wishes Mrs. Miles a speedy recovery.

After getting off the phone, the detective immediately calls Helen in Vermont. She is able to confirm Miles' recent hip fracture and subsequent surgery.

It takes two hours for Mrs. Miles' orthopedist to return the detective's call, but he is finally able to verify that he did surgery on her right hip in early March. He also says she has required crutches since the operation and has been seeing him regularly since then.

Detective Stiles is now confident that Sara Miles can not be the assailant they are seeking. Next on his list is Mr. Dominic Vikander.

Stiles finds a spotless criminal record for Vikander, then he obtains a warrant for his employment, phone, bank, and credit card records. The detective notes that he is a 59-year old operations manager working for Paragon Pharma in Lincoln, Nebraska. He calls the company's human resources department and sends a copy of the warrant as requested.

"How long has Mr. Vikander been with your company, ma'am?"

"According to my files, it's been 11 years now."

"Okay. Has he been on vacation this year so far? And has he taken any other time off in 2019?"

"Let me check. His last vacation took place between mid-December and early January. Since then, he has had perfect work attendance."

"Does he work five days a week?"

"Yes, he does."

"And has he had any problems on the job?"

"No, sir, I don't see any."

"Well, thank you for your time, ma'am. So long."

Detective Stiles then reviews Dominic Vikander's other records for the last several months. He sees no calls to California or the West Coast. His credit card and bank records also show no suspicious transactions.

Finally, the detective looks at the files on Mr. Martin Curry. He is the brother of Shelby Curry, who was raped and murdered in 1973. Mr. Curry works as a security guard in Carson City, Nevada, and the criminal record of this 52-year-old is immaculate.

The firm near Carson City that employs Curry gives Detective Stiles his recent employment history. Mr. Curry has worked at the same bank for the past year and a half, with no time off since last Christmas and New Year's holidays.

Telephone records demonstrate no calls to or from California in the last six months, and credit card information also points to no California purchases. His bank statements reveal no unusual transactions.

Our detective gives a courtesy call to Mr. Curry to inform him of Thomas Spizer's guilt many years ago. Curry is grateful to finally get some closure on his sister's violent demise.

Detective Stiles is now able to report to his lieutenant that Mrs. Miles, Mr. Vikander, or Mr. Curry can not be the Black Bird Killer.

37

Lt. Rhombus obtains warrants for all the appropriate records on Marcus Park, the brother of Mycenae victim Leslie Park. A complete background check reveals that he is a 58-year-old pharmacist in San Diego, meaning he was only 10 when his sister was murdered in 1971.

His criminal file shows one report of possible spousal abuse several months ago. His wife had minor scratches, but he claimed that SHE actually attacked HIM. Rhombus notes that he outweighs his wife by 30 pounds. In addition, there was a speeding ticket for going 86 miles per hour about a year ago. Other than that, he has had no traffic infractions, and he has never been arrested or jailed.

Recent telephone records indicate several calls to the Los Angeles and San Francisco areas this year and a few calls in February and March to the Quai Natia area. Otherwise, there have been no other calls to places north of Los Angeles in 2019.

Given the aforementioned information, the lieutenant opts to call Dr. Park.

"Hello, is this Dr. Marcus Park?"

"Yes. This is he."

"Dr. Park, this is Lt. Rhombus of the Quai Natia Police Department. Do you have time for a few questions?"

"I need to be back at work in about ten minutes. What is this about?"

"Well, I can call you back. Or you can come to the police station to give me your statement."

"Oh, that's okay. Let's take care of it now."

"It should only take a few minutes or so. First, let me ask you about the domestic disturbance report a few months ago."

"The true story is that it was my wife who tried to attack me. And you can see from the records that she dropped all charges."

"And why did she file a complaint on you in the first place?"

"Let's just say she thought I was knocking boots with the pharmacy manager. It was all an unfortunate misunderstanding."

"Are you and your wife doing well now? Any recent disturbances?"

"As well as can be expected, and no."

"I also want to offer my condolences for your sister Leslie's death in 1971. And it may interest you to know that we have confirmed Thomas Spizer as the serial murderer in Mycenae."

"I knew it! He was always the main suspect, but the police never had enough evidence. Did they arrest him finally?"

"Mr. Spizer was killed in a stabbing in 2009, Dr. Park. The assailant was never found."

"He's dead? Thank God! I hope it was a painful death! That animal deserved it."

The pharmacist then chokes up as he tries not to cry.

"But I know his death won't bring my poor sister back. I miss her."

"I am very sorry for your loss," says Lt. Rhombus, trying to console him.

"What else can I do for you, sir?"

"I am currently investigating several unsolved murders in the Quai Natia area. I need to ask you where you have been in the last several months."

"Why, am I a suspect?"

"You are only a person of interest at this time, Dr. Park."

"If you must know, I have been in San Diego ever since I returned from a seminar I attended in San Francisco in February."

"Do you mind if I call your wife to attest to this?"

"If you must. You can call her at her office at this number."

"Thank you," says Rhombus as he writes down her number. "And can you explain some phone calls you made in February and March to the Quai Natia region?"

"Yes. I was calling a friend from college. He had some questions on two new medicines prescribed by his family doctor."

Lt. Rhombus jots down the friend's name and number.

"I appreciate your time, Doctor. Have a good afternoon."

Once he hangs up, Rhombus calls Mrs. Park, who is able to corroborate her husband's story for the last several months. The lieutenant also contacts Park's friend in Quai Natia, who confirms the pharmacist's account.

The records of Mr. Xavier Tapping are now reviewed. He is a 56-year-old computer engineer. He was only 10 when his sister Lynette was raped and murdered in 1973. He obtained a bachelor's degree in computer science, although at age 29. In Central Oklahoma, Tapping attained his graduate degree in cybersecurity in 1996.

In his police record, there are only a few traffic infractions, including one speeding ticket. In the last four months, Mr. Tapping has made various phone calls in and to the Central Coast of California, which includes Quai Natia. Recent credit card purchases in the same region are also noted. There are no suspicious transactions in his bank statements.

Over the next several hours, Lt. Rhombus is not able to contact Mr. Tapping. He only has a cell phone, which has been going straight to voicemail.

The lieutenant rings Detective Stiles.

"Eli, I will be paying a visit to Mr. Xavier Tapping in a few hours. Please find out and text me the phone and address of his current workplace."

"You got it, Rex. Should I come with you?"

"That will not be necessary for now. I will call you when I return."

"Understood. Have a nice trip!"

38

Motoring north in his black Dodge Durango, the inimitable Quai Natia lieutenant is heading to the city of Sacramento. Around 6 p.m., he arrives in the state capital. Driving through a placid neighborhood, he reaches his destination at 314 Galaxy Place. It is a one-story brown and red home with no lawn.

Taking off his sunglasses, he knocks on the front door. An expressionless six-foot man with salt-and-pepper hair opens the door.

"Can I help you?" he says gruffly.

"Good evening, sir. I am Lt. Rhombus of the Quai Natia Police Department. Are you Xavier Tapping?"

"I am Tapping," he responds grimly, with piercing brown eyes.

"May I come in for a few minutes?"

"I think not. Unless you have a warrant."

"No, but I can get one. I have been trying to call you on your cell phone for the last few hours. Have you been receiving my calls?"

"I don't answer any calls without a caller ID," he says brusquely.

"That explains it. And do you have a home phone?"

"I see no reason to have two phones, Lieutenant."

"Understood. I would like to ask you a few questions about your deceased sister, Lynette."

He looks down and crosses his arms before saying, "She has been dead for years. What is your interest now? You police never caught her murderer."

"That is one reason I'm here. We have confirmed that Thomas Spizer was the serial killer in Mycenae."

The expression or lack thereof on Mr. Tapping's face changes little.

"Huh. So that guy was the killer. I always wondered why they never convicted him. Is he finally rotting in jail now?"

"No. He was the victim of a fatal stabbing about 10 years ago."

"The bastard finally got what was coming to him. The world is a better place now. Is that all you came for?"

"I have some other questions about a more current matter. Again, may I come in for a few minutes?"

"Like I said, not without a warrant. I have talked with enough cops since my sister died."

"Sir, I am also investigating several murders in the Quai Natia area. Can you tell me how long you've lived here in Sacramento?"

"Why? Am I some sort of a suspect for these murders?"

Rhombus withholds the truth. "Not at this time. Can you please answer the question?"

Impatiently, Tapping says, "Almost two years. Moved here from Central Oklahoma. Now, I have to go."

"Very well. I may be in contact with you soon, Mr. Tapping."

The testy man shuts the door without saying another word.

Disturbed by the suspect's behavior, Lt. Rhombus returns to his car and checks his cell phone. There is a text from Detective Stiles with the phone and address of the Sheeld Corporation. He calls the business and is told that the facility manager and a few employees are still there. The receptionist assures the lieutenant that the manager will remain on site until he arrives.

Twenty minutes later, Rhombus reaches Tapping's place of work. He asks to talk to the person in charge after flashing his badge. A pleasant 30-something with titian hair appears a few minutes later and extends her hand.

"Hi, Lt. Rhombus. I am Lucinda Otencio, the facility manager. How can I assist you?"

"Good evening, Miss Otencio. I am here to ask you about one of your employees, Mr. Xavier Tapping."

"That would be fine. Follow me to my office."

Sporting an amaranthine dress, she walks with perfect posture as he follows. Soon, they both sit down at her desk and she punches the keyboard of her computer for a few seconds.

"Yes, Mr. Tapping works for us in cybersecurity. He was hired less than two years ago, and he has been a very reliable employee."

"Have you had any difficulties with him since he's been here, miss?"

As she brushes some hair from her face, she answers, "Not that I know of, Lieutenant. He is usually on time and his job performance has been good. He only takes the occasional vacation."

"Could you tell me the last time he holidayed?"

"He took some time off last December for three weeks. No vacation so far this year."

"Are you saying that he has been working full-time this entire year?"

"As far as I know. But let me look at our records."

After Miss Otencio checks her computer, she says, "Mr. Tapping works four days a week and Friday mornings. He has had very good attendance this year – no workdays have been missed, except for one Friday, when he called in sick."

"Oh. Please tell me what day that was."

"It looks like the Friday two weeks ago."

"All right, let me note that. Miss Otencio, would you say he is a friendly fellow?"

"He is polite, but he usually keeps to himself. I have never met his family."

"One more thing, miss. Is he right-handed?"

"Hmm. I'm not positive, but I'll be back in a minute."

She speaks to some employees in another room.

Upon returning, she says, "It is verified. He is left-handed -- his colleagues says so and I also just looked at some of his writing."

"You have been very helpful, Miss Otencio. Thank you."

"Lt. Rhombus, should I be concerned with Xavier, with you asking all these questions about him?"

"Not at this time. I am just following up on some leads in an investigation."

"I see. Can you tell me more about it?"

"Sorry – it is an active case."

"Oh, I get it. Police business."

"Yes, you are correct. Thank you for understanding. Also, Miss Otencio, please note that this meeting between us is strictly confidential."

"I understand, Lieutenant. My lips are sealed."

"Good day, Miss Otencio. Thanks again for your time."

As Lt. Rhombus makes his way back to Quai Natia, he is fully aware that Xavier Tapping may well be the Black Bird Killer. He plans to either visit Mr. Tapping again at his home, this time with a search warrant, or force him to go to Quai Natia for further questioning.

Rhombus recalls the background check he did earlier on Tapping. It shows that his father resides in a retirement home, and his mother died of kidney disease a few years back. He has no children and no living siblings. And his wife Greta died many years ago for unclear reasons.

Given Mr. Tapping's discourteous behavior and minimally cooperative attitude, the lieutenant believes the suspect will probably refuse to answer more questions, even if he is arrested. Realizing this likelihood, Rhombus decides to first call his father Sherwood Tapping, who lives in Sioux Falls, South Dakota.

39

Lt. Rhombus is back in his office early the next morning, planning to talk to Mr. Sherwood Tapping. However, he first contacts the Sioux Falls Police Department to pick up Mr. Tapping and take him to the local precinct. He is taking this course of action to prevent Mr. Tapping from calling his son Xavier soon after their conversation – such a call may tip off Rhombus' primary suspect.

After Mr. Sherwood Tapping arrives at the police station in Sioux Falls, the lieutenant gets on the phone.

"Good morning, Mr. Tapping. This is Lt. Rhombus of the Quai Natia Police Department. I apologize for any inconvenience I am putting you through this morning."

"Hello, Lieutenant. That is quite all right. I already had my breakfast."

"I am glad. Sir, I just need to ask you a few things about your son Xavier."

"That's fine, Lieutenant. Is he is any trouble?"

"Mr. Tapping, my team is investigating some crimes in this area and the name of your son came up. I have some routine questions for you."

"Go right ahead. But I haven't heard from him for about two months now."

"First of all, I offer my sympathy for the violent death of your daughter Lynette many years ago."

"Thank you. That was a long time ago, but it never gets easier. I know she's in heaven now."

"I also want to inform you that her killer has been identified, and he was stabbed to death by some unknown person in 2009."

"Well, I'm happy that he got what he deserved. What was his name?"

"Thomas Spizer."

"Spizer. Yeah, I remember that name came up, but the Mycenae police couldn't prove it was him."

"I can reassure you that we now have definitive evidence. Hopefully, knowing this information will help you sleep a little better."

"A little. Now, what is this about my son?"

"Sir, can I ask you how your son took your daughter's murder?"

"He was close to Lynette, but at age 10, he couldn't really accept the reality. Only after a month or so did he realize she was not coming back. As a result, he became quite sad and solitary."

"That's too bad. How did he do in high school?"

"I would say fair."

"And did he go to college immediately after high school?"

Mr. Tapping sighs. "He tried, but he had to drop out because he wasn't able to focus. It's as if his ambition in life went away in his teens."

"I'm sorry to hear that. So did he work after he graduated from high school?"

"He did different jobs here and there – waiting tables, delivery work, things like that."

Tapping coughs for a few seconds then continues.

"One day, he was talking to his pharmacist about medicine he was prescribed for his insomnia. Xavier became interested in how the pharmacy worked, so he went through a course to become a pharmacy technician."

"Mr. Tapping, how old was he then?"

"Around 21. He liked that job and the people there, and he was always looking for some new medicine to help him sleep better. In fact, he met his wife Greta at the pharmacy."

"Oh, did she work there too?"

"No, you misunderstand. She was picking up a prescription for her mother and Xavier attended to her. Anyway, they got married the next year. They were happy together, until she learned a year or two later about her mother."

"What about her mother, Mr. Tapping?"

"She was diagnosed with Huntington's disease, which is a brain condition that has no cure. All you can do is treat some of the symptoms."

"I presume that Greta became sad because of her mother's illness."

"Yes, of course, but that wasn't all. The doctors asked Greta if she wanted to be tested for the gene for Huntington's. You see, each child of a person with Huntington's disease has a 50 percent chance of inheriting the gene and the disease."

"Those aren't good odds, sir. Did Greta ever decide on getting the test?"

"She thought about it for a long time and also discussed the matter with Xavier. Finally, her curiosity got the best of her and she agreed to the genetic test. And it turned out that she did have the gene for Huntington's."

"That's very unfortunate, Mr. Tapping. What did she do?"

"Well, she had no symptoms, which usually start in your 30's or 40's. But her mother got progressively worse and ended up dying about two years later."

"Do you know how your daughter-in-law coped with her mom's death?"

"As she was mourning her mother, Greta became more and more depressed, knowing it was only a matter of time before she would suffer a similar fate."

"Because she had the Huntington's disease gene?"

"Yes. Sad to say, if you have the gene, you are guaranteed that the disease will eventually affect you."

"Sir, with that incredible burden, did she seek help from a psychologist or psychiatrist?"

"She did eventually see a psychologist, but not soon enough. Xavier found her with her wrists slit in the bathtub. At the hospital, she was pronounced dead."

Thunderstruck, Lt. Rhombus is silent for several seconds.

"That's quite a tragedy, Mr. Tapping. I can only begin to imagine how your son felt. First his sister, then his wife. He must have been devastated."

"He was. And they never had any kids, since they didn't want to risk passing on the disease."

"I understand their difficult decision, sir. How old was Xavier when his wife took her own life?"

"About 25."

"And did he ever remarry?"

"No. But I think he has been dating some lady for the last year."

"That's nice. I have been told that Xavier works with computers now."

"You're right, and it is really quite a story. My son became interested in computers because Greta was quite the computer geek. So after she died, he went to college to get a computer degree."

"You don't say."

"Yup. He told me that since he would be working on something she loved to do, his wife would always be with him in some manner."

"He is quite the romantic. And does he have any hobbies?"

"He likes to play pool and hike. He is a pretty good swimmer. That's about it."

"Out of curiosity, has your son ever been interested in birds or aircraft."

"Nah. Never."

"All right. Well, you have been very generous with your time, Mr. Tapping. Many thanks. I will have an officer take you back to your home now, and this person will stay with you for a day or more. Please do not contact your son Xavier for the time being."

"Lieutenant, if you would, let me know if my boy is in any trouble, okay?"

"You have my word on that. Have a good morning, sir."

Lt. Rhombus asks one of the Sioux Falls police officers to escort Mr. Tapping to his retirement home. He also instructs the officer to closely watch the senior citizen for the next 24 hours or so, in order to restrict his use of the telephone and computer email until further notice.

40

Two fortnights have passed since Jackson Moreau was discovered buried at Olympic Torch Golf Links. Three murders and one assault later, Lt. Rhombus and his team have a solid suspect, but proving he is the elusive serial murderer will not be a slam dunk.

After the light rainfall in the morning, the smell of petrichor fills the air. Still in his office at the police station, Lt. Rhombus awaits his team members. He is sporting his usual dark pants and blazer.

One by one, they arrive. Detective Novo is first, followed by Dr. Paris, who dons an eggplant dress and light blue sweater. A mildly winded Detective Stiles finally walks in and apologizes for being a little tardy.

"How goes your knee pain, Reynold?" asks the lieutenant.

"At the moment, I don't even notice it. I have felt good ever since the orthopedist injected some steroids into the knee yesterday. But let's see how long this pain holiday lasts."

"Do you miss the rugby field?" the doctor asks sincerely.

"Very much, but I'll survive," says Novo as he grins at Paris.

Everyone present knows that the main suspect is now Xavier Tapping, as the other possible perpetrators have been ruled out in the last 24 hours. Mr. Tapping fits the killer's profile fairly well, and the motive of the Black Bird Killer appears to be the elimination of the progeny of confirmed serial killer Thomas Spizer. Stiles starts off the discussion.

"Let me first convey that Xavier Tapping is the brother of Lynette Tapping, a coed raped and murdered by Thomas Spizer in

1973. He lived in Central Oklahoma between 1992 and about two years ago. Remember that Thomas Spizer was killed in Kansas City in 2009 and Sammy Spizer (aka Samuel Pitcairn) had his fatal car accident in Dallas in 2017."

"Kansas City or Dallas is only three to four hours from Central Oklahoma by car," points out Lt. Rhombus.

"That sounds about right, R-double. Less than two years ago, Xavier Tapping moved to Sacramento, which is less than four hours from Quai Natia and two hours from San Jose by car."

"As a result, we can say that Mr. Tapping has lived in the general vicinity of where Thomas Spizer, his son Sammy, and the recent four murder victims were killed," says Detective Novo.

"Correct," says the lieutenant. "And we also know that the Black Bird Killer is left-handed, likely male, and a good swimmer. Tapping has all these characteristics."

"At this juncture, Rex, Mr. Xavier Tapping is our leading suspect by far. Did you find out anything of interest regarding his family?" asks the doctor.

Rhombus responds, "His mother died of kidney disease a few years ago, and his father lives in a retirement home. Mr. Tapping has no siblings, and he married his wife Greta when he was about 22."

"Are they still together?" asks Novo.

"That is no longer possible, Detective. Greta inherited the gene for Huntington's disease from her mother. As Dr. Paris knows, this progressive disease has no cure and you can only manage some of the symptoms. And Greta knew that having the gene meant it was only a matter of time before she would start having problems herself."

"You are right," says Paris. "The gene is on chromosome number four, and it guarantees that this degenerative brain disease will eventually affect you. Did she receive appropriate counseling?"

"When Greta's mother eventually died of Huntington's disease, Greta finally started seeing a psychologist. But despite this assistance, she was unable to overcome her grief and depression – she ended up killing herself about two months later."

"That's a somber story, Rex. Xavier must have been overwhelmed. First his sister is murdered, then his wife commits suicide. He also became fully aware of how a medical condition can be easily passed from one generation to the next."

"I agree, Doctor. Let me also say that Mr. Tapping has made calls to and within the Quai Natia area in the last several months, and credit card purchases in the region have also taken place."

"Were any of those purchases for scuba masks or nitrogen gas?" asks Detective Novo.

"I am afraid not," says the lieutenant.

"R-double, at this time, I would like to remind everyone that our original list of suspects consisting of certain siblings of the Mycenae victims was based on a premise. This supposition was that the Black Bird Killer has known that Thomas Spizer's family tree demonstrates a strong tendency toward violence. And our serial killer wants to prevent more violence by eliminating Spizer and his progeny."

"I do remember that, Eli."

"In other words, the murderer we seek is aware of Spizer's direct descendants as well as the violence displayed by his relatives."

"That would have to be true, Detective."

"Consequently, we are presuming that Mr. Xavier Tapping has this knowledge."

"I guess we are. What are you getting at, Eli?"

"Rex, it is my belief that Mr. Tapping's computer prowess has enabled him to gain this crucial information. And his computer expertise has been indispensable in the plotting of these recent crimes."

"How so, Detective?"

"First of all, I assert that he has needed to hack into well-protected databases to acquire valuable information about Thomas Spizer. For example, he probably accessed the Mycenae police records in the 1970's to help him conclude that Spizer was the serial killer. Similarly, Xavier Tapping likely used his skills to find that Mr. Spizer's brother and son committed violent crimes."

"That makes sense," says Lt. Rhombus. "What else?"

"I strongly suspect that Tapping hacked into the vital records departments of several states to look at the birth certificates. They would have revealed that Thomas Spizer fathered Sammy Spizer, Carl Zimmerman, and Winston Banks."

"Your contention is reasonable, Eli. Could you think of another example of him using his computer skills?"

"Sure. I would also say that Mr. Tapping was the one who broke into the Constellation Fertility Center files a few months ago. This data told him that Jackson Moreau was the donor offspring of Winston Banks."

"To sum it up, Detective Stiles, you are saying that Xavier Tapping has used his computer expertise to achieve three goals: establish Thomas Spizer's guilt in the Mycenae murders, uncover the tendency towards violence in Spizer's family tree, and identify the descendants of Mr. Spizer. Is that correct?"

"You are spot-on, R-double."

"But Eli, accomplishing what you have just described requires very specialized knowledge. Do you feel that our suspect has the proficiency to have pulled all that off?" asks Lt. Rhombus.

"Actually, I do, given his extensive education and experience in the computer world, including cybersecurity."

"So you are maintaining that Mr. Xavier Tapping has been surveilling Thomas Spizer and his progeny for some time now, by way of these cybercrimes?"

"Yes, I am. Remember: He completed his cybersecurity education in 1996 and has been working since then in that specialized field. Don't you agree that he should be capable of everything I have just illustrated?"

"If you put it that way, I would have to concur, Detective. Is there anything you wish to add, Danica and Reynold?"

Both shake their heads.

At that point, Lt. Rhombus gets up, stating, "Let's take five. And Danica, please check if the San Jose medical examiner has finalized the cause of death on Mr. Winston Banks."

Everyone stands and slowly files out of the room.

41

With the entire team back at Lt. Rhombus' office, Dr. Paris announces, "I am now able to give you the official cause of death for Mr. Winston Banks. There is a specialized forensics lab in San Jose, so the final analysis of the alveolar fluid has become available sooner than I expected. As a result, the San Jose forensic pathologist is able to verify that nitrogen gas asphyxiation is the official C.O.D. for our fourth victim."

"Thank you, Doctor. I am sure none of us are surprised at those important results. But on a positive note, as we discussed the other day, we have probably identified all the potential future targets of the Black Bird Killer. They are the known living descendants of Thomas Spizer – Billy Moreau and Nina Cîrstea. And both are under police protection."

"That is good news. But what about the black bird lapel pins? Have we linked them in any way to Mr. Tapping?" asks Detective Novo.

Paris answers, "I regret to say that we have not."

"By the way, Eli, in your review of the Mycenae police files, do you remember if any of the murder victims majored in zoology, biology, or aerospace engineering? Those fields relate to black birds in some way, as we have noted," says Novo.

"When I evaluated the available records, those majors were not mentioned," replies Detective Stiles.

There is quiet for a few seconds.

"All right," says the lieutenant. "Let us all assume for now that Xavier Tapping did commit these reprehensible murders. If so, after fatally stabbing Thomas Spizer in 2009, why do we suppose he waited until 2017 to resume his killing spree?"

Dr. Paris believes she has an answer.

"Rex, I think we all agree that the vicious murder of Thomas Spizer in 2009 was motivated by pure revenge. But I propose that the subsequent homicides, which have only occurred in the last two years or so, have been driven by some occurrence as recently as 2017."

"What type of occurrence are you contemplating, Danica?"

"There are many possibilities. Mr. Tapping could have read a book or seen a documentary on serial killers. Maybe a friend introduced the idea of serial murderers' sons and grandsons becoming psychopaths. And so on."

"Fascinating idea, Doctor. In effect, you are suggesting that the Black Bird Killer didn't start planning the murders of Thomas Spizer's direct descendants until 2017. And Samuel Spizer was his first target."

"Yes. Those are my thoughts exactly."

"Danica, that is very plausible," says Stiles.

Novo comments, "I totally concur."

"Very well," continues Lt. Rhombus. "Now there is a final practical issue I must raise. Can anyone tell me how Mr. Xavier Tapping could be our serial killer if he has been working full-time in Sacramento for the last several months?"

Dr. Paris has no immediate answer, and neither does Detective Stiles. But Detective Novo offers his hypothesis. He takes out his notepad and reminds everyone that the homicide dates were March 9th, 16th, 22rd, and 29th or 30th.

"My notes show that the first two murders happened on Saturday morning, and the fourth one either Friday or Saturday. The assault on Billy Moreau happened on a late Friday afternoon."

"And the third murder?" asks Rhombus.

"Sometime between 10 p.m. Thursday and 8 a.m. Friday. And we know that Mr. Tapping has Friday afternoons off, right? And he doesn't work weekends."

"All of that sounds accurate. Where are you going with this, Reynold?"

"Because most of the crimes occurred on weekend days, Tapping could have simply driven to Quai Natia or to San Jose and back without being missed at work."

"That's right! But what about Carl Zimmerman, who was killed either Thursday night or Friday morning two weeks ago?" asks Paris.

Novo responds, "If Mr. Zimmerman was murdered Thursday night, Mr. Tapping could still have made it back to work by Friday morning. But if the crime occurred Friday morning, I have no explanation."

There is a brief hush in the room before the lieutenant declares, "I believe I have the answer. Xavier Tapping called in sick one day this year, and that was two weeks ago on a Friday!"

"There you have it. He could have driven to Quai Natia on that Thursday evening or Friday morning two weeks ago to murder Mr. Zimmerman," says Detective Novo.

"And people at his office would be none the wiser," adds Detective Stiles.

Lt. Rhombus concludes, "So we can all see now that Mr. Tapping had the opportunity to commit all four recent murders and the assault on Billy Moreau."

Dr. Paris asks, "Rex, do you think we have enough circumstantial evidence to get a search warrant for Tapping's home? We have little in terms of direct physical proof right now."

"I hope so. I will contact Judge Wilson momentarily. With any luck, we can get both search and arrest warrants, although I doubt the latter, knowing the judge."

"I have a good feeling about this, R-double. Let's keep our fingers crossed."

The three leave Rhombus' office as he prepares to make a call.

42

After phoning the busy office of Judge Wilson, Lt. Rhombus is forced to leave a message. As he waits for a call back, he ponders something Detective Stiles said in their meeting.

Soon, he calls the Nebraska Office of Vital Records. He is told that he would need a warrant to gain access to the information he seeks. He gets the same response from the Missouri Bureau of Vital Records, the Kansas Office of Vital Statistics, and the vital records offices of Wyoming, South Dakota, Minnesota, Iowa, and Colorado.

An hour later, the judge's office returns the lieutenant's call.

"Hello, Judge Wilson. How has your golf game been?"

"It's coming along, Lieutenant. And your fencing? Derek told me you had to cut your last bout short."

"Duty called me away, sir."

"I can totally understand that. Now, tell me about the progress in your investigation."

The findings thus far in the search for the Black Bird Killer are summarized by Rhombus.

"Lieutenant, the proposed motive, opportunity, and circumstantial evidence appear sufficient to establish probable cause. But you are lacking any direct proof linking Mr. Tapping to the crimes at this time."

"I am afraid you are right. And that is why the search warrant would be very helpful. I would be looking for a card from the Just Win! tavern, sand from the beach at Biscay Bay or the Olympic Torch golf course, or anything that could place the suspect at the crime scenes."

"Would there be other items of interest?"

"Of course, a black bird lapel pin or a tank of pure nitrogen gas would be the holy grail."

"I think we can agree on that. I will grant you the search warrant to include the home and nearby automobile of Mr. Xavier Tapping. But the arrest warrant is unsubstantiated at this time."

"That is very reasonable, Judge. Thank you. And sir, I have another request. I am looking for certain birth certificates in the Midwest. The offices handling these records in Nebraska, Missouri, Kansas, and the other states adjacent to Nebraska require warrants for the information."

"What are you hoping to discover, Lieutenant?"

"As far as we have determined, the confirmed Mycenae serial killer Thomas Spizer lived or worked in Nebraska, Missouri, Kansas, and possibly the neighboring states in his adult life. As I have told you, we have found all or at least most of his direct descendants. Who I am looking for is anyone we may have missed."

"I see your point. And these persons you're searching for may be potential targets for the Black Bird Killer?"

"Exactly. If I can identify them, we can protect them."

"I admire your mental acumen, Lieutenant. You have your warrants."

"Thank you again, Judge. Good day."

After obtaining the warrants, Lt. Rhombus contacts his two detectives. He then calls the vital records offices in the aforementioned eight Midwest states and asks them to look for any birth certificates listing Thomas Spizer as the father. He instructs them to check the time period from 1970 to 2009.

En route to Sacramento, search warrant in hand, Detectives Stiles and Novo discuss their plan. They have already arranged for two Sacramento Police Department officers to meet them later.

"We have to assume Mr. Tapping is possibly armed, so let's not underestimate him," says Novo.

"I am with you there," says Stiles, checking his Glock 35 pistol and its magazine. "We are looking for anything that can place him in any of the murder scenes or connect him to any of the murders. Only then can we arrest him, understood?"

"Roger that, Eli."

Two uniformed officers are already outside Mr. Tapping's home when the two detectives arrive. After shaking hands with the officers, Detective Stiles gives them examples of items they are looking for. He also reminds them to respect the suspect's property when possible.

Stiles knocks on the front door and identifies himself and the search team. No one hears a sound for almost half a minute before Tapping opens the door. He is suspicious as he sees the uniforms of the officers.

"Can I help you?" he says grimly.

"Mr. Xavier Tapping, I have a search warrant for these premises as well as your car. Please step aside and give us your car keys."

Alarmed by the intrusion, Mr. Tapping states, "I can't believe this! Am I under arrest?"

"You are under investigation for a series of four murders in the Quai Natia area and San Jose. You are not under arrest at this time."

Tapping is watched by an officer in the living room as the other three search the one-story house and his Volvo.

Over an hour later, nothing of significance is recovered by the other officer. But Detective Novo enters the living room with some items in hand.

"Look at what I dug up: a matchbook from the Just Win! pub, and a tee from the Olympic Torch golf course. Do you smoke, Mr. Tapping?"

"On occasion. Is that a crime?"

"No, but when were you last at the Just Win! tavern?"

"I don't recall exactly. Maybe two months ago. Is that illegal?"

"Not unless you murdered someone and tied his body onto a pool table there," says the detective.

Tapping doesn't say a word.

"Now, when was the last time you played golf at Olympic Torch Golf Links, Mr. Tapping?"

"It's been a while. Maybe six months."

"And were you there about a month ago?"

"I get it. You're trying to pin those recent murders on me."

"Are you ready to confess now?"

The suspect is now clearly salty and glares at Novo, strenuously denying the crimes.

A few minutes later, Detective Stiles joins Detective Novo, the officers, and Mr. Tapping in the living room.

"I discovered this in the garage."

He presents a box of rope, which looks like that used to tie Matt Pitcairn to the pool table and Carl Zimmerman to the navigation buoy.

Stiles then signals to Novo and says, "Mr. Xavier Tapping, you are under arrest for the murders of Jackson Moreau, Matt Pitcairn, Carl Zimmerman, and Winston Banks."

Detective Novo handcuffs him and reads him his Miranda rights. Mr. Tapping offers little resistance as he is taken into custody. Detective Stiles then tells one of the officers to seize the suspect's computer tower.

Several minutes later, Stiles says, "Thank you, Officers, for your help. Detective Novo and I will take our suspect to Quai Natia for processing."

"No problem, Detectives. We'll file our report with our precinct."

As the officers leave, Novo locks up the residence as Detective Stiles leads the accused to the vehicle. All are quiet as they travel south toward Quai Natia. After a few hours, Xavier Tapping is booked and then placed into a Quai Natia precinct holding cell.

43

It is a little after 11 a.m. the next morning, and
Assistant District Attorney Margaret Eisen makes her appearance at
the police precinct. A statuesque brunette with hazel eyes, she is
wearing a charcoal business suit and dark blue pumps.

She has already filed a criminal complaint in court against Mr.
Xavier Tapping, charging him with four counts of first-degree
murder. After reviewing various police reports, she joins Lt.
Rhombus in his office. The lieutenant has just contacted the Sioux
Falls police to end the monitoring of Mr. Sherwood Tapping.

"It's good to see you again, Rex. I am happy to know that you
may have finally apprehended the so-called Black Bird Killer. Many
in town have been wondering when the next murder might happen.
But hopefully, we have enough to convict Mr. Xavier Tapping."

"Good morning, Margaret. Detective Stiles thought we had
probable cause last night to arrest him. Our search of his home
turned up items placing him at the Just Win! tavern and the Olympic
Torch golf course. His records also show phone calls to and from the
Quai Natia area in the last month or so."

"It has also come to my attention that you found some
suspicious rope at Tapping's home."

"Yes, our forensic laboratory technicians have compared it to
the rope used to tie Carl Zimmerman to the navigation buoy and
Matt Pitcairn to the pool table. And it's a match in terms of the type
of the rope."

"Rex, does Mr. Tapping have a good alibi for any of the murders?"

"He has refused to say anything so far."

"So the accused is choosing to keep us in suspense. Maybe he'll be more talkative with his defense attorney coming at 11:30."

"Do you know who that would be?"

"Yes, you may remember him – Mr. Rick Pouncey. By his reputation, he will fight for his client to the bitter end."

"Margaret, after reviewing the reports so far, what do you think about our chances of convicting Mr. Xavier Tapping?"

"The case against him is mostly circumstantial now. The matchbook and tee could have been taken by Mr. Tapping at any time. And we don't necessarily know if the rope that you recovered was connected to the ones used on those two murder victims."

"The lab is checking the rope for anything we can use – blood or sand, for example. Detective Novo will also be looking into how common the rope is and how many people have access to it."

"I am anxious to get that information. And Rex, I notice that no nitrogen tanks, breathing masks, or black bird lapel pins were discovered at the suspect's home or in his car."

"That is disappointing but true. He could have moved them to another location after I paid him a visit recently. Or he may have used a different nitrogen container and mask for each murder, discarding them after each crime."

"What about his credit card and bank records? Did you come across any purchases for the nitrogen gas and masks, or even the lapel pins?"

"We did not, Margaret. I surmise that he has been smart enough to buy them with cash. And yes, we have checked local stores for purchases of pure nitrogen gas and scuba or non-rebreather masks in the last several months. Tapping is not listed in their records."

"I see. What about Billy Moreau's friend, Charlee? Can she possibly identify the person who assaulted Billy?"

"When Danica spoke with her, the grade-schooler said she did not get a good look at the perpetrator's face. But she may recognize something about him in a police lineup."

"I will arrange the lineup, with Mr. Tapping's lawyer and myself present. But keep in mind that young children are often unreliable as witnesses. Do you have anything else, Rex?"

"No, not at this time."

"Well, let's keep in mind that no other eyewitnesses have come forward, and the accused is not even close to a confession. We also have no fingerprints, identifying DNA, or murder weapons at the crime scenes."

"I believe you are saying we need more direct evidence."

"That would definitely help. Have you shown Mr. Xavier Tapping's picture to the Just Win! tavern owner and staff? And to employees at the Olympic Torch Golf Links?"

"Yes, we already did. No one recalls him being in either place recently."

"How about video footage? Is it available at either location?"

"At the tavern, they only record during business hours. As for the golf course, cameras are limited to the clubhouse, restaurant, and golf cart storage areas during hours of operation."

"There's a start. I know it's a mind-numbing task but –."

"Say no more. I will have Detective Stiles review the videotapes at the bar as soon as he can. And Detective Novo will check the golf course tapes as well."

"Rex, I have another thought. Your reports state that Mr. Tapping has made phone calls to Quai Natia and the vicinity. You should check if any of the calls were made to residences."

"I know what you're driving at, Margaret. I will pursue that myself to see if he may have any accomplices. Also, Tapping's computer may be a gold mine when our computer expert is able to break through its security system."

"Let me know about your team's headway, Rex. I will talk to Mr. Pouncey after he sees the accused."

Rick Pouncey, wearing a Van Dyke beard, sports a brown tweed jacket and dark blue trowsers. He arrives at 11:30 a.m. sharp to see his client. After meeting for half an hour, he sets up the arraignment on the complaint for the next day.

Assistant District Attorney Eisen sits down with Mr. Pouncey to discuss what the accused will plead.

"Margaret, I think you are wasting your time on my client. The matchbook and golf tee do not put him at the crime scenes at the times of those two murders. That rope can be purchased by almost anyone. And the rest of your criminal case is purely based on circumstantial evidence."

"Surely you know that we can convict on that alone."

"I believe that will be an uphill climb, Counselor. In the end, you will likely fall short in trying to convince a jury. He will be entering a plea of not guilty tomorrow."

"Off the record, in your opinion, do you feel he is telling the truth?"

"Actually, yes. His sister was brutally murdered, and he clearly would have the motive to kill Thomas Spizer. But taking out all of his descendants? Also, his sister was killed in 1973. That means that a whopping 36 years passed between her death and the murder of Spizer."

"Mr. Tapping may not have had the means to exact revenge before 2009."

"That may be a tough sell for any jury, Margaret. And note that eight years separated his alleged murders of Thomas Spizer and his son Sammy in the past."

"I realize that. But he will not be on trial for those two murders. And we are still working on several leads."

"Just don't forget to disclose any new evidence to yours truly."

"You know I will, Counselor."

44

Soon after arriving at the bustling Just Win! tavern in the suburb of Pamplona, Detective Stiles asks about the establishment's videotape footage. Viola the owner directs him to a cozy room where he can view the tapes.

For hours, he stares at the recordings. He initially focuses on the time just before the body of Matt Pitcairn was discovered three weeks prior. His progress is slow as molasses, with no luck in identifying Xavier Tapping.

He lets out a sneeze, thinking it is simply the dust or an allergy. But after an hour or two, he feels a tickle in his throat and a mild fever. As he prepares to go home, the detective calls the computer ace at the police station.

"Ben, any luck getting into that computer of Mr. Tapping?"

"That's a negative, Eli. And given his background in cybersecurity, I was not expecting a cake walk."

"Yeah, I anticipated that as well. Are we allowed to beat the password out of our suspect?" he asks sarcastically.

"I wish it was that simple, Detective. But I believe something called the Fifth Amendment prohibits that."

"I know. I guess that's the price of the rule of law."

"I'll call you or Lt. Rhombus when I get past the computer's security system. By the way, you sound like you're coming down with something."

"Could be. I'm heading home now to get some shut-eye."

"Rest up, Detective."

At the Olympic Torch golf shop, Detective Novo is told that the last tee time scheduled for Mr. Tapping was seven months ago. None of the staff recalls seeing him in the last month or two.

The detective inspects the security tapes around the time of Jackson Moreau's murder about a month ago. Most of the footage is around the clubhouse and restaurant areas, and Novo sees nothing of importance.

Back at the precinct, Lt. Rhombus looks back at the recent telephone records of Mr. Tapping, and the only residence he has called in Quai Natia is that of Patrick Psaki. The criminal record of Mr. Psaki only shows a few parking tickets. Nonetheless, Rhombus gives him a ring.

"Good day, Mr. Psaki. I am Lt. Rhombus of the Quai Natia Police Department. Do you have a few minutes?"

"Sure, sir. What do you need?"

"Our records indicate that Mr. Xavier Tapping called you five weeks ago and nine weeks ago. Is that your recollection?"

"Hmm. That sounds about right."

"How do you know Mr. Tapping?"

"We both worked at the Sheeld Corporation in Sacramento before I transferred to the Monterey office about three months ago."

"And have you been to the Just Win! tavern or Olympic Torch golf course with him recently?"

"I've never picked up a golf club, Lieutenant. But we got together at that bar when he called nine weeks ago. Why do you ask?"

"Do you remember him being anxious or acting out of the ordinary?"

"Not that I recall. He was fairly upbeat and was curious how I liked living in Quai Natia."

"Sir, has he been in any trouble as far as you know?"

"You mean like trouble with the law?"

"Yes, or any other difficulties you can think of."

"No, not since I have known him. What are all these questions about, Lieutenant?"

"I am investigating the local murders you may have read about, and Mr. Tapping is a suspect."

"Oh, with the strange crime scenes. The dead man found buried in the bunker. And the one tied to the pool table."

"Correct, and two others as well."

"Well, I am surprised that you are considering Xavier. He doesn't strike me as a murderer."

"Finally, Mr. Psaki, can you tell me where you were on these dates and approximate times?"

Rhombus lists the dates and times of the recent four murders and the assault on Billy Moreau.

"My wife and I are empty nesters, so I was probably with her at home."

"Would you mind if I speak with her now?"

"I have nothing to hide, Lieutenant. Here's the number of her friend's house. She should be there."

"I appreciate your time, Mr. Psaki. Thank you."

"No problem."

Lt. Rhombus hangs up and calls Mrs. Psaki. She is able to give support to her husband's narrative on the dates of the murders.

An hour later, Rhombus receives a call from the manager of the Missouri Bureau of Vital Records.

"Good afternoon, Lieutenant. This is Natalia. That was quite a project you gave us. But we only turned up one birth certificate, that of Winston Spizer, listing Thomas Spizer as the father. Winston was born on August 16th, 1976."

The lieutenant recalls that Winston later changed his last name to Banks.

"Great! And who is the mother on the certificate?"

"Sir, Kendra Banks is listed as the mother."

"Natalia, I want to express the thanks of the Quai Natia Police Department for the efforts of you and your bureau on this important matter."

"You're welcome, Lieutenant. Good luck on your investigation."

The Kansas Office of Vital Statistics gets back to the lieutenant later that day.

"Hello, Mrs. Zappa. This is Lt. Rhombus."

"Lieutenant, I supervised the search for those birth certificates you asked about. Based on our files, between 1970 and 2009, the only one that shows Thomas Spizer as the father belongs to Sammy Spizer. He was born October 1st, 1977 and the mother is listed as Melina Spizer."

"Are you sure there is no one else?"

"Yes, sir. That's what our files indicate."

"That is fine work, Mrs. Zappa. I am sure you and others put a lot of time into this task. The Quai Natia Police Department and I are grateful for your efforts."

"No problem, Lieutenant. Glad to help. You have a good day."

45

News headlines this morning center around the arrest two nights ago of the possible Black Bird Killer. At the courthouse, many concerned citizens are present in the gallery as Mr. Tapping, Mr. Pouncey, and Mr. Foles, one of Ms. Eisen's deputy district attorneys, stand before the magistrate judge.

"Docket number 112285. The State of California versus Mr. Xavier Tapping. Four counts of murder in the first degree," says the court clerk as she hands a file to the judge.

"What a way to start the day," deadpans the judge. What is your plea, Mr. Tapping?"

"You got the wrong guy."

"I'll take that as a not guilty."

"Not at all guilty, Your Honor."

"Well, that's a first, Counselor."

Mr. Pouncey says, "Mr. Tapping is a law-abiding member of the Sacramento community. His police record demonstrates nothing worse than a speeding ticket, Your Honor. And the criminal case against him is almost all circumstantial."

"Mr. Foles?"

"Your Honor, Mr. Tapping has killed four innocent citizens in the last four weeks, and likely two more in the last 10 years. All the recent serial murders involved appalling crime scenes. Other than his job, he has no strong ties to the community. I fervently request remand without bail."

"Say no more, Mr. Foles. As for you, Mr. Pouncey, you can give your arguments to the trial judge. I am not granting bail to someone possibly responsible for these egregious serial murders. The defendant is remanded," declares the judge, pounding his gavel.

Later that morning and in the early afternoon, the vital records offices of Wyoming, South Dakota, Minnesota, Iowa, and Colorado contact Lt. Rhombus. He is told that there are no birth certificates in those states between 1970 and 2009 with Thomas Spizer as the father.

Finally, the lieutenant calls the office in Nebraska, where the Mycenae serial murders took place.

"This is Lt. Rhombus from the Quai Natia Police Department. Can I please speak with your manager or supervisor?"

"Hello, Lieutenant. Let me get him for you. He should be nearby."

Less than a minute later, the manager comes to the phone.

"Good morning, Lt. Rhombus. This is Tyree Smith, the manager of this department. I was just about to call you."

"I guess my timing is good, sir. What have you been able to find out for me?"

"We got two hits on that search you requested."

"Two?" asks Rhombus with some surprise.

"Yes, that's correct. There is a Carl Vikander born on November 22nd, 1975. The father is listed as Thomas Spizer and the mother as Tammy Vikander."

The lieutenant is aware that Carl Vikander's name was changed to Carl Zimmerman when he was about two years old.

"That is good to know. And you said there is someone else?"

"There sure is. On March 21st, 1976, Madison Chastain was born to Abigail Chastain and Thomas Spizer in Lincoln, Nebraska. Huh. That's pretty unusual that in both birth certificates, the child has the last name of the mother."

"It is," says Lt. Rhombus. "There must have been some friction between the parents."

"I guess. Anyway, that's all we came up with, sir."

"Mr. Smith, I appreciate the work of you and your staff. On behalf of everyone here at the Quai Natia Police Department, I would like to thank all of you."

"That's mighty kind of you, sir. I'll relay your thanks to everyone involved. Good luck."

After getting off the phone, Rhombus checks the police database on Madison Chastain. He is retired from the U.S. Army and lives in Cheyenne, Wyoming, with his wife Gwen, son Geoff, and daughter Constance. There are no felonies or misdemeanors in his record, and his last traffic infraction occurred over ten years ago.

The lieutenant calls the last known phone number for Mr. Chastain.

"Good afternoon. I am Lt. Rhombus of the Quai Natia Police Department. Am I speaking to Mr. Madison Chastain?"

"Yes sir. How can I help you? Did you say Quai Natia?"

"That's right. It is a town of about 25,000 in the Central Coast of California."

"Okay. What can I do for you, Lieutenant?"

"Mr. Chastain, we are pursuing a serial killer in my area. In the course of the investigation, we have determined that a man named Thomas Spizer was a serial murderer in the 1970's. He was responsible for 17 murders in the area of Mycenae, Nebraska, from 1970 to 1974. By any chance, have you heard of Mr. Spizer?"

"In fact, I have. My mother says he is my biological father, but they never married and I have never met him. Accordingly, she decided to use her maiden name for my last name."

"That is very sensible."

"But she never said he committed any murders."

"It is possible she never knew, sir."

"Oh, that's true. I guess I should be happy that my mother was not one of his victims. Is he behind bars now?"

"Actually, he was killed in a stabbing in 2009."

"I would say I am glad to hear that, given the pain he has caused others."

"Is your mom doing well, Mr. Chastain?"

"Sir, she called me last week and was in pretty good spirits. She lives in Little Rock, Arkansas, now with my dad. Is that the only reason you're calling, Lieutenant?"

"No, Mr. Chastain. We strongly believe that the Quai Natia serial killer has been targeting the direct descendants of Mr. Spizer. That means you and your children are in possible danger."

"Really? The thought would never have crossed my mind. Nothing unusual has happened here recently."

"Good to know. How long have you lived in Cheyenne, sir?"

"Since early last year, after I retired from the U.S. Army. Before that, I was stationed in South Korea for seven years. My family was with me."

"And before South Korea, did you live in the U.S.?"

"Between 1995, when I joined the U.S. Army, and last year, I was mostly stationed overseas. I met my wife, who was in the Nurse Corps, during my service in Italy."

"Do you have any siblings, Mr. Chastain?"

"Yes, a brother and a sister. But they were born to a different father. Do you think they're in harm's way, Lieutenant?"

"Not likely, since they are not in the family tree of Mr. Spizer."

"Oh, that's right. Good news for them."

"We have apprehended a suspect in the Quai Natia area murders, but to be on the safe side, I want to provide you and your family with police protection for the time being."

"Thanks. That would be fine with me."

"One more thing, Mr. Chastain. I will leave it up to your discretion whether you should tell your mother about Mr. Thomas Spizer and his past crimes."

"Lieutenant, if it's all the same to you, let's just keep that information between ourselves."

"I totally understand. We will let you know once the Quai Natia murderer is convicted and put behind bars. And thank you for your service to this country, Mr. Chastain."

"It was my honor, sir."

46

Two days pass before the preliminary hearing takes place at the Superior Court of Monterey County. Assistant District Attorney Eisen presents the evidence against Mr. Xavier Tapping, including testimony from Lt. Rhombus, Detective Stiles, Dr. Paris, and Detective Novo. The defense cross-examines the prosecution's witnesses but declines to offer its own witnesses at this time.

When all is said and done, the judge finds probable cause is sufficient, and the accused is bound over for trial by petit jury on the four counts of murder one. A date for the arraignment on the information is established.

Afterwards, the assistant district attorney meets with the lieutenant.

"Rex, we set up a police lineup yesterday that included Mr. Tapping. Charlee, the witness seeing Billy Moreau's attacker running away, and her mother were present on the other side of the one-way mirror."

"What was the result, Margaret?"

"Sadly, the grade-schooler was not able to identify Tapping as the assailant. For this reason, she was not involved in the preliminary hearing today."

"I can understand that."

"Meanwhile, I am still concerned about the paucity of direct proof against the defendant. Mr. Pouncey recognizes that our evidence against Mr. Tapping is mostly circumstantial. Now that may be sufficient, but Pouncey feels confident that I don't have a leg to stand on. The district attorney has also voiced his concerns to me."

"What are you alluding to, Margaret?"

"Just make sure that all of our facts are accurate and that no stone has been left unturned."

"Absolutely. Also, recall that we are still trying to access Tapping's computer files. He refuses to give us the passcode."

"I am well aware, Rex. Let's be sure all our ducks are in a row."

"Will do, Margaret."

An hour later, Lt. Rhombus recalls the list of 149 persons who bought nitrogen gas tanks or scuba/non-rebreather masks from local stores in the last several months. He is aware that none of them has a criminal history, save for one with tax fraud. But he is struck by an idea.

With Detective Stiles at home due to a cold, he taps Officer Zwicker to assist him and Detective Novo. After getting the necessary warrants, they conduct a painstaking review of the employment, phone, credit card, and bank records of all 149 people.

Of these 149, only three have taken time off work recently. These three took vacations out of California, with airline databases confirming these trips. For all persons, there have been no recent large bank withdrawals. Credit card purchases show nothing unusual. And telephone records reveal no suspicious activity.

Next, they call the 149 men and women to seek alibis on the dates of the murders. Unable to reach six of them by phone, Novo and Zwicker pay them a visit. Ultimately, everyone can account for their whereabouts on the dates of the recent homicides. As a result, Lt. Rhombus is more convinced that Xavier Tapping is the guilty party.

Nevertheless, he prepares to review the Mycenae police files once again. For this, he asks for the assistance of Dr. Paris and Detective Novo, both of whom are already somewhat familiar with them. They work for the next day or so, searching for anything missed by Detective Stiles in his previous review.

Finally, after looking over all of the Mycenae serial murder files, Paris states, "Eli did a good job in the summary of these records."

"I would concur, Danica," says Novo.

"But I notice something of interest here," adds Rhombus.

The doctor and detective ask, "What do you mean?"

"Didn't Eli say that none of the coed victims majored in zoology, biology, or aerospace engineering?"

"Yes, he did. Do you see otherwise?"

"On this page, there is the information for the victim Geena St. John, and her major field of study is not listed."

Dr. Paris and Detective Novo look at the computer screen to which Lt. Rhombus is pointing.

"You're right. Eli must have missed this, or he assumed she didn't major in zoology, biology, or aerospace. Another possibility is that her major was undeclared at the time. Whatever the case, Miss St. John went to Creighton University," says the doctor.

Novo calls the university and discovers that Miss St. John did in fact have a major in zoology and a minor in mathematics. Everyone present realizes that her major field of study potentially indicates some connection to black birds.

"Let's read a little more about Geena St. John," says the lieutenant.

The files show that she was 20 years old when she was raped and murdered in 1974. She is survived by a brother named Max, age 17 at the time of Geena's passing. Her parents were in their late 30's when she was killed.

"17 years old in 1974 means age 62 now. A little too old for Max to be our serial killer. Don't you agree?" asks Paris.

"Probably. That age is just above Eli's suggested threshold of 61 years old as I recall," says Rhombus. "But I don't think it would hurt to check him out, would it?"

They search the computer for a Max St. John in Nebraska and nearby states. One is found in Minneapolis, Minnesota, with a deceased sister Geena. His rap sheet is clean. And he works in an advertising firm.

Detective Novo states, "His occupation does not suggest extensive computer know-how."

"But Rex, look at his wife's job. Software engineer!"

"That is a little concerning, Danica. Still, he lives 2000 miles away. And no criminal history is listed."

"He is not our best suspect. But it might be worth getting a warrant for his work, phone, credit card, and bank records."

"I can't help but agree. I will call Judge Wilson first thing in the morning. Now, is there any other new information on our current review of the Mycenae police files?"

"I am satisfied," answers Dr. Paris. "And it may turn out that Eli's oversight was not a big deal."

"Have a good evening, Doctor and Detective. I will contact you tomorrow after I see the remaining records on Mr. Max St. John."

47

The recent financial, telephone, and employment records of Max St. John are analyzed after Lt. Rhombus obtains the required warrants the following morning. Mr. St. John has not recently called California, nor has he made purchases in the Golden State. On top of that, the advertising company employing him in Minnesota describes consistent work attendance for the year, with only a few weeks off taken in early February.

Lt. Rhombus' findings are passed on to Dr. Paris and Detective Novo, and everyone concurs that Xavier Tapping must be their man. Rhombus informs Assistant District Attorney Eisen of the lack of new evidence. She acknowledges his team's efforts and continues her court preparation with her deputy district attorneys.

At this point in time, Lt. Rhombus gives his good friend an update on the happenings of the last few days.

"Bianca, do you have a few minutes?"

"Hi there, Rex! I need to be at an appointment soon, but I have some time right now. Are you about to tell me that you have caught the Black Bird Killer?"

"Perhaps. Our best suspect has been arrested and the trial will start sometime next week."

"I can't wait. Is the accused connected to Thomas Spizer?"

"He is Mr. Xavier Tapping, the brother of one of Spizer's victims in the Mycenae area serial murders."

"Rex, I am sure you have good reason to believe Mr. Tapping is the one."

"Actually, he is continuing to claim his innocence, which is bothersome. He is not interested in any plea bargain. And most of our criminal case against him is based on a lot of circumstantial evidence."

"Who are the prosecuting and defense attorneys?"

"Ms. Margaret Eisen and Mr. Rick Pouncey. She has won a good share of murder cases with no direct proof, and he always gives it his all."

"I am well aware of her reputation for excellence -- she should do fine. I have little experience with Mr. Pouncey."

"Still, I have a small hunch that we are missing something. For some reason, I don't feel fully at ease."

"You know, sometimes I also have a sense that I may have overlooked some aspect of a criminal investigation. In those instances, what I simply do is make a subtle adjustment in my reasoning process."

"Do you mean reframing your approach to some degree?"

"You get the idea."

"I will consider what you just said. Thank you for your words of wisdom."

"Glad to be of service. I have to go now, so I will talk to you soon."

"Until next time, Bianca."

Detective Stiles remains at home with a low-grade fever, and he receives a friendly phone call.

"Eli, I hope you are doing okay. Rex, Reynold, and I looked over the Mycenae police files once again. The lieutenant wanted to double-check everything before the upcoming trial begins."

"You don't say! Did I miss something?"

"Yes, a small fact. It turns out that one of the Mycenae murder victims majored in zoology, indicating a possible link to the black bird lapel pins. She is survived by a brother who is now 62. Consequently, we did a complete assessment of his records. But after this review, we concluded that he can not possibly be the Black Bird Killer."

"Whew! I thought you were going to say I made a major boo-boo."

"No. I can say you are clear of that. We are now waiting on a few more legal matters before the main jury trial begins."

"Sounds good, Danica. I have a good feeling that Mr. Tapping is our serial killer. Resting at home has helped a lot, so I should be much better in a day or two."

"Is there anything else we may be missing, Eli?"

"I can't think of anything at the moment, but you can count on hearing from me if I do."

"All right, Detective. Get well. And that's an order!" she says tongue in cheek.

48

It is a restless night for Lt. Rhombus as he tosses and turns in bed. The details of the serial murders are rattling around in his head. And somehow he is not satisfied that he has done enough to assure his suspect's conviction. After getting up and taking two melatonin pills, he is able to drift into a light sleep.

An hour later, he suddenly awakens and turns on his bedside lamp. On a notepad, Rhombus scribbles some material before dozing off.

Unexpectedly, the lieutenant's energy level is good after he gets up several hours later. After his morning routine, he places his notepad in his jacket pocket as he leaves for work. On his way to the police station, he calls Assistant District Attorney Eisen.

"Good morning, Margaret. How close are we getting to trial?"

"Hello, Rex. The next step is the arraignment on the information, to be followed by any motions by the prosecution or defense if the defendant is still pleading not guilty."

"In your communications with Mr. Pouncey, has there been any interest in a plea agreement?"

"Not to date. If you have no new evidence and no new motions are filed soon, the jury selection process and voir dire should commence sometime after the arraignment coming up."

"Unfortunately, we still have no good eyewitnesses or solid physical evidence. And our computer lab cognoscente has not yet gotten past Mr. Tapping's computer security system. He says that most all of the files have been encrypted thanks to the accused's extensive computer background."

"Are you working on any clues, Rex?"

"Actually, an idea came to me last night and it may affect our case against Mr. Tapping. And from what you just told me, it appears we still have some time before the trial."

"Can you tell me about this possible breakthrough?"

"At this time, I would not call it that -- it may or may not amount to anything."

"You are aware of discovery and making the defense team aware, right?"

"I am on both questions."

"That's fine, Rex. May you have success in your endeavor. I will be all ears for anything useful you may turn up."

"I will keep that in mind. Have a fine day, Margaret."

Lt. Rhombus now decides to look at the murders from a slightly different perspective. Once at his office, he hears the ticktock of the clock as he concentrates with laser focus on the Mycenae serial murder records one last time.

Knowing that Detective Stiles is still under the weather and Dr. Paris is busy at the hospital, he enlists the help of Detective Novo. Over the next 36 hours, they pursue another avenue in their investigation of the Black Bird Murders.

Two days later, the lieutenant meets with the assistant district attorney. He presents to her some new facts he has uncovered.

"That is a touchy situation, Rex. Whether it helps our criminal case or not will depend on factors as yet undetermined. How do you suggest we deal with it?"

"I believe our best chance at getting a conviction will require further action on my end. So here's my proposal."

The two discuss Rhombus' plan and concur that it is the best option.

The day of the arraignment on the information arrives and Mr. Tapping continues to say he's innocent. Over the next several days, no new motions are filed by the assistant district attorney or the defense team.

Jury selection is the next order of business. In the course of three days, the attorneys question a jury pool of over a hundred in the voir dire phase. Dozens of potential jurors are dismissed, some because of peremptory challenges. After the process is complete, both sides agree on 12 jurors and two alternate jurors.

It is now time for the prosecution and defense teams to prepare their witnesses for the impending trial. As the trial date approaches, what has been made public regarding the Black Bird Murders has been limited to the black bird lapel pins, unusual crime scenes, and mild head trauma in all four victims. And from day one, at Lt. Rhombus' request and by court order, the autopsy results and cause of death have been withheld from the community.

49

The scent of oak wood in the air permeates the courtroom as the prosecution and defense attorneys, defendant, and spectators file in. The 12 jurors arrive and enter the jury box. In the audience are some of the murder victims' widows, some of their relatives, and Lt. Rhombus and his team.

About 15 minutes later, everyone responds to the bailiff's announcement: "All rise! Department One of the Superior Court, Monterey County, Criminal Division, is now in session. The Honorable Judge Emmett Nicklaus now presiding."

After the heavyset and bespectacled judge takes the bench, he exclaims, "Good morning. Everyone may be seated, except the jury."

The jurors are sworn in by the court clerk, after which the judge gives them general guidelines.

"Your Honor, today's criminal case is the State of California versus Mr. Xavier Tapping," states the bailiff.

After the prosecution and defense teams tell Judge Nicklaus they are ready, he points toward the prosecution table.

"Your Honor, members of the jury. My name is Margaret Eisen, and my co-counsel and I represent the State of California."

Standing tall in her licorice black skirt suit, she proceeds with her opening statement, describing how she will prove that Mr. Xavier Tapping planned and committed the murders of Jackson Moreau, Matt Pitcairn, Carl Zimmerman, and Winston Banks beyond a reasonable doubt.

Next, Mr. Rick Pouncey, the defense counsel, makes his opening statement, intending to establish Mr. Tapping's innocence. A somewhat squatty fellow, he makes up for his average stature with a strong voice.

After the statements are completed, the judge says, "Prosecution, you may call your first witness."

"Your Honor, I wish to call Lt. Rex Rhombus to the stand."

The lieutenant walks with aplomb toward the witness box.

Judge Nicklaus states, "The witness will remain standing as he is sworn in by the courtroom clerk."

"Please raise your right hand. Do you solemnly state that the testimony you may give in the case now pending before this court shall be the truth, the whole truth, and nothing but the truth, so help you God?"

"I do," says Rhombus as he sits down.

Assistant District Attorney Eisen begins by saying, "Good morning, Lt. Rhombus. Are you leading the investigation into the recent Quai Natia area serial murders, also known as the Black Bird Murders?"

"Yes. But I answer to my captain."

"Understood. How long have you worked in Quai Natia?"

"I moved here from Washington State in 2013. Since then, I have headed the homicide unit of the Quai Natia Police Department."

"Thank you, Lieutenant. Now, can you please tell the court how you have managed to relate the recent murder victims to each other."

"Yes. In a word, consanguinity."

"Please expand on that, Lt. Rhombus."

"Certainly. There is only one common link among the four murder victims: They are all genetically related to Mr. Thomas Spizer. He was responsible for a brutal series of rapes and murders in the area of Mycenae, Nebraska, between 1970 and 1974."

"So all the recent victims of the Black Bird Killer are sons or grandsons of Mr. Spizer?"

"Fundamentally, that is correct. But the story is more complicated."

"We have plenty of time, Lieutenant. Please continue."

"To start off, let me just remind everyone that four individuals have been murdered in the last five to six weeks by the so-called Black Bird Killer. The first recent murder victim was Jackson Moreau, the second murder victim was Matt Pitcairn, the third recent victim was Carl Zimmerman, and the fourth victim was Winston Banks."

"Thank you, Lt. Rhombus. Those are the names of the persons for whom the defendant is being charged with first-degree murder."

"Agreed. Now, I would like to go back to the 1970's. Thomas Spizer raped Tammy Vikander (later Zimmerman) in 1975, and she gave birth to Carl. She opted to raise Carl as her son, and Carl Zimmerman was our third murder victim."

Ms. Eisen follows with, "So the third recent victim was essentially the biological son of Thomas Spizer."

"That is correct. Moving to 1976, Thomas Spizer and Kendra Banks had a child out of wedlock. This child was named Winston Banks, who was our fourth murder victim."

"I see. Thus, the fourth recent victim was the son of Mr. Spizer."

"Right again. In 1977, Thomas Spizer married his wife Melina and they had a son Sammy. Sammy would later change his name to Samuel Pitcairn, who later had a son Matt Pitcairn, our second victim."

"Therefore, the second recent victim was the grandson of Thomas Spizer," says the assistant district attorney.

"Exactly, Ms. Eisen. Finally, we know that the fourth recent victim, Winston Banks, donated sperm while he was in college. From that donor sperm, the donor offspring was Jackson Moreau, our first murder victim."

"Lieutenant, based on what you just said, our fourth recent victim (the sperm donor) was the biological father of the first victim (the donor offspring). And since we already know that the fourth recent victim was the son of Thomas Spizer, it is clear that the first recent victim was the grandson of Mr. Spizer."

"You are spot-on, Madam Assistant District Attorney. All four murder victims of the Black Bird Killer were direct descendants of Mr. Thomas Spizer. To sum it all up, Jackson Moreau and Matt Pitcairn were grandsons of Spizer, while Carl Zimmerman and Winston Banks were Spizer's sons."

Ms. Eisen is silent for several seconds. She then says, "We all need to take a deep breath now. That is a remarkable family tree you have constructed, Lt. Rhombus. You have carefully identified Thomas Spizer as the common ancestor of the four victims of the Black Bird Killer."

The assistant district attorney pauses for a moment.

"Lieutenant, in addition to these four victims, do you believe the defendant has committed other murders?"

"As it happens, I do. My team suspects that he was responsible for Thomas Spizer's stabbing death in 2009 and Sammy Spizer's/Samuel Pitcairn's fatal hit-and-run car accident in 2017."

"In other words, you are blaming Mr. Xavier Tapping for the deaths of the serial killer Thomas Spizer, his son, and the four recent local victims, all of whom are genetically related to Thomas Spizer."

"I could not have put it any better, Ms. Eisen."

"Thank you, sir. But let it be clear that Mr. Tapping is only on trial now for the four murders in the last six weeks or so."

Ms. Eisen now turns to the jury and asks if any juror needs Lt. Rhombus to repeat any of his testimony. The jury appears attentive and focused, and each juror shakes his/her head.

The assistant district attorney then announces, "To assure that everyone in the jury is clear about Lt. Rhombus' testimony, we have prepared this exhibit."

Mr. Foles, one of the deputy district attorneys, places a large whiteboard display on a tripod in front of the court. It demonstrates how Thomas Spizer is genetically linked to all of the Black Bird Murder victims.

"Your Honor, the prosecution offers People's Exhibit A into evidence. May I please publish this to the jury?"

After the judge reviews the display, he has it shown to the defense counsel.

"Mr. Pouncey?"

"No objections, Your Honor."

"Exhibit A is so admitted," says Judge Nicklaus.

The bailiff moves the display to a location in full view of the jury members. As the jurors look over the exhibit, their nods indicate how their understanding of the facts has been enhanced. After some oohs and aahs are heard from the spectators also viewing Exhibit A, Ms. Eisen continues with her witness.

"Now, tell me about motive, Lieutenant. Why would the accused want to kill Thomas Spizer and his progeny?"

"It all stems back to the Mycenae area serial murders in the 1970's, all committed by Mr. Spizer. The defendant is the brother of one of the victims, Lynette Tapping. And we have evidence that he has murdered his sister's killer as well as the various descendants of this killer."

"Lt. Rhombus, I can understand Mr. Tapping wanting revenge against Thomas Spizer, who raped and murdered his sister. But why kill Spizer's direct descendants?"

The lieutenant responds, "Various studies claim that serial killers have a genetic defect that can be transmitted to their offspring. So by eliminating all the progeny of serial killer Thomas Spizer, the defendant believes he is preventing future violence by Spizer's descendants."

"Objection, Your Honor!" exclaims Mr. Pouncey. "The witness is not a geneticist or psychologist."

"Sustained. I will allow a little latitude, Ms. Eisen, but be careful," says Judge Nicklaus.

"Thank you, Your Honor. Lieutenant, have the close relatives of Mr. Spizer committed acts of violence in the past?"

"Actually, yes. As Detective Stiles will explain later, Spizer's brother Jeremy murdered his girlfriend and his son Sammy was convicted twice for assaulting his wife. Xavier Tapping is aware of these violent crimes in the family tree of Thomas Spizer."

"In your opinion, Lieutenant, does this history of violence in Mr. Spizer's first-degree relatives support Mr. Tapping's belief that Spizer's progeny will commit violent acts in the future?"

"Your Honor, same objection," says Mr. Pouncey.

"Sustained. Move on, Ms. Eisen," commands the judge.

"Yes, Your Honor. Lt. Rhombus, if the defendant has planned to kill all of Mr. Spizer's direct descendants, why was Billy Moreau, the first recent victim's young son, not murdered like the others?"

"Well, he was attacked and suffered a mild concussion. In our opinion, at the time of the assault, the assailant's conscience stopped him from kidnapping and then killing the young victim."

"Thank you for clearing that up, Lt. Rhombus."

Before Ms. Eisen can continue her questioning, the judge interrupts her.

"Your testimony so far has been intensive, Lieutenant. Let's all take a brief recess so everyone can take it all in," says Judge Nicklaus as he taps his gavel against the sound block.

50

Half an hour passes before the courtroom is back in session. The judge is forced to quiet the audience as their whispering is becoming quite audible. Returning to the witness stand, the lieutenant affirms the oath once again. And Assistant District Attorney Eisen is ready to continue with her witness.

"Lt. Rhombus, can you tell me where the defendant was living when the various murders occurred?"

"Sure. When Thomas Spizer was stabbed to death in Kansas City, Mr. Xavier Tapping resided in Central Oklahoma. He was still living there when Samuel Pitcairn was killed in Dallas."

"And how far are those cities from Central Oklahoma?"

"Only about three to four hours by car."

"So a relatively short distance. And where has the defendant lived during the time of the recent four murders?"

"He has resided in Sacramento for the last one and a half to two years, less than four hours by auto from Quai Natia and only two hours from San Jose."

"Quai Natia and San Jose are where the four local murders took place, correct?"

"Yes."

"Lieutenant, do you agree that the defendant was physically able to travel to the murder sites at the times of all the recent murders?"

"I would say so, Ms. Eisen. Therefore, he had the opportunity to commit all the recent homicides."

"Thank you, Lt. Rhombus. Nothing further. Your Honor, I would like to reserve the right to recall the lieutenant to the stand at a later time if needed."

"That would be fine, as long as his additional testimony is crucial to the trial."

"Yes, Your Honor."

"The defense may now cross-examine the witness," says the judge.

Mr. Pouncey, in his dark brown suit and eggshell dress shirt, approaches the witness.

"Thank you, Your Honor. Lieutenant, that is quite a story there. How did you come about it?"

"My team slowly put the pieces together during our investigation."

"It is impressive. But your case against my client is wholly circumstantial, isn't it? You have no good eyewitnesses or videotapes that place Mr. Tapping at any of the crime scenes, do you?"

"Actually, there is one witness. A grade-schooler saw the perpetrator running away from young Billy Moreau, who was assaulted. But she did not get a good look at his face."

"Like I said, you have no reliable eyewitnesses. Lt. Rhombus, do you have any physical evidence placing Mr. Tapping at any of the crime scenes?"

"Yes. We found a matchbook from the Just Win! tavern, the location of the second crime scene, at Mr. Tapping's home."

"Mr. Tapping has admitted going to the Just Win! tavern as a customer, has he not?"

"That he has."

"As a result, the book of matches does not place him at the second crime scene at the time of the murder, does it?"

"No, it does not. In our search of Mr. Tapping's house, we also discovered a tee from the golf course where the first victim was killed."

"But the accused has played golf there. And does the tee prove he was there at the time of that murder?"

"No."

"Finally, you recovered some rope in my client's residence. Can you prove that Mr. Tapping used that type of rope to tie the second victim to the pool table? Or the third victim to the navigation buoy?"

"The rope that turned up at Mr. Tapping's home is the same type used on Matt Pitcairn, the second victim. It also matches the rope used to tie down the third victim, Carl Zimmerman."

"But Lieutenant, isn't this rope commonly available in many home improvement, hardware, and general stores throughout the country?"

"It is available."

"Thus, almost anyone could have bought this rope and tied down those two victims. Am I right?"

"Well, I wouldn't say anyone."

"I move to strike the witness' last statement, Your Honor. I will rephrase."

"The last statement of Lt. Rhombus will be so stricken. The jury will disregard it," commands Judge Nicklaus.

"Lieutenant, the rope that turned up at the defendant's home is readily available in many stores. Are you able to say with certainty that it was Mr. Tapping who used that type of rope to tie down those two victims?"

"No, I am not."

"Thank you, Lieutenant. Based on what Lt. Rhombus just testified, it is clear that no physical proof places the defendant at any of the crime scenes at the times of the murders. And I believe that raises significant reasonable doubt that the accused did in fact commit these crimes."

"Objection! Argumentative, Your Honor," asserts Ms. Eisen.

"Sustained. Is there a question in the offing, Mr. Pouncey?"

"Yes, Your Honor. Lt. Rhombus, how old was the defendant when Thomas Spizer was killed?"

"Mr. Tapping was 10 when his sister was killed in 1973, so he was 46 years old when Spizer was stabbed to death in 2009."

"If my client murdered Mr. Spizer as you are claiming, why do you suppose he waited until 2009 to kill his sister's murderer?"

"He didn't get his bachelor's degree in computer science until 1992, and his cybersecurity master's degree wasn't obtained until 1996. So he didn't have the means to fully research and monitor Thomas Spizer until the mid-to-late 1990's."

"And what about the eight years that elapsed between the fatal stabbing of Thomas Spizer in 2009 and the subsequent murder of his son Sammy in 2017?"

"We believe that Mr. Tapping's plan to murder the progeny of Thomas Spizer, starting with his son Sammy, was inspired by some event in 2017 or a little before."

"Do you know what this event was, Lieutenant?"

"It must have been something that convinced Mr. Tapping that serial killers have a genetic predisposition and can transmit their 'killer genes' to their descendants. For example, he may have read a book or seen a documentary. It could have been a lecture or seminar he attended. Or he may have even discussed the matter with an expert in the field of serial killers."

"In other words, there is no specific event that you know of, do you?"

"That is correct."

"Thank you. Nothing further, Your Honor."

"Prosecution?" asks the judge.

"Brief redirect, Your Honor," says the assistant district attorney. "Lt. Rhombus, despite the lack of direct physical proof against the defendant, is it still your contention that he is guilty of the four recent serial murders?"

"Yes, very much so. In our investigation, we have established clear motive, intent, the opportunity to commit the crimes, as well as a compelling sequence of events."

"Thank you, Lieutenant."

"You may step down from the witness box, Lt. Rhombus," says Judge Nicklaus.

51

"Madam Assistant District Attorney, you may now call
your second witness."

"Thank you, Your Honor. I call to the stand Detective Eli Stiles."

He prefers wearing a casual blazer with matching stretch pants, but Stiles is dressed in a dark suit and blue tie for the formal occasion.

Ms. Eisen gets up from her counsel table and asks the detective to outline the profile of the Quai Natia serial killer.

"We have firm evidence that the Black Bird Killer is a left-handed man who is a computer expert and able swimmer."

"Detective Stiles, let's take those characteristics one at a time. How do we know the assailant is a left-handed man?"

"Well, the culprit is probably male because the vast majority of American serial killers are men. Plus the strength and endurance needed to bury the first victim in a golf bunker and transport the third victim to the navigation buoy in the bay most likely point to a man."

"Well put, Detective. And how do you know he is left-handed?"

"That is our conclusion based on the pattern of the knots used to tie our second victim to the pool table and our third victim to the navigation buoy."

"Are you a knot expert, Detective Stiles?"

"Not really. But we obtained the expert opinion of a forensic knot specialist, Katana Gibbs, who can testify if needed."

"Very well. I am sure the court will accept your sworn testimony at this time. Now, how do we know that the recent serial killer is a good swimmer?"

"He would have to be, given that he was able to transport the third victim, Carl Zimmerman, from the beach to a buoy 300 yards away in Biscay Bay."

"But couldn't the murderer simply have taken a small boat to the buoy and then tie down the victim's body there?"

"That is possible, Ms. Eisen, but all of Mr. Zimmerman's clothes were quite damp when he was found."

"What you say makes sense, Detective. At any rate, what about the defendant? Is he a capable swimmer?"

"Yes. Mr. Tapping's father communicated this to Lt. Rhombus."

"Thank you. I remind the jury that we now have evidence that the Black Bird Killer is a left-handed male who is a good swimmer. And the accused, Xavier Tapping, fits this profile to a tee."

Ms. Eisen pauses for a few seconds.

"Now, I would like to go over the proof you have that the Quai Natia area serial murderer is adept in computers. Have you had much experience with computer systems, Detective Stiles?"

"Yes. I majored in computer science at the University of Illinois before changing to criminal justice."

"So why do you believe the Black Bird Killer has considerable expertise in computers?"

"To plan the various murders, the perpetrator has needed to hack into various secure computer systems."

"And does the defendant have this proficiency?"

"Xavier Tapping obtained his bachelor's degree in computer science in 1992 and his graduate degree in cybersecurity in 1996. It is easy to conclude that his formal training has given him extraordinary skills working with computers, including the ability to hack into protected databases."

"At this point, I want the jury to note that the defendant possesses the required know-how to get into protected computer systems."

Ms. Eisen then looks at the jury for several seconds, making sure they are paying attention.

"Detective Stiles, can you show me how these skills helped the accused identify his targets and plan their murders?"

"I can. Let me start with how Mr. Tapping drew the conclusion that Thomas Spizer was the serial murderer who killed his sister Lynette."

"Are you saying the defendant knew about Mr. Spizer as the Mycenae killer many years ago?"

"Yes, I am."

"How did he know, Detective?"

"First of all, the defendant hacked into the Mycenae Police Department files. They told him that Thomas Spizer fit a witness' description of the Mycenae killer and was the main suspect."

"Please go on."

"Next, Mr. Tapping gained access to the police records of Thomas Spizer, his brother Jeremy, and his son Sammy. He found that Thomas was accused of domestic violence in the past, Jeremy was killed while being arrested for the murder of his girlfriend, and Sammy was charged with domestic abuse several times and served prison time twice."

"And given the above information, what did the accused determine?"

"With the eyewitness' account and the familial tendency toward violence, Mr. Tapping put two and two together to deduce that Thomas Spizer was the Mycenae serial killer."

Ms. Eisen follows with, "It is very important that the jury understand this. The defendant knew years ago that Thomas Spizer was the serial murderer in Mycenae, Nebraska. Detective Stiles, do we now have incontrovertible evidence that Mr. Spizer was in fact the Mycenae killer?"

"We are 100 percent sure at this time."

Several seconds pass before the assistant district attorney continues.

"Lt. Rhombus has eloquently described how all the Black Bird Murder victims are direct descendants of Thomas Spizer. Detective Stiles, can you tell me how the accused put together this detailed family tree?"

"Yes, I can."

"Please explain it to us, if you would."

"Sure. We can start with the vital records departments of Nebraska, Kansas, and Missouri, states in which Mr. Spizer lived or worked as an adult. Mr. Tapping gained access to their computer systems and files. Afterwards, he searched for the birth certificates listing Thomas Spizer as the father."

"And what did those records tell him?"

"He immediately learned that Sammy Spizer, Carl Vikander, and Winston Banks were sons of Thomas Spizer. Later, Sammy Spizer changed his name to Samuel Pitcairn and Carl Vikander's name was changed to Carl Zimmerman."

"What was the defendant's next course of action, Detective?"

"Mr. Tapping looked into the public records of Samuel Pitcairn and learned that his son was Matt Pitcairn. As a result, Mr. Tapping became aware that Matt Pitcairn was the grandson of Thomas Spizer."

"So, at this juncture, the defendant was able to identify four of Thomas Spizer's descendants – Samuel and Matt Pitcairn, Carl Zimmerman, and Winston Banks – who would become his targets for murder."

"That is correct, Ms. Eisen."

"Finally, how did Mr. Tapping find out that the remaining recent murder victim, Jackson Moreau, was related to Thomas Spizer?"

The detective answers, "Again using his computer know-how, Mr. Tapping got into the phone records of Winston Banks, who moved to California. He noted that Banks donated sperm to the Constellation Fertility Center. Soon after, he hacked into the fertility center's computer system to determine that the donor offspring of Winston Banks was Jackson Moreau."

"In other words, since Jackson Moreau was found to be the biological son of Winston Banks, and Thomas Spizer was the known father of Winston Banks, the defendant concluded that Jackson Moreau was essentially the grandson of Mr. Spizer."

"Ms. Eisen, you are exactly right."

"There you have it, members of the jury. With his extraordinary computer skills, Mr. Xavier Tapping was able to construct the family tree relating the vicious serial killer Thomas Spizer to all four recent victims of the Black Bird Killer."

The victims' widows and family members nod in approval.

"I just have a few more questions for you, Detective. Have you actually confirmed with the Constellation Fertility Center that Jackson Moreau was born using the sperm of Winston Banks?"

"I have."

"Have you verified that the birth certificates of Sammy Spizer (later Pitcairn), Carl Vikander (later Zimmerman), and Winston Banks list Thomas Spizer as the father?"

"Yes."

"And do public records of Samuel Pitcairn show Matt Pitcairn to be his son?"

"Affirmative, ma'am."

Ms. Eisen asks the jury to review Exhibit A, which lays out the genealogy chart of Thomas Spizer.

"Thank you, Detective Stiles. Your Honor, I move that People's Exhibit B be introduced into evidence. It summarizes the detective's testimony on how the defendant constructed Thomas Spizer's family tree."

Mr. Foles presents another large whiteboard exhibit to the court.

"Any objection, Mr. Pouncey?" asks Judge Nicklaus after both have had time to peruse the display.

"None, Your Honor."

"Very well. People's Exhibit B is so admitted."

"Your witness," Ms. Eisen says to Mr. Pouncey.

Mr. Pouncey stands and quickly walks toward the witness.

"Hello, Detective Stiles. Did you ever determine who broke into the Constellation Fertility Center's computer system?"

"No."

"And do you have reports of computer security breaches at the Mycenae Police Department or in the vital records offices of Missouri, Kansas, or Nebraska?"

"No, however --."

"A no is sufficient, Detective," says Mr. Pouncey as he cuts Stiles off. "Nothing further for this witness."

The defendant's attorney returns to his counsel table.

"Your Honor, I would like to redirect."

"Go ahead, Ms. Eisen."

"Detective Stiles, given your expertise in computers, if an organization's computer system suffers a security breach, will the company's personnel always be aware of the problem?"

"They may detect it, but many breaches occur without the knowledge of the organization involved."

"Thank you, Detective. Nothing further, Your Honor."

"You are excused, Detective Stiles," says Judge Nicklaus.

Stiles feels fairly good about his testimony. He sits in the audience for a minute before seeing a call on his phone display. After the detective leaves the courtroom to answer the call, he is followed by Lt. Rhombus.

"A solid testimony, Eli. I don't think I could have done better."

"Thanks, R-double. Danica should be up next – I am confident she will knock it out of the park."

52

Another short break is ordered by Judge Nicklaus, during which Dr. Paris and Ms. Eisen discuss the doctor's upcoming testimony. Afterwards, everyone reenters the courtroom and the bailiff declares the resumption of the trial.

The comely medical examiner is called to the witness stand by Assistant District Attorney Eisen. She is sworn in by the bailiff before taking a seat next to the judge. Her coffee brown pant suit and vanilla blouse complement her chestnut hair and brown eyes.

"Good afternoon, Dr. Paris. Are you the forensic pathologist involved in the so-called Black Bird Murders?"

"Yes, I am. Except for the most recent homicide in San Jose."

"That's fine. Have you been in contact with the San Jose medical examiner?"

"I have."

"Very well. Can you please tell me about the cause of death of the recent victims."

"Based on the autopsies, I conclude that each victim was incapacitated by blunt force head trauma, followed by death by asphyxiation."

"Doctor, what is asphyxiation?"

"It means inadequate oxygen supply to body tissues."

"Basically, one does not get enough oxygen to breathe."

"That's right."

"Was there clear evidence of asphyxiation in all the homicide victims?"

"Yes, there was. Postmortem findings included enlarged internal organs and venous congestion. Blood analysis showed lactic acidosis. All these indicators point to asphyxiation."

"So the victims were smothered to death?"

"Actually, no. Smothering indicates that air movement through the nose and mouth is blocked. That did not occur in our victims."

"How do you know?"

"I found no major bruises around the nose and mouth."

"I understand. How about strangulation?"

"Since no ligature marks were seen, we can rule out strangulation. Ms. Eisen, there are other ways to deprive someone of oxygen."

"Such as?"

"One common example is inhalation of carbon monoxide gas. This gas binds to our red blood cells' hemoglobin much more strongly than does oxygen. As a result, the oxygen is displaced and not delivered to the body's tissues."

"Thank you for the biology lesson, Doctor. But in the end, the local murder victims met their demise due to something uncommon, did they not?"

"Yes, Ms. Eisen. The ultimate cause of death in the Black Bird Murders was asphyxiation due to pure nitrogen gas inhalation."

"In English please, Dr. Paris."

"Allow me to explain. The alveoli are small air sacs that are the final branches of our lungs' airways. We measured very high levels of nitrogen in those sacs in all the victims. These results are only possible if the victims were forced to inhale pure nitrogen gas."

"But doesn't air usually contain nitrogen?"

"Yes, most of air is composed of nitrogen, about 78%, while most of the rest is oxygen."

"If that is so, how does pure nitrogen gas harm you?"

"When you inhale pure nitrogen, it dilutes out the oxygen you should be breathing in. As your oxygen levels drop precipitously, the central nervous system is suppressed and your breathing becomes irregular and slow. You die within two to three minutes, leaving high levels of nitrogen in your alveoli."

"I guess too much of anything, including nitrogen in the gas you breathe, is not good for you."

"That is a good way to put it, Ms. Eisen. Also, when the local victims were forced to inhale pure nitrogen, they were still breathing out carbon dioxide as usual."

"And why is that important, Doctor?"

"It is important because carbon dioxide did not build up in the blood of the victims. For this reason, they did not experience the hypercapnic alarm response."

"Can you please explain that to the court?"

"I would be glad to. The hypercapnic alarm response is the panic you usually feel and react to when you are running out of oxygen. But this panic only occurs if carbon dioxide levels rise in your blood."

"But carbon dioxide did not accumulate in the blood of the victims. Is that right, Dr. Paris?"

"That is correct. Since these carbon dioxide levels did not increase, the murder victims felt no sense of panic as they inhaled pure nitrogen. Meanwhile, their oxygen levels were rapidly dropping."

"Doctor, to be crystal clear, are you saying that the murder victims did not suffer any significant distress as they were forced to inhale pure nitrogen gas?"

"That is exactly right. The recent victims became unconscious due to the blow to the head, followed by a rapid drop in oxygen levels as they were exposed to pure nitrogen gas. Death followed soon after. But if it's any consolation, they did not suffer as they passed away."

Several of the victims' family members noticeably choke up.

"Very enlightening, Doctor. Do you believe the Black Bird Killer wants to minimize suffering in his victims for some reason?"

"Yes, I do. I think he feels these four victims were mostly innocent descendants of an evil man. But in his mind, they would inevitably turn out to be psychopaths or at worst serial killers."

"Members of the jury, we now have definitive proof that the rarely used method of forced nitrogen gas inhalation took the lives of all four local victims."

The assistant district attorney takes a brief pause.

"Dr. Paris, how could the killer administer the pure nitrogen gas?"

"He rendered each victim unconscious with the blow to the head. Then he applied a face mask with a good seal connected to a tank of pure nitrogen."

"Did each victim struggle when the mask was forced upon him?"

"All the murder victims, being unconscious due to the head trauma and experiencing no hypercapnic alarm response, would not have resisted."

"So their deaths were essentially painless, except for the head blows?"

"Yes, I would say so."

"Thank you, Doctor. I believe we could all agree that these cruel murders were relatively pain-free but reprehensible nonetheless. Nothing further, Your Honor," says Ms. Eisen as she returns to the prosecution's table.

53

"You may cross-examine the witness, Mr. Pouncey," says Judge Nicklaus.

"Thank you, Your Honor. Dr. Paris, good afternoon. Are you able to offer us an alternative explanation for the recent deaths?"

"No, I am not."

"But isn't pure nitrogen gas asphyxiation rare?"

"It sure is. Still, the test results are unmistakable."

"Okay. Doctor, is it true that you have recovered no murder weapons and have detected no identifying fingerprints or DNA at the crime scenes?"

"That is correct."

"With the exception of the head bruises, were there any signs of violence when the bodies were discovered?"

"No. Only the contusions."

"And was a scuba diving mask, non-rebreather mask, or tank of nitrogen gas found in the police's search of the defendant's home and car?"

"No, none of those items were seen. But Mr. Tapping may have moved them to another location when Lt. Rhombus first visited him without a search warrant."

"At any rate, there is no physical evidence to tie my client to the murders of the four victims. Is that correct, Doctor?"

"There are the golf tee, the matchbook from the tavern, and the rope we came across at Mr. Tapping's home."

"But hasn't Lt. Rhombus already testified that those articles do not necessarily put the defendant at the crime scenes at the times of the murders?"

"Yes."

"Thank you, Dr. Paris. Now, let's turn to the black bird lapel pins you found at all the crime scenes. Can you demonstrate that my client placed them on the victims?"

The doctor, her shoulder-length hair somewhat crumpled with a look of concern across her face, answers, "No, at this time, I can not."

There are audible gasps from the spectators, including the families of the victims.

Mr. Pouncey asks, "Do you have any idea what the images of the black birds signify?"

"A local ornithologist believes they are crows, but he admits the images aren't detailed enough."

"In your opinion, what do you feel they tell us about the killer?"

"He is possibly a bird-lover. Or his sister killed in Mycenae had a special liking to black birds."

"Dr. Paris, in your investigation, did any of the young women killed at Mycenae have an interest in or study birds in particular?"

"I can not comment on their personal interests. But one of the victims majored in zoology. None majored in biology."

"Was this zoology major the defendant's sister?"

"No, she was not," admits the doctor.

"So, are you saying that there is no clear link between my client and the black birds seen on the lapel pins?"

Paris answers, "None that we have ascertained. Another possibility is the black birds indicate a certain military aircraft called the SR-71 Blackbird."

"And does my client have or did any of the Mycenae victims have any association with aircraft, flying, or the military?"

"Not that we're aware of."

"Hmm. That's a head-scratcher, Doctor. Let me then remind the jury: We are looking for the so-called Black Bird Killer, but the prosecution has identified no connection between the defendant and black birds."

Everyone, including Dr. Paris, is speechless.

"Thank you, Doctor. No further questions," says Mr. Pouncey.

Seeing her raised hand, Judge Nicklaus asks, "Redirect, Ms. Eisen?"

"Yes, thank you, Your Honor. Dr. Paris, I have done some research into the symbolism of crows, and I learned that they can represent many things. These include transformation, change, intelligence, individuality, creativity, as well as darkness and death."

"That is what I also understand, Ms. Eisen."

"Great! Consequently, is it not possible, even probable, that the black bird lapel pins simply are markers of death for the Black Bird Killer?"

"Yes, I would say that is very likely."

"Thank you, Doctor. Finally, did the serial killer probably use a different nitrogen tank and different mask for each victim."

"Yes, that is the most likely scenario."

"Therefore, is it reasonable that the perpetrator discarded these items after each of the murders?"

"I would say yes. That would make the most sense."

"So Dr. Paris, given the above sequence of events, would it be surprising that there were no nitrogen tanks or non-rebreather/scuba masks discovered in the defendant's home or car?"

"No, it is not at all surprising."

"Nothing further, Your Honor," says Eisen.

At this point, Judge Nicklaus gives Dr. Paris permission to leave the witness stand.

"Any more witnesses, Madam Assistant District Attorney?"

Ms. Eisen turns to Lt. Rhombus in the audience, and he shakes his head. She then looks at the judge, saying, "The prosecution rests, Your Honor."

"Very well," says the judge. "That will be all for today. The defense may call its first witness tomorrow morning at 9 a.m. sharp. This court is adjourned."

54

Judge Nicklaus enters the courtroom at precisely 9 the next morning, with his reputation for punctuality intact. The murder victims' families and friends appear apprehensive as everyone rises from their seats at the bailiff's request.

"The criminal case of the State of California against Mr. Xavier Tapping is back in session with the Honorable Judge Emmett Nicklaus presiding."

The judge then directs the defense to call its first witness.

"Dr. Eamon Teixeira, Your Honor."

The defense's medical expert is sworn in.

Mr. Pouncey asks, "Good morning, Dr. Teixeira. You have heard Dr. Paris' assessment as to the cause of death in the serial murders. Do you agree?"

"I reviewed Dr. Paris' autopsy reports and the various body fluid tests that were run on three of the murder victims. I also scrutinized the alveolar fluid tests."

"Why only three victims, Doctor?"

"Because the fourth victim was killed in San Jose, where a different medical examiner was in charge."

"Understood. Did you look over the San Jose reports as well?"

"Yes, I did. From my evaluation of all the data, I concur that each of the four victims of the so-called Black Bird Killer suffered a concussion as well as death due to asphyxiation."

"Anything else, Dr. Teixeira?"

"However, I am not sure that pure nitrogen gas was the cause of the loss of oxygen."

Dr. Paris and most people in the courtroom are astounded by his statement.

"And why not?"

"Because the laboratory they used to check alveolar nitrogen content is not currently accredited to do so. Its accreditation expired last month."

There is suddenly a hullabaloo coming from discontented members of the audience.

"Order in the court!" commands the judge, after which he strikes the sounding block with his gavel several times.

Onlookers gradually settle down over the next 30 seconds.

An irked Ms. Eisen immediately says, "Sidebar, Your Honor."

Judge Nicklaus signals to the assistant district attorney and main defense attorney, and they both approach the bench.

Ms. Eisen contends, "Judge, I was not made aware of this information by Mr. Pouncey. If I was, we would have had the tests run again by another laboratory."

Mr. Pouncey claims, "I only obtained it this morning, Your Honor. And the prosecution should be aware of the status of any laboratory they use."

Judge Nicklaus ruminates for a moment before telling both attorneys to return to their counsel tables.

He then says to the jury, "The tests run by the laboratory in question will be repeated by a currently accredited one. The new results will be made available to the jury as soon as possible."

The judge now turns toward the defense table.

"Do you have anything further for Dr. Teixeira, Mr. Pouncey?"

"Yes, Your Honor. Doctor, have you heard about the transmission of some 'serial killer gene' to one's progeny?"

"There has been some writing about that, but no rigorous studies support it. I believe it is just speculation until proven."

"Thank you, Dr. Teixeira. Nothing further, Your Honor."

As Mr. Pouncey sits down, Judge Nicklaus says, "Ms. Eisen, you may cross-examine."

"Thank you, Your Honor. I will be brief, Doctor. If the alveolar fluid analysis by the new laboratory shows the same results as the ones now, do you agree with the cause of death being pure nitrogen gas asphyxiation?"

"Yes, I do."

"Thank you. No more questions for this witness."

After Dr. Teixeira steps down from the witness box, the defense calls two character witnesses to demonstrate the defendant's good reputation and moral conduct. They are his friend, Patrick Psaki, and his work supervisor, Lucinda Otencio.

Both describe Xavier Tapping as somewhat introverted but also having a generally calm demeanor. Neither has seen the defendant display any violent activity. After their testimonies, there is no cross-examination of either witness by Ms. Eisen.

At this time, Mr. Pouncey announces, "Your Honor, the defense calls Mr. Xavier Tapping."

Suddenly, there are murmurs coming from the gallery. Assistant District Attorney Eisen is mildly surprised to see the defendant called to the stand. And she is aware that the defense counsel knows the risks but apparently feels his testimony is essential to win the case.

The accused walks slowly to the witness box and is sworn in. He appears stoic with a piercing gaze.

"Good day, Mr. Tapping. Can you tell us what you do for a living?" asks Mr. Pouncey.

"I work in cybersecurity for the Sheeld Corporation in Sacramento."

"Have you been accused of any crime in the past?"

"Not until recently, no."

"Now, on the dates of the four recent murders, do you remember where you were?"

"I believe they all occurred on weekends, and I was in or near Sacramento on those days."

"Can anyone corroborate your whereabouts for us, Mr. Tapping?"

"Yes. I have seen my girlfriend Sally the last several weekends."

"Finally, Mr. Tapping, did you murder any of the four recent victims: Jackson Moreau, Matt Pitcairn, Carl Zimmerman, or Winston Banks?"

"Absolutely not. I don't even know them."

"Thank you. Nothing further, Your Honor."

55

Assistant District Attorney Eisen steps toward the witness stand.

"Hello, Mr. Tapping. I would like to remind you that the recent murders occurred on March 9th, March 16th, March 22nd, and either March 29th or 30th. Was your girlfriend with you on those days?"

"Yes, most of them, but I was sick on the weekend of the 22nd so I asked her to stay away."

"Was she with you the entire day and night on the other three or four days I listed?"

The defendant, becoming somewhat irritated, says, "I don't recall the exact hours she was with me."

"Let me specifically ask you about the hours from approximately midnight to 8 a.m. on March 9th and 16th, when the first two murders occurred."

"She may have spent the night with me on those days, but I am not sure."

"Mr. Tapping, is it possible that on those dates, she was not with you during those hours I just referred to?"

"I suppose it's possible," the accused mumbles.

"I didn't get that. Please speak up, Mr. Tapping."

Reluctantly, he says, "It's possible," with a louder voice.

Subsequent susurrations from the audience force the judge's hand, as he bangs his gavel on the bench.

"If everyone is unable to quiet down, I will remove each and every one of you from this courtroom."

The audience complies and settles down, and Ms. Eisen continues her cross-examination.

"Mr. Tapping, do you remember calling in sick to your office on the morning of Friday, March 22nd?"

"Yes."

"Your office supervisor, Miss Otencio, stated that you have had a perfect attendance record for 2019, EXCEPT for your sick day on the 22nd of March. Is that right?"

"I guess that's true if that's what she said," he says sternly.

"I find it remarkable – no, let's say highly suspicious – that on the only workday you could not attend this year, the murder of Carl Zimmerman occurred. Is it not more likely that you feigned illness that day, giving you the opportunity to drive down to Quai Natia and heinously kill Mr. Zimmerman?"

Some definite unease is seen on the defendant's face.

Ms. Eisen presses him further, asking, "Mr. Tapping, is that what really happened that day?"

"I already told you. I was ill at home that day and all weekend."

"Can your girlfriend attest to that? Did you see her at all during that weekend?"

"I did talk to her, but I didn't see her."

"Did you see anyone that weekend, Mr. Tapping?"

After several seconds, he responds, "I am not sure."

"Let the record show that the defendant has no alibi whatsoever for the day Mr. Zimmerman, the third victim, was killed."

In her French heels, the assistant district attorney paces for a short while between the jury box and the witness stand.

"Mr. Tapping, how long have you worked with computers?"

"Since about the early to mid-1990's."

"And you have both a bachelor's degree in computer science as well as a master's degree in cybersecurity, correct?"

"Yes," he says, without emotion.

"With your experience, would you say you have the capability to gain access to the computer files of almost any organization if you choose?"

"I have never done such a thing."

"That is not what I asked. I asked if you have the skills to hack into computer systems of large organizations, hypothetically."

"Objection, Your Honor. Asked and answered," contends Mr. Pouncey.

"Overruled," says Judge Nicklaus. "Answer the question, Mr. Tapping."

Tapping looks at his attorney, who subtly nods.

The accused follows with, "Yes, I have the expertise to do that."

"Would you say that you have the ability to get into, for example, a police database or a medical center computer system if you wanted to?"

"I already said yes," says the deflated defendant.

Some gabble is heard from the onlookers.

"Now, Mr. Tapping, I would like to turn to the subject of your deceased wife, Greta. Why did you never have children?"

"We chose not to."

"Is that the only reason? Remember, you are under oath. And we have spoken to your father in Sioux Falls."

"If you must know, she had the gene for Huntington's disease. And we didn't want her to pass it on to anyone."

"I am sure that was a difficult decision, Mr. Tapping. In other words, you did not want any of your children or grandchildren to inherit a terrible medical condition that your wife had. Is that right?"

"Yes."

"So if the descendants of Thomas Spizer already inherited his mental illness of psychopathic behavior, wouldn't you want to do away with them?"

The defendant displays increasing anxiety.

"Objection, Your Honor!" exclaims Mr. Pouncey. "Argumentative."

"Withdrawn, Your Honor," says Ms. Eisen calmly.

"Finally, Mr. Tapping, out of revenge, have you ever wanted to kill the man who viciously raped and murdered your innocent sister?"

He is silent but clearly tense.

"Have you dreamed of murdering the monster who violated and brutally ended the life of Lynette?"

The defendant becomes more restless and fidgety before angrily responding, "Of course! Anyone that barbaric should be put to death! But I – ."

Before the defense can object, Eisen interrupts Tapping's statement by saying, "Thank you. You have answered my question. Nothing more, Your Honor."

A frustrated Mr. Tapping lets out an audible "Aaargh!"

"Your Honor, permission to redirect?" asks Mr. Pouncey.

"Proceed," says the judge.

"Mr. Tapping, the prosecution asserts that you have killed the four recent victims since they are the progeny of Thomas Spizer, who murdered and raped your sister. Did you ever have the intent to kill Mr. Spizer or his descendants?"

The accused tries to calm down before he answers. Almost half a minute later, he responds.

"I was only told less than two weeks ago that it was Thomas Spizer who definitely murdered my sister. She was killed many years ago, and I have tried to forget that terrible event."

"Did you murder Thomas Spizer and his sons and grandsons?"

"No, I did not. Killing them would not bring my sister back."

"Thank you, Mr. Tapping. I am very sorry for the loss of your sister, as well as your wife and mother. Nothing further."

"You may step down, sir," says the judge to the exasperated defendant.

The defense attorney follows with, "Your Honor, I wish to call my last witness, Sally Liu."

The accused's girlfriend is sworn in, and she backs up the story of the defendant. However, on cross-examination by Ms. Eisen, Ms. Liu is not clear on specifically what hours she was with Mr. Tapping on the dates of the murders. And she admits not seeing him on the day Carl Zimmerman's body was recovered in Biscay Bay.

After her testimony is completed, the judge declares, "The court will adjourn for today. Closing arguments will be presented by the prosecution and the defense tomorrow morning."

All begin their egress from the courtroom after Judge Nicklaus strikes the sound block with his gavel and leaves the bench.

Once outside the courtroom, Lt. Rhombus speaks briefly with Assistant District Attorney Eisen.

"Margaret, isn't it unusual for the defendant to testify in his own trial?"

"You are right, Rex. When the main defense counsel took this calculated risk, he tacitly acknowledged that he needed the defendant's testimony to win the case. And Mr. Tapping's brief expression of anger on the stand did not help his cause."

"I can see that. And another thing: How important is it that the lab we used is not currently accredited? Aren't the results on the alveolar fluid content still valid if the same results are found by another lab?"

"It is only a technicality, Rex, and your lab's alveolar fluid test results will stand if another lab confirms them. If that happens, the cause of death also will not change."

"So why did the defense bother to bring it up in court?"

"Mr. Pouncey raised the issue to suggest that your investigation team is careless and not following protocol. The incident did not help us, but it was not a game changer."

"I get you."

"But on the flip side, Mr. Pouncey took the risk that the jury would see through his grandstanding."

"I see. Margaret, how do you think the trial has gone otherwise?"

"As well as I could expect, except for the mystery of the black birds on the lapel pins. I also wish we had more direct evidence, as I've said before."

"What I am still working on may give us just that."

"Okay, Rex. I will be waiting. And make sure to arrange another laboratory to repeat those tests as soon as it can."

"I'll take care of it, Margaret, in two shakes of a lamb's tail."

56

There is a hush in the courtroom the next morning as the clock strikes 9. The bailiff declares, "The trial of the State of California against Mr. Xavier Tapping is in session. Please take your seats."

Judge Nicklaus directs the prosecution to present its closing argument. After standing up from her counsel table, Assistant District Attorney Eisen approaches the jury.

"In the 1970's, Mr. Thomas Spizer horrifically murdered 17 young college women, including Lynette Tapping. The defendant Xavier Tapping had clear motive to kill the man who brutally raped and murdered his sister Lynette. But he didn't stop there. Mr. Tapping, with his exceptional knowledge of computers, later decided to use his expertise to systematically track down and then eliminate the progeny of the monster Thomas Spizer.

"When his wife inherited the gene for Huntington's disease, Mr. Tapping came to understand how an illness can spread to the afflicted's offspring. In a similar way, he came to believe that the psychopathy of serial murderers could also be inherited. Supporting his belief were the violent acts already carried out by Thomas Spizer's brother Jeremy and son Sammy. So he truly felt he was doing the world a favor by murdering all direct descendants of Thomas Spizer.

"These progeny include the four murder victims for which the defendant is being charged for first-degree murder. At least some of these four descendants of Thomas Spizer had a history of impulsive behavior, but they had not committed any crimes. The accused, however, felt it was only a matter of time before they would become psychopaths. As a result, Mr. Tapping set out to kill these individuals, but he did not wish them to suffer. Thus, he subdued each victim with a blow to the head, followed by a relatively painless death using pure nitrogen gas.

"Other than his girlfriend, the defendant has no alibi for the dates of the recent murders. On March 22nd, the date of Carl Zimmerman's homicide, Mr. Tapping claims he just happened to call in sick to his office. And this was his only sick day of 2019 so far! Coincidence? I think not.

"Some would say we should feel sorry for Mr. Tapping, who has lost his sister to a murderer, and his wife and mother to different illnesses. Some may even say he is justified in some way in carrying out these homicides. But who gives him the right to be judge, jury, and executioner? In a society where law is all that separates us from chaos and anarchy, he must be held responsible. And as the jury of your peers, you can send this message of accountability by strongly finding Xavier Tapping guilty of these horrendous crimes."

Assistant District Attorney Eisen makes eye contact with each juror before walking back to her table. There is a brief silence before Mr. Pouncey stands up and then moves toward the jury box.

"Bravo, Ms. Eisen. I must commend you for your brilliant sleight of hand. Ladies and gentlemen of the jury, if you listened carefully to what she said in the last few minutes, Ms. Eisen would want you to believe that there is already a mountain of evidence that proves Mr. Tapping is unequivocally guilty. Nothing is further from the truth.

"What has the prosecution shown us? Mr. Xavier Tapping has the knowledge and means to hack into various computer systems to monitor Thomas Spizer's progeny. What if he did? Does that prove my defendant actually did so? It certainly doesn't prove he committed murder.

"Ms. Eisen claims Mr. Tapping believes that serial killers can 'transmit' their 'killer genes' to their descendants. But how can she be sure that he in fact has that belief?

"There is no physical evidence or good eyewitness to place my client at any of the crime scenes at the times of the murders. And what is the connection between the black bird lapel pins, the signature of the serial killer, and my client? None has been demonstrated by the prosecution.

"Don't let Ms. Eisen's smoke and mirrors strategy fool you. Mr. Xavier Tapping is not guilty until proven otherwise. The burden of proof falls on the prosecution. And I am certain that the assistant district attorney has not established my client's guilt. You have no choice but to find Mr. Xavier Tapping not guilty on all counts. Thank you."

Mr. Pouncey quietly turns and walks back to the defense's table.

"Rebuttal, Your Honor," says Ms. Eisen.

"Proceed, Madam Assistant District Attorney," says Judge Nicklaus.

Eisen walks to the front of the jury box.

"Because of the scarcity of direct physical evidence, the prosecution's case is largely circumstantial. But remember that circumstantial evidence is sufficient to convict in many murder trials. And just think about the following as you begin your deliberations: If the defendant is guilty, as I believe we have established, can you afford to take the chance of allowing a serial killer to go free?"

After glancing at the jury one more time, Ms. Eisen slowly walks back to her table.

Judge Nicklaus then directs the jury members regarding their task at hand.

"Ladies and gentlemen of the jury, you have heard all the testimony from both sides. I will now give you some instructions, after which you will take a short break before you begin your deliberations. I expect all of you to discuss the facts presented to you without bias and determine the innocence or guilt of the defendant, Mr. Xavier Tapping."

He adds, "Be sure to consider the credibility of the witnesses. If you find the defendant guilty, it must be determined beyond a reasonable doubt. Finally, if you can not reach a verdict by day's end, we will sequester you."

The jury is then guided out of the courtroom. After all of them take in a snack, they retire to the jury room to begin deliberations.

After an hour and a half of lively and sometimes heated discussion, all jury members agree to a preliminary vote. The tally is 7-5 in favor of acquittal. Six jurors dominate the debate, three passionately arguing on the side of conviction and three opposing. But everyone is willing to further review the details in the primarily circumstantial case of the prosecution.

A central issue is why the defendant took his only sick day of the year on the day Carl Zimmerman was murdered. Plus Mr. Tapping has no alibi for that entire weekend. Those favoring a conviction contend that a simple coincidence would be implausible.

The demeanor of the defendant on the stand did not win him any friends in the jury. However, the pro-acquittal group generally feels that the lack of direct physical proof poses reasonable doubt.

Regarding the lack of laboratory accreditation pointed out by the defense, the jurors agree that the ploy was just meant to distract them from the real substance of the trial.

A few hours into deliberations, only two jurors have changed their initial votes. A unanimous verdict is not in sight, and they are all excused for a late lunch at 2 p.m.

Upon reconvening at the jury room an hour later, everyone seems energized. The chosen foreperson is insistent that they reach a verdict that day. And all the jury members appear motivated to do so.

Finally, about four hours later, the assistant district attorney gets word that the jury has reached a verdict. She had been asked by

Lt. Rhombus to contact him before the decision was to be announced.

"Hi Rex. The jury is about to return to the courtroom for the verdict."

"Thank you for calling, Margaret. I was actually about to call you. Do you remember that I was working to get more support for our case against Mr. Tapping?"

"Yes. But it might be too late now."

"On the contrary, it is of the utmost importance. I now believe Xavier Tapping is NOT our man."

"Really? Can you tell me about your new findings?"

They discuss the new evidence, after which Ms. Eisen makes an urgent call.

"Yes, this is Assistant District Attorney Eisen. I would like to meet with Judge Nicklaus immediately."

Fifteen minutes later, in Judge Nicklaus' chambers, Ms. Eisen and Mr. Pouncey are present.

"The verdict is about to be read, Counsels. What pressing issue merits this meeting?"

"Your Honor, I will now make you privy to the new developments from Lt. Rhombus' continuing investigation."

"Go ahead, Ms. Eisen."

She informs the judge about the brand-new facts provided by the lieutenant.

"What do you think our next course of action should be, Ms. Eisen?"

"In light of the new information, I am now willing to drop the charges against Mr. Xavier Tapping, Your Honor."

"Are you absolutely sure that your prosecution of the new suspect will be successful?"

"I am quite confident, Judge."

"And you, Mr. Pouncey?"

"Sir, I will be more than glad to tell my client he is free to go."

"So be it. I will dismiss the charges against the defendant – my office will inform the jury immediately. Ms. Eisen, you and Lt.

Rhombus may proceed with your legal action regarding the new suspect."

"Thank you very much, Your Honor."

After leaving the judge's office, Ms. Eisen calls the lieutenant about the case against Xavier Tapping being dismissed. Without delay, Lt. Rhombus summons his team for an emergency meeting at the police precinct conference room.

57

It is not quite twilight at the precinct, and Dr. Paris and Detective Stiles are unaware of the meeting just held at Judge Nicklaus' chambers. They anticipate that their lieutenant will be updating them on the status of jury deliberations. Detective Novo is still on the way.

Lt. Rhombus enters the conference room and announces, "Good evening, everyone. If you don't mind, I will get down to brass tacks. As the jury's verdict was about to be revealed, a decision by Judge Nicklaus was made at the eleventh hour. The charges have officially been dismissed against Xavier Tapping. The judge feels that new evidence has exonerated him."

Paris and Stiles both display a look of bewilderment.

"This is quite unexpected. What new proof was found, Rex?" asks the puzzled doctor.

At that moment, Detective Novo and Officer Zwicker walk in.

"Eli Stiles, we have a warrant for your arrest for the murders of Jackson Moreau, Matt Pitcairn, Carl Zimmerman, and Winston Banks."

They handcuff the detective as he acquiesces. His firearm is confiscated and he is read his Miranda warning.

Gobsmacked, Dr. Paris is at a loss for words.

"R-double, this must be a mistake!" exclaims Stiles, clearly dumbfounded.

"I will look into this, Eli. There must be an explanation," responds the lieutenant calmly.

Detective Stiles does not put up a struggle as he is led out of the room.

Lt. Rhombus gets a cup of water for the incredulous medical examiner and then shuts the door. He gives her a few moments to consider the dramatic turn of events.

"Danica, only a few people, including Judge Nicklaus and Assistant District Attorney Eisen, are aware of what I am about to tell you."

"Rex, did you know about this arrest? And it is not a mistake?"

"You are right on both counts. And you were not involved in the plan for reasons that will become apparent."

Tensely sipping some water, she sits back in her chair, waiting for an explanation.

"A few days before the trial, Ms. Eisen was not positive that we had enough to convict Xavier Tapping. So she asked me to find more proof if possible. As you know, we meticulously looked over the 149 recent local purchasers of nitrogen gas and special masks. We also reviewed the Mycenae serial murder files again."

"Yes, I remember. And we still concluded Mr. Tapping was the perpetrator."

"I agree. But despite all that, my gut told me that something was not right. For this reason, I organized an effort to revisit the files on the Mycenae area murders. But this time, I looked at the crimes from a slightly different angle – I decided to investigate any siblings of the Mycenae victims who were BORN AFTER the killings."

"Huh. I never thought of that. How did you manage to find these siblings?"

"Well, I called on Detective Novo to assist me. Eli was still nursing a cold, while you were occupied at the hospital. We looked up the mothers of the 17 murder victims, and Novo and I called all but one of them."

"What did you find, Rex?"

"These 17 mothers gave birth to a total of seven children after 1974, the year of the last Mycenae homicide. Of course, these seven individuals have every right to be vengeful siblings of the Mycenae victims. And doing the math, all of them are now age 44 or younger."

"And Eli is one of those seven siblings?"

"Not so fast. We did complete background checks and looked at employment records to eliminate three of them as suspects. Another two were taken off the list after we obtained warrants and checked recent phone, bank, and credit card records."

"That leaves two."

"Correct. One of them, David Moussa, is the brother of Ingrid Moussa, a Mycenae murder victim in 1971. He resides in Daly City, less than three hours from Quai Natia. Mr. Moussa works for a software company and has never been arrested. But he has made credit card purchases and phone calls in the Quai Natia region, and he is a lefty."

"Wow! Is he one of the 149 who bought nitrogen gas or a non-rebreather/scuba mask recently?"

"No, he is not. But we visited him at his office in San Francisco."

"So has he been arrested?"

"That's a negative, Danica. He has a solid alibi for all the murders."

"If that is so, then who is left?"

"The remaining person is named Edward St. John, one of the brothers of victim Geena St. John."

"She was the student who majored in zoology, right?"

"Bingo! And we have already looked into her other brother, Max. As you probably recall, we ruled him out as the possible killer."

"Does that make Edward St. John our primary suspect now?"

"Yes it does. Mrs. St. John gave birth to Edward in Peoria, Illinois. But she and her husband retired and moved to Portugal several years ago. Accordingly, we arranged for the Minneapolis police to pick up Edward's brother Max."

"Really? Why didn't you just contact him on his cell?"

"I was looking ahead, in the event that he might call and warn his brother Edward after our talk. Also, we have not contacted Edward's parents – I didn't want them to tip off their son either."

"Very smart, Rex."

"Thank you. Once he was at the police precinct, I gave Mr. Max St. John a call. He went on to describe how Edward went to college at the University of Illinois at Champaign, after which he went to the police academy in Springfield. After serving in the police force in Springfield for two years, he transferred to the St. Louis Police Department in 2008."

"That partial biography is very familiar."

"It sure is, Danica."

Suddenly, the truth dawns on Dr. Paris. "That is the story of Eli!"

"You're right on the money, Doctor."

"Thanks. But Edward St. John is not Eli Stiles."

"Unless he actually is, Danica," Rhombus says cryptically.

After a few moments, the doctor realizes the initials of Edward St. John are virtually those of Eli Stiles. "Is it possible, Rex?"

"More than possible – Edward St. John must be the same person as Eli Stiles. But I wanted to get unambiguous proof, without tipping off Detective Stiles."

"I have an idea. Does Max use the same phone number for Edward/Eli as we have for him?"

"Good thinking. But the numbers are different. So Detective Stiles probably has a second cell phone."

"How about listening in on a phone conversation between Max and Edward/Eli? Wouldn't that provide the evidence we need?"

"It probably would, but there is a risk that Eli would sense something is amiss, then he would become suspicious."

"True. Did you have another option?"

"Happily, I did. We checked with the Illinois circuit courts of the counties in which Edward resided: Peoria, Champaign, and Sangamon. Alas, we found no name change petitions for Edward St. John."

"What about the circuit court for St. Louis?"

"You read my mind, Danica. Lo and behold, the St. Louis Circuit Court gave us verification that Edward St. John officially changed his

his name to Eli Stiles in 2017!"

Dr. Paris exclaims, "This is unbelievable! Did the court records state the reason for the name change request?"

"The only reason given was he wanted a fresh start, including a name change, as he was preparing for a big move to California."

"2017. That was the year Samuel Pitcairn/Sammy Spizer was killed in the car accident. Did the name change occur before that?"

"Danica, he was already known as Eli Stiles at the time of the accident. Therefore, I surmise that he changed his name soon after he decided to eliminate the progeny of Thomas Spizer, starting with Samuel Pitcairn."

"That makes sense, Rex. If he was planning to murder Spizer's descendants, he predicted correctly that the investigation would eventually lead to Thomas Spizer, the Mycenae killings, and the female victims. So he had to remove any association between himself and his sister Geena."

"My thoughts exactly."

"Rex, how did Max feel about his brother's name change?"

"As it happens, Max had not been aware of it! His only communications with Edward/Eli since 2017 have been by cell phone, and Eli has used his birth name in their conversations.

"But doesn't his brother have Eli's home or work phone in California?"

"According to Max, Eli has said he is working undercover in a special police unit. As a result, he is not able to divulge details about his home or office."

"Actually, I am impressed at Eli's facade. If I was Max, I would not have suspected anything. But now that he is cognizant of the facts, what is stopping Max from warning Eli that we know his true identity?"

"I was afraid of that possibility, Danica. I simply could have threatened Max with an arrest for obstruction of justice if he told his brother, but that may not have prevented it."

"You're right – his loyalty to his brother may be very strong."

"That is true. So I opted to take no chances – Max St. John has remained in police custody, with no phone or email privileges. But now that Mr. Stiles is under arrest, I can release his brother Max."

"I understand, Rex, and I totally agree with your decision. It is now clear that Eli changed his name in 2017, to one with virtually the same initials no less. But I am still hearing of no crimes so far."

"Be patient, Danica. First, let me remind you that St. Louis is only four hours by car from Kansas City. Also, it is only a 90-minute flight or a 10-hour drive from St. Louis to Dallas."

"Let me get this straight, Rex. Both Xavier Tapping and Eli had a sister murdered by Thomas Spizer in Mycenae, Nebraska. They both lived relatively close to where Thomas Spizer and his son Sammy were killed. And both are computer savvy."

"Correct on all points, Doctor. Also, we know that Eli is left-handed, physically fit, and a good swimmer. All these characteristics fit our killer's profile."

"Mr. Tapping has those traits as well."

"No argument there. Yet another similarity between them is both moved to California in 2017, with Eli landing in Quai Natia and Tapping in Sacramento. In essence, they both relocated to the general vicinity of the recent murders."

"Based on circumstantial evidence, that would make Xavier Tapping just as likely as Eli to be the murderer at this point, right?"

"Except for one thing. You'll recall that Eli's sister Geena majored in zoology at Creighton University, while Tapping's sister had a major in accounting."

"So you think Eli's sister's zoology major gives us a link to the black bird lapel pins?"

"Precisely. Furthermore, Eli's brother told me that their sister Geena had a great love for animals and birds in particular."

"But Rex, as in the criminal case against Xavier Tapping, all we have is circumstantial evidence against Eli. Are you that sure that he is responsible for the local serial killings?"

"There is a little more to the story, Danica. I will be back soon," says Lt. Rhombus as he leaves the room to make a call.

58

"Good evening, Margaret. A short while ago, Eli Stiles was apprehended, and I am now getting Dr. Paris caught up on all the details. I also just contacted the Minneapolis Police Department to release Eli's brother Max from police custody."

"I'm glad. Did Detective Stiles offer any resistance?"

"As we expected, he was caught completely off-guard. And Detective Novo and Officer Zwicker provided the show of force to ensure a non-violent arrest."

"Very good, Rex. I will inform Judge Nicklaus and Mr. Pouncey, who will arrange for Mr. Tapping's release in a few hours."

"Shall I meet you in your office tomorrow morning?"

"I'll be expecting you around 11. Have a good evening."

The lieutenant returns to the conference room, where Dr. Paris still can't understand how Detective Stiles could be the Black Bird Killer.

"Are you doing all right, Danica?"

"A little on edge. But I will be better once you show me the proof that clearly implicates Eli."

"Point taken. I knew we clearly needed more physical evidence to cement our case against him. Thus, I convinced Judge Wilson to give me a search warrant for his place."

"And how were you able to conduct the search without him knowing?"

"It was simply a matter of timing. While you, Eli, and I were in the courtroom two days ago for our testimonies, Detective Novo and

Officer Zwicker were carefully but neatly combing through Detective Stiles' apartment."

"Do you believe Eli is aware of this search?"

"I think not. Novo was able to pick the lock of the front door, and both were instructed to leave almost everything in place and undisturbed."

"Under those circumstances, Eli should be oblivious to the event. Rex, did they find a smoking gun, such as a black bird lapel pin, nitrogen tank, or scuba mask?"

"Those would have been the ultimate prizes, Danica, but we were not so fortunate."

"But you did come away with some incriminating evidence, right?"

"Probably. A crack hammer with traces of blood."

"That is very suspicious. Has the blood already been analyzed?"

"Hallie from the lab tells me the blood on the hammer is all Type O positive. As you might remember, our first murder victim's blood type is A positive, but that of the other victims is O positive."

"And what is Eli's blood type? And the blood type of Billy Moreau, who was assaulted?"

"Danica, our records show that Eli is B positive, while Billy is A positive."

"Then the blood type on the crack hammer matches three of the victims. But when will the DNA analysis be ready?"

"Results should be available tomorrow."

"I will be waiting with bated breath, Rex. But one thing bothers me. What made you sure enough to drop charges against Mr. Tapping and arrest Eli?"

"That's a good question. By any chance, do you know of a fellow by the name of Ben Montenegro?"

"Not personally. Isn't he the head of the computer forensics lab here?"

"You are absolutely right. Mr. Montenegro, our computer scientist extraordinaire, was finally able to gain access to Mr. Tapping's computer files, but only hours after jury deliberations began. I am sure the difficulty was due to the accused's cybersecurity expertise."

"Is that why he was not an expert witness in the trial?"

"You are exactly right, Doctor. But once he was able to scrutinize Mr. Tapping's encrypted files, our computer guru did not find anything linking the homicides to him."

"I get it. Still, it makes you wonder why Tapping didn't just give us the access codes – he apparently had nothing to hide."

"That may be true. He knew of his innocence, so he simply might have been very confident that he would be acquitted. However, it is also likely that he wanted to avoid some embarrassment."

"What are you referring to, Rex? What is in those encrypted files?"

"In Mr. Tapping's computer, Mr. Montenegro found a plethora of pornographic images and videos."

"Ah, the truth comes out. But are there minors in those pictures and videos?"

"I haven't seen them myself, but Ben said the subjects appeared to be 18 or older."

"I know that child pornography involves persons under 18 in California. What about other states, such as Oklahoma?"

"Also 18 -- it's a federal statute. As a result, we can say that Mr. Tapping is legally clear of any wrongdoing."

"As for Eli, I presume our computer expert will be trying to get into his computer files now."

"He will be working on that very soon. As you probably know, with Eli in custody, we can confiscate his PC without the risk of him fleeing. And given Detective Stiles' unblemished rap sheet and the magnitude of the charges, we need to be 1000 percent sure that he is our man."

"Rex, what if Mr. Montenegro can't get into Eli's computer?"

"We will cross that bridge when we get to it, Danica."

59

Assistant District Attorney Eisen files charges for four counts of murder one against Eli Stiles the following morning. She schedules his arraignment on the complaint for the day after.

Meanwhile, Lt. Rhombus confronts Mr. Stiles and his attorney Camila Hill at the county jail. He goes over the evidence against his former detective and asks him to explain the blood on the crack hammer.

The accused is silent, following the advice of his attorney. He also refuses to give the password or passphrase to his computer. As the meeting ends, Stiles, usually the epitome of confidence, looks at Rhombus with a brooding and sullen expression.

An hour later at the forensics computer lab, Mr. Montenegro has so far been unable to fully access Mr. Stiles' computer data. He updates the lieutenant on his slow progress.

"Hello, Lieutenant. As you know, it took some time to gain access to the computer records of our previous suspect, Xavier Tapping. Being in cybersecurity, he encrypted his entire hard drive."

"That was to be expected. And what of Mr. Stiles?"

"He has a computer background as well, but he only encrypted some of the files. I am now attempting to get into those hidden folders."

"Have you seen anything incriminating in the files you have opened thus far?"

"Unfortunately no, Lieutenant."

"Thank you for your dedicated efforts, Ben. Please call me as soon as possible with any further headway you make."

"Hopefully it will be sooner rather than later. Bye for now."

At 11 a.m., Dr. Paris accompanies Lt. Rhombus and Detective Novo as they meet the assistant district attorney.

Ms. Eisen says, "The arraignment on the complaint is set for tomorrow. We are waiting on Mr. Montenegro regarding the encrypted information in Mr. Stiles' computer. And the DNA test results on the bloody hammer are pending."

"Those computer files and the DNA results could make our criminal case against Eli essentially airtight," states Novo. "But I am curious about the crime scenes of the recent murders. Why do you think they were so unusual, Lieutenant?"

"For one thing, I am convinced that the killer clearly wishes to gain attention for the crimes. And for another, I believe he feels that our four local victims had the right to die at locations where they had good times while they were alive."

"I see what you mean. Jackson Moreau enjoyed golf, Matt Pitcairn frequented that tavern to play billiards, Carl Zimmerman swam and scuba dived for fun, and Winston Banks excelled in high school football."

Lt. Rhombus adds, "In other words, the Black Bird Killer has a heart, in a way. We might even call him a 'kind killer'."

Dr. Paris agrees, saying, "It would appear. Also, he likely didn't go through with the kidnapping/murder of Billy Moreau because of his youth. But he probably has plans to murder him in the future."

"But why was Eli more violent in the slayings of Thomas and Sammy Spizer?" asks Eisen.

"Margaret, I believe it is a simple matter of proportionality. Thomas Spizer raped and murdered 17 women, so he deserved a painful, violent death. His son Sammy was guilty of domestic violence at least twice, so his death involved some but less suffering."

Ms. Eisen then reminds everyone, "Let's not forget that murdering people who may or may not become criminals is not forgivable under any circumstances."

"That is the current norm in our society, Margaret."

"And whether or not Mr. Stiles felt guilty in committing the homicides, he still designed them carefully. He even tried to get away with them by framing Xavier Tapping."

A few moments of reflection by the group are suddenly interrupted as Rhombus' and Paris' cell phones ring almost simultaneously.

"Lt. Rhombus, this is Ben Montenegro at the computer lab. I finally succeeded in breaking through the encrypted files in Eli Stiles' computer. They clearly reveal a wealth of information that he has collected on Thomas Spizer, his son Sammy, and the four local murder victims."

"That is outstanding work, Ben. Can you give me some details?"

"Sure. The records demonstrate a copious amount of data on the persons I listed, including photographs, addresses, employment data, phone records, and bank and credit card information. They go back over a year."

"By any chance, did the encrypted data also include particulars on other possible future targets for Eli?"

"Yes, there are similar files involving a few other individuals. Do you need their names?"

"Please."

He relays a list of people to the lieutenant, who is not surprised.

"Ben, I really appreciate your tireless work and diligence in our investigations of Mr. Tapping and now Mr. Stiles. Your excellent reputation is well-deserved."

"You're very welcome, Lieutenant."

While Lt. Rhombus has been on the phone with Mr. Montenegro, Dr. Paris has been talking to the crime lab.

"Dr. Paris here."

"Good morning. This is Hallie from the lab. We have final results on the blood from the crack hammer. It contains the DNA of Carl Zimmerman and Winston Banks."

"That is exceptional news. And no one else?"

"Only those two people, Doctor."

"Much obliged, Hallie. Have a fantastic day."

After Rhombus and Paris share the findings with Eisen and Novo, everyone breathes a little easier.

Detective Novo then asks, "Danica, why do you believe there was blood from only two of the victims on the crack hammer?"

She answers, "It's possible that Eli used a different hammer or heavy object for the other victims. Equally likely is he wiped off the blood of the other victims more carefully. At any rate, we're just fortunate that you and Officer Zwicker found the specks of blood on the hammer in the first place."

"I am glad to help," says the detective.

Ms. Eisen states, "Well, our case to convict looks very strong. I will meet tomorrow with the accused and Ms. Hill after the arraignment. Can anyone think of anything else?"

"Margaret, I know you will do the right thing. But once Eli is convicted, I suggest we give him a small amount of leniency in his sentence. For one thing, he has served as an excellent Quai Natia detective until recently. And for another, he did try to minimize the suffering of the four local murder victims."

"That is very thoughtful, Rex. Let me discuss that matter with my colleagues. Have a good day, everyone."

60

Eli Stiles pleads not guilty at his arraignment the following day. To no one's surprise, given the four counts of first-degree murder, the magistrate judge orders that Stiles be remanded without bail. Assistant District Attorney Eisen then informs the defendant's attorney that there will be no preliminary hearing until they meet with her later that day.

Several hours later, at the county jail, Eli Stiles and Ms. Hill await Ms. Eisen in the meeting room. He is handcuffed and a guard is present. The door opens as the assistant district attorney enters.

Eisen begins by saying, "Mr. Stiles, you were given a summary of our criminal case against you by Lt. Rhombus yesterday."

"Go on, Counselor," says Ms. Hill.

"At this time, I have additional evidence proving you are the Black Bird Killer. In our search of your home, we came upon some blood on a crack hammer. That blood contains the DNA of two of the victims, Carl Zimmerman and Winston Banks."

Ms. Hill asks to see the search warrant, and Ms. Eisen obliges.

"We have also managed to gain access to your computer files, including the encrypted ones. A lot of specific information about the four local murder victims, as well as Thomas Spizer and Sammy Spizer/Samuel Pitcairn, was discovered."

His attorney tells Mr. Stiles that the warrant papers appear to be in order.

"The next step would be a preliminary hearing, after which I expect we go to trial. For your egregious crimes, I will be seeking the death penalty. And given the new evidence, I am extremely confident you will be convicted."

"Maybe I'll just take my chances with the jury," utters the defendant.

"You have the right to do that, but I am now giving you a one-time opportunity. Until now, you have had a record of exemplary service as an officer of the law. For this reason, I am offering life in prison without the possibility of parole, with certain conditions."

Ms. Hill whispers something to her client.

He asks, "How can I be sure you are telling the truth about the hammer and computer files you say you found?"

"In trial, you and your attorney can challenge any of my witnesses and findings. But you know the truth, Mr. Stiles. And my offer expires in ten minutes."

"What are the conditions, Ms. Eisen?" asks Ms. Hill.

"I have spoken to the widows of two of the four murder victims, as well as the parents of the other two victims. Mr. Stiles must give an earnest apology to all of them in a courtroom."

"Will others be allowed in the courtroom?"

"Only the judge and bailiff."

"Is that the only stipulation?" asks Ms. Hill.

"We also require Mr. Stiles to briefly meet with Lt. Rhombus to answer a few questions he has about the murders."

"Ms. Eisen, allow me to speak with my client for a few minutes."

The assistant district attorney leaves the room and waits outside.

Eight minutes later, Ms. Hill tells Ms. Eisen, "My client accepts your offer, Counselor."

"I am glad, and I will make the arrangements. By any chance, would Mr. Stiles be willing to meet with Lt. Rhombus now?"

"Let's get it over with," says the former detective.

Fifteen minutes later, Rhombus, appearing crestfallen, walks into the room and sits across the table. Stiles proceeds to confess to the four murders.

"I am very sorry to lose an excellent detective and a friend, Eli. First, I need to be sure how you killed the four local victims."

"I knocked each one out with the blow to the head, then I took each of them to my car to breathe in pure nitrogen gas. The gas canister and mask apparatus were discarded after each crime."

"And how did you get the idea of nitrogen gas?"

"A premed buddy of mine in college mentioned it once, and I figured it would be a relatively painless way to die."

"I know that your sister Geena was killed seven years before you were born. At what time did you make the decision to kill her rapist and murderer?"

"At the University of Illinois, my good friend Rebecca was sexually assaulted. That incident brought back painful memories about my sister. After a lot of thought, I decided that I needed to make Geena's murderer pay for his atrocities."

"I see. And when did you make up your mind about killing the direct descendants of Thomas Spizer?"

"At first, my only intention was to get revenge on the murderer of my dear sister. After doing away with Spizer, I continued to monitor his progeny out of curiosity."

"Using your computer skills?"

"Yes. But for a while in early 2017, I dated a very smart criminal psychologist. She convinced me that psychopathic behavior is almost certainly inherited. By chance, many of Spizer's sons and grandsons were living in this general area. So after I took care of Samuel Pitcairn in Dallas, I moved to Quai Natia."

"Did you ever tell this girlfriend about your plans?"

"No. She wouldn't have understood."

"Eli, as you are aware, Thomas Spizer's son Sammy was guilty of domestic violence on at least two occasions, and Spizer's brother Jeremy probably brutally murdered his girlfriend."

"That's right. And it turns out that most or all of the four local murder victims had already displayed impulsive and/or aggressive behavior in the past. It was only a matter of time before all of Thomas Spizer's descendants would become psychopaths, and possibly serial killers."

"Understood. Can you explain the bizarre murder scenes?"

"I wanted these homicides to be memorable to the public, events they would never forget. I also felt it would be appropriate for the victims to die at locations that gave them happiness when they were alive. Of course, the lapel pins commemorate my sister, who had a special affinity for ravens."

"Your brother told me that Geena was a bird enthusiast. Why were ravens her favorite?"

"All I recall is she thought they were very intelligent, acrobatic, and adaptable."

"The mystery of the black birds is revealed. Finally, do you have the intention to harm anyone else?"

"Knowing you, I'm sure you are already aware of the Chastains. And I was considering the children of Jackson Moreau and Carl Zimmerman for a later time."

Lt. Rhombus stands up and gives the handcuffed prisoner a sincere handshake.

"Good luck, Eli."

"I don't regret what I did, R-double. I couldn't risk any of them becoming a monster like Thomas Spizer."

"Eli, you will have the chance to clarify your actions and apologize to the victims' loved ones very soon."

"And Rex, please tell Danica and Bianca that I am sorry if I let them down."

"I will be sure to relay your message."

He leaves the room as Mr. Stiles sits with a faraway look in his eyes.

61

Lt. Rhombus promptly notifies Assistant District Attorney Eisen, Dr. Paris, and Detective Novo about Eli Stiles' confession. He also outlines the recent sequence of events for Lt. Durso, who understandably becomes very dismayed and saddened by Mr. Stiles' criminal activity. Then, as he had promised, the lieutenant makes a call to the Sioux Falls retirement home where Sherwood Tapping resides.

"Hello, Mr. Tapping?"

"Yes. Please speak up. My hearing is not the best."

"This is Lt. Rhombus from Quai Natia, California. Do you remember me?"

"Let me think. Didn't we talk about my son recently?"

"You are right, sir. I just wanted to be the first to tell you that we found the murderer in our investigation and your son is innocent."

"That's wonderful to hear, but I could have told you that. Xavier is a good boy."

"I am sure he is. Have a very good afternoon, Mr. Tapping."

"Thank you for calling, sir."

Later that afternoon, Eisen, Paris, and Novo join Rhombus in his office.

"So it was definitely a raven on the lapel pins. Eli wanted to memorialize his deceased sister as part of his nefarious deeds, as she admired that particular feathered friend," says the lieutenant.

The assistant district attorney states, "Everything is becoming very clear now. But I am at a loss to explain something. How do you suppose the four local murder victims ended up in the area of Quai Natia?"

"That is an excellent question, Margaret."

"Maybe the climate attracted them. Or the ocean," posits the doctor.

"The reasons could have been job opportunities and a relatively low crime rate," suggests Detective Novo.

"Or it simply may have been fate," says Lt. Rhombus.

Everyone ponders the different possibilities for several moments.

"Not to change the subject, but does anyone else here somewhat empathize with Eli?" asks Dr. Paris.

"I do," says the lieutenant. "But Eli made his own bed, and he will have to lie in it."

Ms. Eisen adds, "His motive may have been justifiable to him, but he should never have taken the law into his own hands."

"That he did, and with conviction. He will have a long time to look back at his actions," says Rhombus.

"I also feel sorry for Mr. Tapping, who had to go through the entire ordeal. Plus he has lost his sister, his wife, and his mother."

"Danica, I called his father a few hours ago to give him the good news regarding his son. And I have something in mind, Margaret."

"Pray tell, Rex."

"Eli nearly succeeded in framing Xavier Tapping for the serial murders. For all the trouble he has been put through, perhaps we can make it up to Mr. Tapping with a small gesture."

"And what would that be?"

"As you are aware, Hanna Moreau offered a reward for the capture and successful prosecution of her husband's killer. I was thinking that we could give some portion of that to Mr. Tapping. Would that be proper and legal, Margaret?"

"I like your idea, Rex. Let me look into it and talk with Mrs. Moreau."

On that note, the lieutenant takes out four small bottles of chilled sparkling mineral water from his personal fridge.

Each one opens then raises a bottle, with Lt. Rhombus declaring, "Here's to the memory of the four recent murder victims, who were targeted solely because they were blood relatives of an evil man."

The other three respond, "Hear, hear!" as they all clink bottles and sip their drinks.

"But thanks to our efforts, we have prevented at least five other individuals from suffering the same fate."

"Five?" asks Detective Novo. "Aren't Billy Moreau and Nina Cîrstea the only living progeny of Thomas Spizer?"

"Not quite. It's a long story, but I discovered about two weeks ago that Spizer also had a son Madison in early 1976 when he dated a person named Abigail Chastain. And Madison now has a son Geoff and a daughter Constance."

"Are they all right?"

"I am happy to say they have been fine and under police protection in Cheyenne, Wyoming."

"Do you have any suspicion as to why they haven't been recent targets of Eli?"

"The main reason is they lived in Europe and Asia for many years until returning to Wyoming only last year."

"Good for them," says Novo. "In all likelihood, if Eli was not caught, the Black Bird Murders would have probably resumed outside California."

Dr. Paris then asks, "Rex, why do we think Eli hasn't pursued young Nina Cîrstea, Carl Zimmerman's daughter? She has lived in Utah with her mother for three years now."

"Danica, I believe the reason lies in what you just said -- her youth. In the same way that Eli could not go through with the murder of young Billy Moreau, he probably couldn't imagine killing a preschooler like Nina."

All nod in agreement as they drink their effervescent beverages.

"But Eli admitted to me that he was considering their murders for a future date."

"Thanks to us, he will never get that chance," says Detective Novo.

A few minutes later, Officer Zwicker interrupts the gathering.

"Pardon the intrusion, everyone, but you might want to hear this. There is a report of a male corpse at Perez Parque with no clear signs of injury."

"Will you be on the scene soon, Officer?"

"Yes, I am on my way now. But there is something else -- a black bird lapel pin was found attached to his shirt."

Everyone in the office looks at each other, wide-eyed and dumbfounded.

62

Without delay, Lt. Rhombus puts down his bottle and calls the county jail.

"Can I please speak with the correctional officer watching Mr. Eli Stiles?"

Dr. Paris, Ms. Eisen, and Detective Novo are on the edges of their seats as the lieutenant waits on the phone.

"Good evening, Officer. This is Lt. Rhombus. Is Mr. Stiles in your custody at this time?"

"That's affirmative. He's in his cell lying down. Is there anything wrong?"

"No, I am just checking on our prisoner. Has he had any visitors or made any phone calls in the last few hours?"

"This slim brunette, probably in her late 40's, came to see him. She said she was his lawyer."

"What is her approximate height and hair color?"

"About 5-foot-7 with dirty blonde hair. She was wearing a dark brown pant suit, and she had ID."

"That sounds like Ms. Hill. And any calls?"

"He made one collect call, about 20 minutes long."

"Officer, please get me a recording of that call."

"I'll get to it right away, Lieutenant."

After hanging up, Rhombus says, "Eli has seen only his attorney and made only one phone call since I saw him a few hours ago. Margaret, would you mind listening to the tape of that call once it's available?"

"No problem. I will head over there now."

"Thank you. And Reynold, please write down this list of the five living direct descendants of Thomas Spizer: Billy Moreau, Nina Cîrstea, Madison Chastain, and his children Geoff and Constance."

He jots down the names on a notepad.

"Those five individuals should still be under police watch. Make sure you alert the police units looking over them."

"Right away, Lieutenant," says Novo.

"Are you going to the crime scene now?" asks Paris.

"Yes, please meet me there, Doctor. For now, I have to assume this murder is connected to the other four."

Twenty minutes later, Lt. Rhombus and Dr. Paris reach Perez Parque. The lieutenant finds Officer Zwicker while the doctor makes a beeline for the corpse.

"Officer Zwicker, what is the situation?"

"A woman walking her dog came across the lifeless body at the edge of the fountain. He's a 51-year-old man named Mariano Galaz. His police record is spotless."

"Do you see any signs of a struggle? Or any murder weapon?"

"No blood or obvious bruises on the body. And we haven't recovered a potential weapon."

"How about motive? Was any jewelry or money stolen?"

"No robbery here, Lieutenant."

"Okay. Thank you, Officer. Try to keep this growing crowd from contaminating the crime scene."

"I'll take care of it, sir."

After Paris performs a brief examination of the corpse, she finds Rhombus.

"Rex, he's been dead for only two to three hours. There is some bruising in the back of the head, as well as a black bird lapel pin attached to his shirt. Sound familiar?"

"It sure does. No other signs of injury? And does the pin match the ones on the other homicide victims?"

"Lacerations, obvious needle marks, and gunshot wounds are absent. The other lapel pins were not exactly identical to each other, so I will have to compare this pin to those."

"Please do that, Doctor. Are you able to perform an emergency postmortem this evening?"

"Under the circumstances, I definitely can. What are you thinking?"

"Hard to say at this point. The priority as far as I'm concerned is to make sure Eli is not involved in any way."

"I agree. I'll give you my assessment in several hours."

63

The various law enforcement entities watching the five surviving descendants of Thomas Spizer are contacted by Detective Novo. He finds that nothing out of the ordinary has recently occurred.

At the county jail, Assistant District Attorney Eisen listens to the recording of the only phone call made by Eli Stiles in the last few hours. All she hears is a benign conversation between a son and his mother.

Lt. Rhombus enlists the help of Detective Novo and Officer Zwicker to track down the living relatives of Mariano Galaz, who was a local architect. They include his father in Los Angeles, brother and sister in Oregon, and a son and daughter who live locally. After various phone calls, it is determined that none of them is clearly related to Thomas Spizer or any of the four recent murder victims.

The results of the general blood tests for the newly deceased show lactic acidosis and a markedly elevated potassium level. No substances of abuse are detected on toxicology screening. After a thorough inspection of the body, in addition to the small head contusion, Dr. Paris finds a small needle puncture site at the medial aspect of the left ankle. On autopsy, the brain, lungs, kidneys, and liver are swollen with venous congestion, but the heart shows healthy coronary arteries.

She concludes that the cause of death is sudden cardiac arrest due to acute hyperkalemia. In other words, the assailant injected the victim with intravenous potassium chloride through a vein in the left ankle area. This action resulted in very high blood levels of potassium, which caused his heart to stop.

Once the probable cause of death is conveyed to Lt. Rhombus, his team checks local pharmacies for recent theft of potassium chloride. Two hospitals report missing vials, and Novo and Zwicker are instructed to review the recent surveillance camera footage near their pharmacies.

While looking over the videotapes at Sacred Heart Hospital, Detective Novo spots a suspicious man leaving the main pharmacy at 10 p.m. four nights ago. He was wearing scrubs and a fanny pack, and a hospital ID badge was visible. The detective questions members of the pharmacy staff and asks if anyone recognizes the man seen on the tape. One of them clearly identifies him as Ted Dobbs, an ICU nurse.

Rhombus is immediately informed and looks at his criminal record, which is clean. After the lieutenant obtains warrants for Dobbs' phone and credit card records, he detects nothing outstanding. Still not convinced of his innocence, however, Lt. Rhombus obtains a search warrant for the suspect's home and car. Novo and Zwicker serve the warrant and find one vial of potassium chloride in the back of the refrigerator. They arrest Mr. Dobbs and Mirandize him.

At the Quai Natia Police Department, Mr. Dobbs is only briefly interrogated by Lt. Rhombus and Detective Novo before he requests a lawyer. An hour later, after consulting with his attorney, Dobbs agrees to confess to the crime and accept a plea bargain. The motive for the murder becomes evident: Mr. Dobbs caught Mr. Galaz sleeping with his wife a week before.

64

Fair white clouds move slowly across the azure sky on this late April morning. At the Quai Natia police precinct conference room, Lt. Rhombus and Detective Novo are joined by Assistant District Attorney Eisen and Dr. Paris. They bring the ladies up to speed on the developments of the last 48 hours.

"Rex, I need to know. Do you believe Mr. Ted Dobbs is in any way associated with Eli in the Black Bird Murders?" asks Ms. Eisen.

"I would say definitely not, Margaret. Danica's assessment indicates that Mr. Mariano Galaz was killed after intravenous potassium was injected into him – a cause of death inconsistent with the Black Bird Murders. In addition, we are unable to put Mr. Galaz in the family tree of Thomas Spizer."

"I agree," says Dr. Paris. "I don't even see a need to check alveolar fluid in this case. But Rex, do you think this homicide can be considered a copycat crime?"

"Looking at all factors, I would say only in part. It is true that Mr. Dobbs mimicked the publicized details of the recent killings: unusual murder scene, mild head injury, black bird lapel pin, and apparent unknown cause of death."

"No argument there."

"And the Black Bird Murders were violent crimes that have been sensationalized by the local media in recent weeks."

"Right you are."

"But Dobbs does not really match the profile of a quintessential copycat criminal: He has no prior criminal history and there is no current record of any mental health problems. As I see it, the murder was essentially a premeditated act of revenge."

"However, don't you think he relished the potential notoriety of being associated with the Black Bird Killer?"

"I do. So let's call Mr. Dobbs a three-quarters copycat killer for now."

Novo comments, "That's a good compromise, Lieutenant."

Paris and Eisen are also amused by Rhombus' suggestion.

"Incidentally, Dobbs' use of intravenous potassium chloride is clearly an effective way to try to hide the cause of death. And his career as an intensive care nurse gives him access and specialized knowledge," mentions Dr. Paris.

"By the way, Rex, have you checked the hospital where he works to see if there have been any unexplained ICU deaths in the recent past?"

"I appreciate the thought, Margaret, but I already asked Reynold to do so. No mysterious deaths have occurred recently at Sacred Heart Hospital."

"You are still razor-sharp after all these years."

"Thank you. I do what I can."

"Rex, I still wonder how we could have missed Eli being the perpetrator until the last week. Did you have any suspicions before the last several days?"

"Danica, there were actually subtle indications throughout the investigation, but I could not be sure until a few days ago."

"Such as?"

"As you also probably noted, Mr. Stiles, like Mr. Tapping, moved to this area sometime in late 2017 and is a lefty, a good swimmer, and deft in computers. How about you, Doctor? Can you remember any strange or curious circumstance involving Eli in the last month or so?"

"Let me think. Admittedly, there is one instance I recall. When I was called about the second victim at the Just Win! tavern over a month ago, I happened by chance to be in the area, so I arrived fairly quickly. But I was surprised to see that Eli had arrived at the crime scene before me!"

The lieutenant says, "That was definitely unexpected. Of course, what convinced me that he was a legitimate suspect was his failure to tell us that the Mycenae victim Geena St. John majored in zoology. In fact, I daresay that he altered the Mycenae police files to show no major field of study for Miss St. John."

"Well, we're all glad that you maintained your objectivity this entire time," adds Ms. Eisen.

"Indeed," remarks Lt. Rhombus.

"So Rex, what happens to our team now that Eli is no longer with us?" asks Dr. Paris.

"Danica, hold that thought."

Rhombus arises and leaves the room. A minute later, he returns with a chiseled dark-haired officer sporting a moustache.

"Ladies, please say hello again to Officer Damon Zwicker. As you may already know, he has worked with me and Detective Novo in our investigations of Xavier Tapping, Eli, and Ted Dobbs. And I am pleased to announce that he should be promoted to the title of police detective within a week."

"Welcome to the team, Officer Zwicker!"

He accepts handshakes from everyone in the room.

"Please, call me Damon. Or Dez."

"Dez? Is that your nickname?" asks Paris.

"My middle name is Edgar, so Dez or D-E-Z caught on with the guys."

"Dez it is!" announces Lt. Rhombus. "Now, if you will all excuse me, I have a fencing match with Mr. Treadwell to resume."

THE BLACK BIRD MURDERS